喚醒你的英文語感！

Get a Feel for English !

喚醒你的英文語感！

Get a Feel for English !

貝塔語言出版 Beta Multimedia Publishing

IRT 語言測驗中心 Language Testing Center

附一片朗讀MP3

英文閱讀越好人物篇

〔閱讀〕讓你更有競爭力，知識力、英語力、考試力，全部向上提升！

從7大領域的28個傳奇人生，讀出與世界接軌的**好知識 + 好英文！**

He was awarded the Nobel Peace Prize for his work on nuclear arms reduction.

Yahoo became one of the most successful companies in the new dotcom age.

She wrote the whole Harry Potter series.

His Ninth was performed in 1824 and Beethoven conducted the orchestra without being able to hear it.

His mature art is full of bright colors and swirling shapes and portraits of his friend

She was named a UN Messenger of Peace, and traveled around the world.

His mature a and swirling

作者：Quentin Brand

序言

我們身處的是一個變化快速又精彩的世界，裡頭住著形形色色的人物。許多人曾經對我們所居住的這個地球有所貢獻，而他們的貢獻持續影響著我們。本書鎖定了世界各地的傳奇男女，介紹他們的人生與成就，他們直接或間接都對人類產生了重大的影響。

書中人物分為七類：政治領袖、音樂家、文學家、藝術家、科學家、企業領袖、運動員。每類各有四個人物，兩存兩歿、兩男兩女。

書中人物都懷抱著理想，而且努力奮鬥來實現這個理想。他們的努力改變了我們對世界的看法，或是大大提升了我們的生活品質。有的人出身貧窮，有的人最後變得富有。相同的是，他們全都有個信念，並全力以赴去實現它。希望各位能從他們的故事獲得啓發。

如何運用本書

閱讀是加強英文最有用與最有效率的方法。這點很幸運，因為閱讀也是最容易獨力完成的事。不過，許多人覺得閱讀英文很難。我來教各位一些閱讀的祕訣。

❶ 首先，閱讀時請著重在看得懂的部分，而不是看不懂的部分。許多人在閱讀時都著重在看不懂的部分。一邊閱讀，一邊在不認識的字底下畫線。這是錯誤的策略，因為這會使你洩氣。所以，一定要著重在你看得懂的部分，而不是看不懂的部分。

❷ 第一次閱讀時，不要指望能把每個部分都看懂。就算你必須把內文讀個幾遍才能搞懂一切，也無所謂，主要是讓自己習慣讀英文。你可以參考文章的譯文來幫助理解。

❸ 每個單元的習題都是設計來幫助各位逐步理解內文，並協助各位學習跟內文主題有關的新字彙。

■ 閱讀理解：幫助各位了解文章大意和架構方式。
■ 重要詞彙：幫助各位認識該單元的困難字彙。
■ 填空：幫助各位熟悉並學會這些字彙的使用方式。
■ 你還可以學更多：鼓勵各位主動學習，並多了解一些與內文主題相關的資訊。書中提供了一些建議，可以利用下列網站進一步上網閱讀：

  ☑ Youtube
  ☑ Wikipedia（維基百科）
  ☑ Encyclopedia Brittanica（大英百科全書）
  ☑ Google（谷歌）

如果你依照這些建議進一步閱讀，你會發現許多重複的字彙。這有助於你記住這些字彙。

最後提供了一些討論問題。你可以利用這些問題來跟朋友或同學聊聊你所讀過的人物，或者寫段文章來談論這些主題。

❹ 各單元的「Word List」為文章中的難字做了註解。書中多元主題的字彙在準備托福考試時相當實用，如果你是要為全民英檢考試做準備，可以針對打上 ★ 星號的字彙做加強。

希望各位會覺得本書有趣、實用、又具啓發性。說不定有朝一日你也會是此類名人傳記書中的一員呢！

目錄 Contents

Part 1

叱吒風雲的領袖人物

Barack Obama

Henry VIII

Aung San Suu Kyi

Indira Gandhi

Unit 1

Henry VIII
亨利八世

人物速覽

- 英國國王
- 1491年生於倫敦格林威治
  （Greenwich, London），1547年卒
  於倫敦
- 英國國教會創始人
- 六任妻子的丈夫

❶ **Henry** was the second son of King Henry VII of England, the first king of the Tudor dynasty. When Henry was 11 years old, his older brother, the next in line to the throne,[1] died. This meant that Henry became the next in line. He married his brother's fiancée,[2] Catherine of Aragon, the daughter of the king of Spain. Neither he nor Catherine wanted to marry each other, but they had no choice as both their fathers wanted the marriage to proceed[3] in order to join their two countries together. Catherine gave Henry a daughter, Mary, who later became Queen of England after her father's death, but Catherine didn't have any other children, which was a great disappointment to Henry.

❷ Henry then fell in love with a woman called Anne Boleyn, a lady in waiting[4] to Catherine. He wanted to marry her, but in order to do so he had to divorce Catherine. Henry asked the pope[5] for a divorce, but the pope refused. In the end, King Henry, who always got what he wanted, sent Catherine home, and married Anne. He threw all the Catholics[6] out of England, confiscated[7] their money and property, and proclaimed[8] himself head of a new Church of England.

Ⓦ Ⓞ Ⓡ Ⓓ Ⓛ Ⓘ Ⓢ Ⓣ

1. throne [θron] *n.* 王位
2. fiancée [ˌfiənˋse] *n.* 未婚妻
3. proceed [prəˋsid] *v.* 著手進行
4. lady in waiting *n.* 宮女；侍女
5. pope [pop] *n.* 教皇；教宗
6. Catholic [ˋkæθəlɪk] *n.* 天主教徒　*adj.* 天主教會的
7. confiscate [ˋkɑnfɪsˌket] *v.* 沒收；把……充公
8. proclaim [proˋklem] *v.* 宣告；公布

❸ In those days, England was a Catholic country. Catholics believe that everyone, no matter who, should obey the pope and follow his rules. Henry was very angry that the pope would not help him, and the fight between the king and the pope about the king's marriage became the most important political issue of the time. The pope argued that because he was God's representative[9] on earth, his power was greater than the king's, but the king argued that his power was greater than the pope's.

❹ Anne, however, could not give Henry what he wanted — a son. She gave birth to a daughter, Elizabeth, who later became queen after her half sister Mary's death. Henry then fell in love with Jane Seymour, who was Anne's lady in waiting. He found a way to accuse Anne of treason,[10] and had her executed[11] so he could marry Jane. Jane gave Henry a son, Edward, who became king after Henry died. However, Jane died giving birth to her child.

❺ Henry's next wife was Anne of Cleves. He married her for political reasons, to make the country safe from attack by Catholics. However, Henry soon found his new wife boring and quickly divorced her to marry another woman called Catherine Howard, one of Anne's ladies in waiting. Catherine was a member of a very old and powerful Catholic family, and

──── Ⓦ ⓞ Ⓡ Ⓓ Ⓛ Ⓘ Ⓢ Ⓣ ────

★ 9. representative [ˌrɛprɪˋzɛntətɪv] n. 代表；代理人
10. treason [ˋtrizn̩] n. 叛逆罪
11. execute [ˋɛksɪˌkjut] v. 處死
12. plot [plɑt] v. 密謀
13. cranky [ˋkræŋkɪ] adj. 古怪的；難以取悅的

Henry soon became convinced that Catherine's family were plotting[12] to kill him. He found a way to accuse her of treason, and she was executed.

❻ Henry's last wife was a rich widow called Catherine Parr. By now, Henry had become very fat, very sick and very cranky.[13] She looked after Henry until he died of his various illnesses.

譯文

❶ 亨利是英國亨利七世國王的次子，亨利七世則是都鐸王朝的第一任國王。亨利 11 歲時，他身為王位繼承人的哥哥過世。這表示亨利變成了王位繼承人。他娶了哥哥的未婚妻──阿拉貢的凱瑟琳，她是西班牙國王的女兒。他和凱瑟琳都不想與對方成婚，但他們別無選擇，因為雙方的父親都希望成就這段婚姻，好讓兩國成為命運共同體。凱瑟琳替亨利生了個女兒瑪麗，瑪麗後來在父親過世後當上了英國女王。但凱瑟琳並沒有再生下其他子女，讓亨利大為失望。

❷ 後來亨利愛上一位叫做安．波琳的女子，她是凱瑟琳的侍女。他想娶她，但如果要這麼做，他就必須休掉凱瑟琳。亨利央請教皇同意離婚，但教皇不肯。最後，總是為所欲為的亨利國王把凱瑟琳送回家去，並娶安為妻。他把天主教徒全部趕出英國，沒收他們的金錢與財產，並自命為新英國國教會的領袖。

❸ 當時的英國是天主教國家。天主教徒相信，不論是誰，都應該服從教皇並遵守他的規定。亨利非常氣惱教皇不幫他的忙，而國王與教皇為了國王的婚姻而彼此對抗，也成了當時最重要的政治問題。教皇認為，他是上帝在人世間的代表，所以他的權力大過於國王。但國王卻認為，他的權力比教皇大。

❹ 然而，安並不能給予亨利他所想望的東西——兒子。她生了一個女兒伊莉莎白，伊莉莎白後來在同父異母的姐姐瑪麗過世後當上了女王。亨利之後愛上了珍‧西摩爾，她是安的侍女。他想出法子指控安叛國，並將她處死，好讓他能娶珍為妻。珍替亨利生了個兒子愛德華，愛德華在亨利過世後當上了國王。不過，珍也因為難產而過世。

❺ 亨利的下一任妻子是安‧克里夫斯。他是為了政治因素而娶她，以保護國家免於天主教徒的攻擊。不過，亨利不久就對他的新婚妻子感到厭倦，很快地休了她，並娶了另一位叫做凱瑟琳‧霍華的女子，她是安的侍女。凱瑟琳出身一個非常古老並有權勢的天主教家族，亨利不久後就相信，凱瑟琳的家族密謀要殺害他。他想了個辦法指控她叛國，並將她處死。

❻ 亨利的最後一任妻子是個有錢的寡婦，名叫凱瑟琳‧帕爾。此時的亨利變得非常肥胖、多病又異常暴躁。她一直照顧亨利，直到他各種疾病纏身而過世。

閱讀理解

配合題，請判斷下列摘要各屬於文章的哪個段落，見範例。

Wife number 3	❹
Wife number 1	
Wives number 4 and 5	
Wife number 2	
Wife number 6	
Henry and the pope	

重要詞彙

連連看，請為每個詞彙找出它的正確翻譯。

- confiscate •
- accuse sb. of sth. •
- fiancée •
- argue that •
- cranky •
- political issue •
- find sth. sth. •
- head of sth. •
- lady in waiting •
- representative •
- execute •
- political reason •
- proclaim oneself sth. •
- dynasty •
- treason •
- the next in line to the throne •

- 指控某人做某事
- 爭論……
- 沒收
- 暴躁的
- 處死
- 末婚妻
- 對……感到……
- ……的領袖
- 侍女
- 政治議題
- 政治因素
- 自命為……
- 代表
- 王位繼承人
- 王朝
- 叛國

填 空

理解文章大意後，請用前項習題中的詞彙來完成句子，有些字須做適當變化。

■ Henry VIII was the second king of the Tudor (01)＿＿＿＿＿＿＿.

■ When Henry's older brother Arthur died, Henry became

(02)＿＿＿＿＿＿＿.

■ He married his dead brother's (03)＿＿＿＿＿＿＿, but he fell in love

with her (04)＿＿＿＿＿＿＿, Anne.

■ The fight between Henry and the pope was the biggest

(05)＿＿＿＿＿＿ of the period.

■ The pope (06)＿＿＿＿＿＿ his power was greater than the king's

because he was God's (07)＿＿＿＿＿＿ on earth.

■ Henry (08)＿＿＿＿＿＿ all the property of the Catholic Church in

England, and he (09)＿＿＿＿＿＿ himself (10)＿＿＿＿＿＿ the

Church of England.

■ Anne Boleyn and Catherine Howard, Henry's second and fourth

wives, were both (11)＿＿＿＿＿＿ (12)＿＿＿＿＿＿ and were

(13)＿＿＿＿＿＿.

■ Henry married his first and fifth wife for (14)＿＿＿＿＿＿ only, to

help his country.

■ Henry (15)＿＿＿＿＿＿ his fifth wife very boring.

■ In his old age Henry became fat, ill and **(16)** _____ .

 你還可以學更多

a) 請利用網路查詢下列關鍵字，以了解更多關於 **Henry** 的資訊：

> ⊘ Some pictures of Henry
>
> ⊘ Henry's wives
>
> ⊘ Some pictures of Henry's wives
>
> ⊘ The Tudor dynasty
>
> ⊘ The Catholic Church
>
> ⊘ The Church of England

b) 請試著用英文討論下列話題：

> 1. 你想不想認識亨利？為什麼？
>
> 2. 亨利為什麼有這麼多妻子？
>
> 3. 他為什麼想要個兒子？
>
> 4. 你覺得哪個妻子最幸運？為什麼？
>
> 5. 你覺得國王應不應該為所欲為？

解 答

 閱讀理解

Wife number 3	❹
Wife number 1	❶
Wives number 4 and 5	❺
Wife number 2	❷
Wife number 6	❻
Henry and the pope	❸

 重要詞彙

accuse sb. of sth.	指控某人做某事
argue that	爭論……
confiscate	沒收
cranky	暴躁的
execute	處死
fiancée	未婚妻
find sth. sth.	對……感到……
head of sth.	……的領袖
lady in waiting	侍女
political issue	政治議題
political reason	政治因素
proclaim oneself sth.	自命為……

representative	代表
the next in line to the throne	王位繼承人
dynasty	王朝
treason	叛國

 填 空

(01) dynasty	(02) the next in line to the throne	(03) fiancée
(04) lady in waiting	(05) political issue	(06) argued that
(07) representative	(08) confiscated	(09) proclaimed
(10) head of	(11) accused of	(12) treason
(13) executed	(14) political reasons	(15) found
(16) cranky		

Indira Gandhi
英迪拉 · 甘地

人物速覽

- 第 5 及第 8 任印度總理
- 1917 年生於印度阿拉哈巴德
  （Allahabad, India），1984 年卒於
  印度新德里（New Delhi, India）
- 印度歷史上首位女總理
- 印度首任總理之女

❶ **Indira Gandhi** was born into an Indian political family called the Nehru family. Her father was a well-educated lawyer and a close friend of the great Indian independence leader, Mahatma Gandhi. At the time of Indira's birth and childhood, India was a British colony.[1] Indira's family were involved in the political struggle[2] for independence. This made her childhood difficult. Her father was often in prison for political activities, and her mother was frequently ill. Indira's involvement[3] in politics started when she created a political movement called Venara Sena, an organization for young Indian girls and boys her own age who wanted independence from the British.

❷ As a young woman, Indira was sent to England to study at Oxford University, and to spend some time in Switzerland for her health. There, she met her future husband, Feroze Gandhi (Gandhi is a common Indian family name). They married when they returned to India, and they had two children together.

❸ After Independence in 1942, Mr. Gandhi became a member of the new Indian parliament,[4] while Mrs. Gandhi became the leader of the main political party in India, called the Indian National Congress. During this time, Indira's father became the first Prime Minister[5] of India. When Indira's

Ⓦ Ⓞ Ⓡ Ⓓ Ⓛ Ⓘ Ⓢ Ⓣ

1. colony [ˈkɑlənɪ] *n.* 殖民地
2. struggle [ˈstrʌɡl] *n.* 奮鬥；掙扎
3. involvement [ɪnˈvɑlvmənt] *n.* 捲入
4. parliament [ˈpɑrləmənt] *n.* 議會；國會
★ 5. Prime Minister [ˈpraɪm ˌmɪnɪstɚ] *n.* 首相；總理

father died in 1964, Indira began to move up in the government. She was created Minister of Information and Broadcasting, and she was elected Prime Minister for the first time in 1966.

❹ In 1971 there was a war between India and her northern neighbor, Pakistan.[6] At that time there were two Pakistans: West and East, separated from each other by North India. West and East Pakistan had different cultures and different languages, and East Pakistan wanted to be independent from West Pakistan. Mrs. Gandhi's solution was to declare[7] war on West Pakistan to help protect East Pakistan's people, and then to give them their own country, now called Bangladesh.[8]

❺ In the first part of her term[9] as Prime Minister, Indira was very popular, especially with the poor, whom she helped with agricultural[10] policies. However, towards the end of her first term, she became more and more unpopular, and this made her very autocratic.[11] In 1975 she declared a state of emergency. This allowed her to remove her political enemies and use the police to stop protests.[12] There was widespread civil unrest[13] and lawlessness[14] in India as a result. Eventually, she lost her position as Prime Minister and was arrested.

Ⓦ Ⓞ Ⓡ Ⓓ Ⓛ Ⓘ Ⓢ Ⓣ

6. Pakistan [ˌpækɪˋstæn] *n.* 巴基斯坦
7. declare [dɪˋklɛr] *v.* 宣布
8. Bangladesh [ˋbæŋɡləˋdɛʃ] *n.* 孟加拉
9. term [tɜm] *n.* 任期
★ 10. agricultural [ˌæɡrɪˋkʌltʃərəl] *adj.* 農業的
11. autocratic [ˌɔtəˋkrætɪk] *adj.* 獨裁的

❻ Indira was elected Prime Minister for the third time in 1980. In the north of India is a province called Punjab. During the 1980s this province wanted independence from the rest of India. Indira refused to give it to them. Some of the separatists[15] were hiding in a temple. Indira called in the army to remove them, and in the following battle, many innocent people, most of them Sikhs,[16] were killed. To get revenge for this incident, two of Indira Gandhi's Sikh bodyguards assassinated[17] her.

譯文

❶ 英迪拉‧甘地出身於名為尼赫魯家族的印度政治家族。父親是一位受過良好教育的律師，而且是印度偉大獨立領袖聖雄甘地的密友。在英迪拉出生時以及小時候，印度是英國的殖民地。英迪拉的家族捲入了獨立的政治鬥爭，這也造成她童年時期的艱苦。她父親經常因為參與政治活動而入獄，母親則長年臥病。英迪拉參與政治是始於她發起名為 Venara Sena 的政治運動，此組織的訴求對象是跟她年齡相仿、並希望從英國獨立的印度年輕少男少女。

❷ 在還是年輕女性時，英迪拉被送往英國牛津大學就讀，並因為健康因素，在瑞士待了一段時間。她在那裡結識了她後來的丈夫費羅茲‧甘地（甘地是印度常見的家族姓氏）。他們在回到印度後結了婚，並生了兩個小孩。

---

12. protest [ˈprotɛst] *n.* 抗議
13. unrest [ʌnˈrɛst] *n.* 不安；動盪
14. lawlessness [ˈlɔlɪsnɪs] *n.* 不服從法律；目無法紀
15. separatist [ˈsɛpəˌretɪst] *n.* 分離主義者；主張獨立自治者
16. Sikh [sik] *n.* 錫克教徒
★ 17. assassinate [əˈsæsn̩ˌet] *v.* 暗殺

❸ 在1942年獨立後，甘地先生成為新印度國會的議員，甘地太太則成了印度主要政黨的領袖，該黨名為印度國大黨。在這段期間，英迪拉的父親成為印度的首任總理。英迪拉的父親在1964年過世，之後英迪拉便開始在政府單位裡竄升。她被任命為資訊暨廣播部長，並在1966年首次當選總理。

❹ 到了1971年，印度和北方的鄰國巴基斯坦開戰。當時有東、西兩個巴基斯坦，被北印度隔開。東、西巴基斯坦有不同的文化和不同的語言，東巴基斯坦想要從西巴基斯坦獨立出來。甘地女士的解決之道是向西巴基斯坦宣戰，並協助保護東巴基斯坦的民眾，然後讓他們擁有自己的國家，也就是現在所稱的孟加拉。

❺ 在她首次擔任總理之初，英迪拉廣受愛戴，尤其是對於在農業政策上受過她幫助的窮人來說。不過，在她首屆任期接近尾聲時，她愈來愈不得人心，並因此變得十分專橫。1975年，她宣布進入緊急狀態。此舉讓她得以掃除政敵，並動用警察來阻止示威。結果內亂與違法行為在印度各地頻生。最後，她失去總理的職位，並遭到逮捕。

❻ 英迪拉在1980年第三度當選總理。印度北方有一省叫做旁遮普。1980年代，該省想要脫離印度其他地區獨立出來，英迪拉拒絕。有些主張獨立自治人士躲進了寺廟，英迪拉下令軍隊加以掃蕩。在後續的戰役中，許多無辜人民遭到殺害，而且多半是錫克教徒。為了替這事件報仇，英迪拉·甘地的兩個錫克教徒保鑣暗殺了她

閱讀理解

配合題，請判斷下列摘要各屬於文章的哪個段落，見範例。

The war between India and Pakistan	❹
Marriage and family	
The state of emergency	
Her family and childhood	
Problems in the Punjab	
Early political career	

 重要詞彙

連連看，請為每個詞彙找出它的正確翻譯。

- independence •
- Minister of Information •
- autocratic •
- bodyguard •
- involvement •
- British colony •
- agricultural policy •
- civil unrest •
- declare war •
- be elected •
- independence leader •
- assassinate •
- Member of Parliament •

- • 農業政策
- • 行刺
- • 專橫的
- • 保鑣
- • 英國殖民地
- • 內亂
- • 宣戰
- • 當選
- • 獨立
- • 獨立領袖
- • 捲入
- • 國會議員
- • 資訊部長

▨ state of emergency •	• 政治活動
▨ political movement •	• 政治運動
▨ Prime Minister •	• 政黨
▨ political party •	• 政治鬥爭
▨ political struggle •	• 總理
▨ term •	• 示威
▨ protest •	• 主張獨立自治者
▨ political activity •	• 緊急狀態
▨ separatist •	• 任期

填 空

理解文章大意後，請用前項習題中的詞彙來完成句子，有些字須做適當變化。

▨ Indira's father was a friend of the **(01)**_____, Mahatma Gandhi, and he was involved in the **(02)**_____ for **(03)**_____ during the days when India was a **(04)**_____.

▨ He was often in prison for his **(05)**_____.

▨ Indira's **(06)**_____ in politics started when she created a **(07)**_____ for young Indian boys and girls.

▨ Mr. Gandhi became a **(08)**_____ after Independence and Indira became the leader of a **(09)**_____.

▨ Indira's first government job was **(10)**_____, and she was **(11)**_____ **(12)**_____ of India three times.

▨ In 1971 India **(13)**_____ on Pakistan.

■ During her first (14)_____, Indira had lots of (15)_____ to help the poor.

■ She became very (16)_____ in her second term, and declared a (17)_____ to deal with the (18)_____ and (19)_____ in India.

■ Indira was (20)_____ by her (21)_____ who agreed with the Punjab (22)_____.

 你還可以學更多

a) 請利用網路查詢下列關鍵字，以了解更多關於 **Indira Gandhi** 的資訊：

- ✓ Some pictures of Indira Gandhi
- ✓ Indira Gandhi's children
- ✓ The war between India and Pakistan in 1971
- ✓ Indira Gandhi's father
- ✓ Indira Gandhi's assassination
- ✓ India's struggle for independence

b) 請試著用英文討論下列話題：

1. 你想不想認識英迪拉？為什麼？
2. 英迪拉在她第二屆任期時，為什麼變得非常專橫？
3. 英迪拉為什麼不讓旁遮普獨立？
4. 你覺得英迪拉的孩子對母親的政治決定有什麼感受？
5. 你想不想去印度旅遊參觀？為什麼？

 解 答

 閱讀理解

The war between India and Pakistan	❹
Marriage and family	❷
The state of emergency	❺
Her family and childhood	❶
Problems in the Punjab	❻
Early political career	❸

 重要詞彙

agricultural policy	農業政策
assassinate	行刺
autocratic	專橫的
bodyguard	保鑣
British colony	英國殖民地
civil unrest	內亂
declare war	宣戰
be elected	當選
independence	獨立
independence leader	獨立領袖
involvement	捲入
Member of Parliament	國會議員

Minister of Information	資訊部長
political activity	政治活動
political movement	政治運動
political party	政黨
political struggle	政治鬥爭
Prime Minister	總理
protest	示威
separatist	主張獨立自治者
state of emergency	緊急狀態
term	任期

 填 空

(01) independence leader

(02) political struggle

(03) independence

(04) British colony

(05) political activities

(06) involvement

(07) political movement

(08) Member of Parliament

(09) political party

(10) Minister of Information

(11) elected

(12) Prime Minister

(13) declared war

(14) term

(15) agricultural policies

(16) autocratic

(17) state of emergency

(18) protests

(19) civil unrest

(20) assassinated

(21) bodyguards

(22) separatists

Unit 3

Aung San Suu Kyi
翁山蘇姬

人物速覽

- 緬甸總理當選人
- 1945 年生於緬甸仰光（Rangoon, Burma）
- 1991 年諾貝爾和平獎（Nobel Peace Prize）得主
- 政治犯

❶ **Aung San Suu Kyi** was born into a Burmese[1] political family. Both her parents were famous Burmese politicians. Her father was the leader of the independence movement, and the founder of the modern Burmese army. He was assassinated the year Burma gained independence from the British. After his death, her mother became an important person in the new Burmese government. She was appointed[2] ambassador[3] to India, and it was in India that Aung San Suu Kyi was brought up and educated.

❷ As a young woman, Aung San Suu Kyi went to England to study at Oxford University. There, she met her future husband, Dr. Aris, an Englishman who was a scholar of Tibetan[4] Buddhism at Oxford. After graduating from Oxford, Aung San Suu Kyi moved to New York, where she worked for the United Nations for three years. She kept in touch with her husband by writing letters to him every day. After that, she returned to London, where she lived with her husband and had two children while she studied for her Ph.D.

❸ In 1988 Aung San Suu Kyi returned to Burma to care for her mother, who was now very old and sick. At this time, there was a lot of social and political unrest in Burma. The Burmese wanted democracy, but the government, who were mostly old soldiers, the same men who killed Aung San Suu Kyi's father, did not want to lose their grip[5] on power. Aung

Ⓦ Ⓞ Ⓡ Ⓓ Ⓛ Ⓘ Ⓢ Ⓣ

1. Burmese [bɝˋmiz] *adj.* 緬甸（人）的　*n.* 緬甸人
★ 2. appoint [əˋpɔɪnt] *v.* 任命；指派
★ 3. ambassador [æmˋbæsədə] *n.* 大使
4. Tibetan [tɪˋbɛtn] *adj.* 西藏（人）的　*n.* 西藏人
5. grip [grɪp] *n./v.* 抓牢；緊握

San Suu Kyi decided to help the Burmese democracy movement. She addressed[6] a huge rally[7] in the capital city of Rangoon, and became leader of the Burmese National League for Democracy. The government put her under house arrest.[8]

④ In 1990 the military junta[9] allowed a general election in the country for the first time. The National League for Democracy won. This meant that Aung San Suu Kyi was now the Prime Minister-elect of Burma. However, the military rulers were very disappointed that their candidate did not win the election and they refused to acknowledge[10] Aung San Suu Kyi as the winner. She was arrested again.

⑤ In 1997, Aung San Suu Kyi's husband, Dr. Aris, was diagnosed[11] with terminal[12] cancer. She asked the junta to allow her husband to visit her in her house for the last time. Many leaders and governments around the world lobbied[13] the Burmese government for her. The government refused, but they offered her the chance to go to England to visit him. Aung San Suu Kyi knew that this was a trick, and that if she left Burma, she would never be allowed back again. She decided to stay in Burma, and never saw her husband again, as he died of his illness in 1999.

⑥ Aung San Suu Kyi, the elected leader of her country, is still under

---

Ⓦ Ⓞ Ⓡ Ⓓ Ⓛ Ⓘ Ⓢ Ⓣ

6. address [ə`drɛs] v. 對……講話
7. rally [`rælɪ] n. 集會；示威活動
8. under house arrest 囚禁在家
9. junta [hoōn'tə] n. （政變後的）軍事政權；臨時政府（源自西班牙文）
10. acknowledge [ək`nɑlɪdʒ] v. 承認

house arrest. She spends her time writing and meditating.[14] Her belief in Buddhism and in non-violent protest makes her strong. She won the Nobel Peace Prize in 1991.

譯文

❶ 翁山蘇姬出身於緬甸的政治世家，雙親都是緬甸的知名政治人物。父親是獨立運動的領袖，以及緬甸現代軍隊的創始人。在緬甸從英國獨立出來那年，他遭到刺殺。在他死後，她的母親成了緬甸新政府的重要人物。她被任命為駐印度大使，而翁山蘇姬正是在印度長大及接受教育。

❷ 翁山蘇姬前往英國牛津大學就讀時，是個年輕女性。她在那裡遇到了未來的丈夫阿里斯博士，這位英國人是在牛津教授藏傳佛教的學者。從牛津畢業後，翁山蘇姬搬到紐約，並在聯合國服務了三年。她跟丈夫保持聯絡的方法是每天寫信。後來她回到倫敦跟丈夫及兩個小孩同住，並攻讀博士學位。

❸ 1988 年，翁山蘇姬回到緬甸，照顧當時年邁又多病的母親。這段時期的緬甸出現了許多社會和政治動亂。緬甸人想要民主，但以軍人為主體的政府卻不想失去所掌握的權力，而翁山蘇姬的父親就是被這批人所殺害。翁山蘇姬決定為緬甸的民主運動盡一份心力。她在首都仰光的盛大集會上發表演說，並成了緬甸全國民主聯盟的領袖。結果政府把她軟禁在家。

11. diagnose [ˌdaɪəgˋnos] *v.* 診斷為
★ 12. terminal [ˋtɜmənl] *adj.* 末期的；終點的
13. lobby [ˋlɑbɪ] *v.* 進行遊說、疏通
14. meditate [ˋmɛdəˌtet] *v.* 冥想

❹ 1990年，軍政府同意舉行首次的全國普選。全國民主聯盟贏得了勝利，這代表翁山蘇姬此時是緬甸的總理當選人。不過，軍隊統帥非常失望他們的候選人沒有贏得大選，拒絕承認翁山蘇姬勝選。結果她再次遭到逮捕。

❺ 1997年，翁山蘇姬的丈夫阿里斯博士被診斷出末期癌症。她要求政府允許她丈夫最後一次到她家探視，全世界有許多領導人和政府也替她向緬甸政府遊說。政府拒絕，但提供她一個到英國探視丈夫的機會。翁山蘇姬知道這是個詭計，只要她一離開緬甸，就一輩子再也回不去了。她決定留在緬甸，並再也沒見過她的丈夫，而他則在1999年因病去世。

❻ 當選國家領導人的翁山蘇姬目前仍被軟禁在家，並把時間用來寫作和沉思。她對於佛教與非暴力抗爭的信仰使她變得堅強。她在1991年贏得了諾貝爾和平獎。

 **閱讀理解**

配合題，請判斷下列摘要各屬於文章的哪個段落，見範例。

Her beliefs	❻
Early political career	
She becomes Prime Minister	
Family and childhood	
Death of her husband	
Student life and marriage	

 重要詞彙

連連看，請為每個詞彙找出它的正確翻譯。

- be diagnosed with •
- military junta •
- acknowledge •
- ambassador •
- general election •
- appoint •
- candidate •
- capital city •
- keep in touch with sb. •
- address sb. •
- democracy movement •
- lose their grip on power •
- lobby the government •

- • 承認
- • 對某人演說
- • 大使
- • 任命
- • 被診斷出
- • 候選人
- • 首都
- • 民主運動
- • 普選
- • 跟某人保持聯絡
- • 向政府遊說
- • 失去所掌握的權力
- • 軍政府

■ put sb. under house arrest •	• 非暴力抗爭
■ rally •	• 總理當選人
■ non-violent protest •	• 把某人軟禁在家
■ terminal cancer •	• 集會
■ Tibetan Buddhism •	• 學者
■ Prime Minister-elect •	• 癌症末期
■ win an election •	• 藏傳佛教
■ United Nations •	• 聯合國
■ scholar •	• 贏得大選

填 空

理解文章大意後，請用前項習題中的詞彙來完成句子，有些字須做適當變化。

■ Aung San Suu Kyi's mother was (01)_____ the first Burmese (02)_____ to India.

■ Dr. Aris was a (03)_____ of (04)_____.

■ In her early life, Aung San Suu Kyi worked for the (05)_____, but she (06)_____ her husband by writing letters.

■ The Burmese government do not want to (07)_____.

■ Aung San Suu Kyi decided to join the (08)_____ in Burma. She (09)_____ a huge (10)_____ in the (11)_____, and became the leader of the Burmese National League for Democracy.

■ Aung San Suu Kyi was (12)_____ for many years and was allowed no visitors.

■ Aung San Suu Kyi won (13)_____ and became the (14)_____ of Burma.

■ The (15)_____ were angry that their (16)_____ did not win, and refused to (17)_____ Aung San Suu Kyi as the winner.

■ Her husband was (18)_____ (19)_____. In spite of many governments around the world (20)_____ the Burmese government, Aung San Suu Kyi was not allowed to see him.

■ Aung San Suu Kyi believes in (21)_____, which means you should never use violence in the struggle for political freedom.

你還可以學更多

a) 請利用網路查詢下列關鍵字，以了解更多關於 Aung San Suu Kyi 的資訊：

- ✓ Some pictures of Aung San Suu Kyi
- ✓ Some pictures of her husband, Dr. Aris
- ✓ The government of Burma　✓ Aung San Suu Kyi's father
- ✓ The United Nations　✓ Burma's struggle for independence

b) 請試著用英文討論下列話題：

1. 你想不想認識翁山蘇姬？為什麼？
2. 政府為什麼要在 1990 年舉行大選？
3. 翁山蘇姬為什麼會贏得諾貝爾和平獎？
4. 你對於非暴力抗爭有什麼看法？
5. 你想不想去緬甸旅遊？為什麼？

解 答

 ## 閱讀理解

Her beliefs	❻
Early political career	❸
She becomes Prime Minister	❹
Family and childhood	❶
Death of her husband	❺
Student life and marriage	❷

 ## 重要詞彙

acknowledge	承認
address sb.	對某人演說
ambassador	大使
appoint	任命
be diagnosed with	被診斷出
candidate	候選人
capital city	首都
democracy movement	民主運動
general election	普選
keep in touch with sb.	跟某人保持聯絡
lobby the government	向政府遊說
lose their grip on power	失去所掌握的權力

military junta	軍政府
non-violent protest	非暴力抗爭
Prime Minister-elect	總理當選人
put sb. under house arrest	把某人軟禁在家
rally	集會
scholar	學者
terminal cancer	癌症末期
Tibetan Buddhism	藏傳佛教
United Nations	聯合國
win an election	贏得大選

 填 空

(01) appointed

(02) ambassador

(03) scholar

(04) Tibetan Buddhism

(05) United Nations

(06) kept in touch with

(07) lose their grip on power

(08) democracy movement

(09) addressed

(10) rally

(11) capital city

(12) put under house arrest

(13) the general election

(14) Prime Minister-elect

(15) military junta

(16) candidate

(17) acknowledge

(18) diagnosed with

(19) terminal cancer

(20) lobbying

(21) non-violent protest

Unit
4

Barack Obama
巴拉克 · 歐巴馬

人物速覽

- 第 44 任美國總統
- 1961 年生於夏威夷火奴魯魯
  （Honolulu, Hawaii）
- 美國首位非裔美籍總統
- 《哈佛法律評論》首位非裔美籍社長
- 2009 年諾貝爾和平獎得主

❶ Barack Obama was born into a mixed race family. His mother was a white American woman, and his father was an exchange student from Kenya in Africa. They met when they were in college, and got married. Two years after Obama's birth, they divorced, and Obama's father returned to Kenya. Obama's mother then married again, this time to a man from Indonesia. After some time, the family moved to Indonesia where Obama spent his early childhood. At the age of 10, he returned to Hawaii where he was brought up by his grandparents.

❷ When he graduated from high school, he went to Columbia University in New York, where he studied political science and international relations. After he graduated, he went to Chicago where he worked as a community officer in the poor neighbourhoods of the city, helping disadvantaged[1] people to get jobs, education and housing. After three years of this, he went to Harvard Law School. He wanted to become a lawyer so that he could help more people. At Harvard, he was elected the first African American president of the *Harvard Law Review*, a very famous journal.[2] This made him famous all over America.

❸ After graduating from Harvard Law School, he returned to Chicago, where, for many years, he was actively involved in local politics helping the poor in Chicago, especially among the African American community. During this time, he met his wife Michelle, who was also working in local politics and civil rights. He was elected to the Illinois Senate[3] as a member

Ⓦ Ⓞ Ⓡ Ⓓ Ⓛ Ⓘ Ⓢ Ⓣ

1. disadvantaged [ˌdɪsəd`væntɪdʒd] *adj.* 因貧窮而處於困境的
★ 2. journal [`dʒɝnḷ] *n.* （雜誌等）定期刊物
3. senate [`sɛnɪt] *n.* 參議院

of the Democratic Party[4] in 1996, and he focused on civil rights, health care and education issues. During his days as a state legislator, he worked with Republican Party[5] legislators on bipartisan[6] issues such as voting reform, civil rights and the death penalty.[7]

❹ In 2004 Obama was elected to the US Senate, as a senator[8] for Illinois State. He won the largest number of votes in the state's history, and became the rising star of the Democratic Party. As senator he focused on issues such as voting reform, weapons control and government transparency.[9]

❺ In 2008, Barack Obama decided to run for president as the Democratic Party candidate. First he had to win the nomination[10] for president from the Democratic Party. This was difficult and took a long time because the other popular candidate was Hillary Clinton, wife of former President Bill Clinton. The campaign[11] was long and hard, but Obama beat Clinton to get the nomination. Then Obama had to beat the Republican Party candidate, John McCain.

❻ Barack Obama's campaign was the first campaign to use the internet to raise money and get support. His message was a message of hope

---

Ⓦ Ⓞ Ⓡ Ⓓ Ⓛ Ⓘ Ⓢ Ⓣ

   4. Democratic Party [ˌdɛmə`krætɪk ˌpɑrtɪ] *n.* 民主黨
   5. Republican Party [rɪ`pʌblɪkən ˌpɑrtɪ] *n.* 共和黨
   6. bipartisan [baɪ`pɑrtəzn̩] *adj.* 兩黨的
★ 7. death penalty [`dɛθ ˌpɛnⱼtɪ] *n.* 死刑
   8. senator [`sɛnətɚ] *n.* 參議員

and a new beginning for the nation and the world. He beat John McCain and was sworn in[12] as the 44th President of the United States. He made Hillary Clinton, his former rival, his Secretary of State. In 2009 he was awarded the Nobel Peace Prize for his work on nuclear arms reduction.

譯文

❶ 巴拉克·歐巴馬出身混血家庭。母親是白種美國女性，父親則是來自非洲肯亞的交換學生。他們相識於大學時期。在歐巴馬出生兩年後，他們離了婚，歐巴馬的父親也回到了肯亞。後來歐巴馬的母親再婚，這次嫁給了一位來自印尼的男子。經過一段時日，舉家搬遷至印尼，歐巴馬早期的童年就是在那裡度過。他在 10 歲的時候回到夏威夷，並由外祖父母撫養長大。

❷ 高中畢業後，他到紐約就讀哥倫比亞大學，讀的是政治學和國際關係。畢業後，他去了芝加哥，並在該市的貧民區擔任社區幹事，協助弱勢民眾謀職、求學與住宿。做了三年後，他到哈佛法學院就讀。他想要成為律師，如此才能幫助更多的人。在哈佛的時候，他獲選為《哈佛法律評論》首位非裔美籍社長，這是一本非常有名的刊物，使他的名聲傳遍了美國。

❸ 從哈佛法學院畢業後，他回到芝加哥，並長年積極參與地方政治，以協助

9. government transparency [`gʌvəmənt træns`pɛrənsɪ] *n.* 政府施政透明化
10. nomination [ˌnɑmə`neʃən] *n.* 提名；任命
★ 11. campaign [kæm`pen] *n.* （選舉等）活動
12. swear in [`swɛr ˌɪn] *ph.* 使……宣誓

芝加哥的貧民，尤其是在非裔美籍的社區。在這個時候，他認識了他太太蜜雪兒，她也在為地方政治與民權而努力。他在 1996 年代表民主黨獲選為伊利諾州的參議員，並全力投入民權、醫療保健與教育等議題。在擔任州議員期間，他曾與共和黨的議員聯手處理兩黨議題，諸如選制改革、民權和死刑等。

❹ 2004 年，歐巴馬代表伊利諾州獲選為美國參議員。他贏得了該州有史以來最多的選票，並成為民主黨的明日之星。在擔任參議員期間，他全力投入選制改革、武器管制和政府施政透明化等議題。

❺ 2008 年，巴拉克・歐巴馬決定參選總統，並成為民主黨的候選人。首先他必須贏得民主黨的總統提名。這並非易事，而且耗費了很長時日，因為另一位聲勢看好的候選人是希拉蕊・柯林頓，也就是前總統比爾・柯林頓的夫人。競選活動既漫長又辛苦，但歐巴馬打敗了柯林頓並獲得提名。歐巴馬接著必須擊敗的是共和黨候選人約翰・麥肯。

❻ 巴拉克・歐巴馬的競選首次使用了網際網路來募款及爭取支持。他所傳達的訊息既是希望，也是國家和世界的新起點。他打敗了約翰・麥肯，並宣誓就職，成為美國第 44 任總統。他還任命先前的對手希拉蕊・柯林頓為國務卿。2009 年，他因在削減核武上的努力而獲頒諾貝爾和平獎。

閱讀理解

請把下列摘要搭配上它所描述的段落,見範例。

High school and college	❷
Illinois State Senator	
His childhood and family	
US Senator	
President Obama	
2008 presidential campaign	

重要詞彙

連連看,請把每個詞彙搭配上它的正確翻譯。

- African American community •
- bipartisan •
- former rival •
- beat (someone in a race) •
- issue •
- campaign •
- civil right •
- exchange student •
- community officer •
- Democratic Party •
- disadvantaged •
- death penalty •
- international relation •

- • 非裔美籍社區
- • (在競賽中)打敗(某人)
- • 兩黨的
- • 競選活動
- • 民權
- • 社區幹事
- • 死刑
- • 民主黨
- • 弱勢的
- • 交換學生
- • 先前的對手
- • 國際關係
- • 議題

■ voting reform	•	•	刊物
■ legislator	•	•	議員
■ nomination	•	•	地方政治
■ mixed race family	•	•	混血家庭
■ local politics	•	•	提名
■ political science	•	•	政治學
■ run for president	•	•	參選總統
■ the rising star	•	•	明日之星
■ government transparency	•	•	政府施政透明度
■ vote	•	•	選票
■ journal	•	•	選制改革
■ weapons control	•	•	武器管制

填 空

理解文章大意後，請用前項習題中的詞彙來完成句子，有些字須做適當變化。

■ Obama came from a (01) _____ because his father was an (02) _____ from Kenya, and his mother was a white American.

■ He studied (03) _____ and (04) _____ in college, and was the president of a famous (05) _____ in law school.

■ For his first job he worked as a (06) _____ in Chicago, where he helped the poor and (07) _____, especially in the (08) _____.

■ He became involved in (09) _____ and joined the (10) _____.

■ He was a (11) _____ in the Illinois State Senate, where he worked on (12) _____ (13) _____ such as (14) _____ and the (15) _____ .

■ He was elected to the US Senate with the largest number of (16) _____ in the history of the state of Illinois, and became (17) _____ of the Democratic Party.

■ As a US Senator he worked on issues such as (18) _____ and (19) _____ .

■ He ran for president, beating the other candidate for the (20) _____ .

■ His (21) _____ used the internet to get support.

■ He (22) _____ John McCain and won the presidency.

■ He made his (23) _____ , Hilary Clinton, Secretary of State.

你還可以學更多

a) 請利用網路查詢下列關鍵字，以了解更多關於 Obama 的資訊：

⊘ Some pictures of President Obama as a child

⊘ Some pictures of the First Family

⊘ The White House

⊘ Michelle Obama

⊘ The Democratic Party

⊘ Hillary Rodham Clinton

b) 請試著用英文討論下列話題：

1. 你想不想認識巴拉克‧歐巴馬？為什麼？
2. 你覺得在混血家庭中長大會是什麼情況？
3. 你會投希拉蕊還是歐巴馬一票？
4. 美國的政治制度跟台灣有哪些不一樣？
5. 假如你是一國之君，你會做哪些事？

解 答

閱讀理解

High school and college	❷
Illinois State Senator	❸
His childhood and family	❶
US Senator	❹
President Obama	❻
2008 presidential campaign	❺

重要詞彙

African American community	非裔美籍社區
beat (someone in a race)	（在競賽中）打敗（某人）
bipartisan	兩黨的
campaign	競選活動
civil right	民權
community officer	社區幹事
death penalty	死刑
Democratic Party	民主黨
disadvantaged	弱勢的
exchange student	交換學生
former rival	先前的對手
international relation	國際關係

issue	議題
journal	刊物
legislator	議員
local politics	地方政治
mixed race family	混血家庭
nomination	提名
political science	政治學
run for president	參選總統
the rising star	明日之星
government transparency	政府施政透明度
vote	選票
voting reform	選制改革
weapons control	武器管制

 填 空

(01) mixed race family   (02) exchange student   (03) political science

(04) international relations   (05) journal   (06) community officer

(07) disadvantaged   (08) African American community

(09) local politics   (10) Democratic Party   (11) legislator

(12) bipartisan   (13) issues   (14) voting reform

(15) death penalty   (16) votes   (17) the rising star

(18) weapons controls   (19) government transparency

(20) nomination   (21) campaign   (22) beat

(23) former rival

Part 2

才情豐沛的音樂家

Jessye Norman

Mozart

Beethoven

Kyung-Wha Chung

Wolfgang Amadeus Mozart
沃夫岡‧阿瑪迪斯‧莫札特

人物速覽

- 作曲家、音樂家
- 1756 年生於奧地利薩爾斯堡
  （Salzburg, Austria），1791 年卒於
  奧地利維也納（Vienna, Austria）
- 從小即展現過人的音樂天賦，被喻為
  神童

❶ Wolfgang Amadeus Mozart was born in Salzburg[1] into a musical family. His father was a professional musician and composer employed[2] by the Archbishop[3] of Salzburg, who was the ruler of the town. Mozart had an older sister called Nannerl. When she was seven years old, their father started to teach her the piano. Mozart, who was three years old at the time, watched curiously and began to practice on his own. He showed great talent, and his father started to teach him as well. Soon, the child Mozart was writing small compositions and showing them to his father. They were so good that his father decided to stop composing and focus on teaching his son.

❷ During the next few years, Mozart and his father and sister traveled widely all over Europe, performing as child prodigies[4] for princes, kings and archbishops. They went to England, Italy, France and Germany. Wherever he went, Mozart impressed people with his great talent for musical performance and composition. He wrote his first opera at the age of fourteen. During these journeys he met many famous musicians and became very famous himself. All of Europe was talking of the wonderful child prodigy.

❸ During the next few years, Mozart tried to find a regular job. This was difficult as there were few positions available for composers and

Ⓦ Ⓞ Ⓡ Ⓓ Ⓛ Ⓘ Ⓢ Ⓣ

1. Salzburg [ˋsɔlzˌbɝg] *n.* 薩爾斯堡（奧國西部的城市）
2. employ [ɪmˋplɔɪ] *v.* 雇用
3. archbishop [ˋɑrtʃˋbɪʃəp] *n.* 總主教；大主教
4. prodigy [ˋprɑdədʒɪ] *n.* 天才

musicians. He got his first job in Salzburg, but was not happy there as the payment was very low, and the Archbishop did not like operas. Mozart wanted to compose operas. He traveled widely around Europe again, this time with his mother, looking for a better job. They were poor, and the little money he made from his concerts had to be spent on traveling expenses. While they were in Paris, his mother fell seriously ill and then suddenly died.

❹ In 1782, Mozart quarreled with his employer and decided to leave Salzburg. He went to Vienna[5] and worked as a freelance[6] musician. He quickly became very popular and famous composing operas and other pieces.[7] He married the daughter of a musician, Constanze, and they had seven children together, only two of whom survived into adulthood.[8] During this period, Mozart worked hard on his music, and made lots of money playing his pieces.

❺ Towards the end of the 1780s, Mozart started to have financial difficulties. He traveled around Europe again looking for a better job but was not able to find one. His music was still very popular with the public in Vienna. In 1878 he composed one of his most famous pieces, called *Eine kleine Nachtmusik*, and it was a big hit.

Ⓦ Ⓞ Ⓡ Ⓓ Ⓛ Ⓘ Ⓢ Ⓣ

5. Vienna [vɪˋɛnə] *n.* 維也納
6. freelance [ˋfriˋlæns] *adj.* 不受雇於人的
★ 7. piece [pis] *n.* 一首；一曲
8. adulthood [əˋdʌlthʊd] *n.* 成年（時期）
9. unmarked [ʌnˋmɑrkt] *adj.* 無記號的；不被注意的

❻ Mozart fell ill in December of 1791, and as there was no money to pay for doctors and medicine, his illness quickly became serious. His wife did her best to look after him, and his friends helped him to continue composing from his bed. He wrote his best works during his last year when he was very ill. He died at the age of 35 and was buried in an unmarked[9] grave with no funeral as there was no money to pay for one.

譯文

❶ 沃夫岡‧阿瑪迪斯‧莫札特出身於薩爾斯堡的一個音樂家庭。父親是職業的音樂家暨作曲家，受雇於薩爾斯堡的大主教，也就是該鎮的首長。莫札特有一個姊姊叫做南妮兒，在她七歲的時候，父親開始教她彈鋼琴。當時三歲的莫札特好奇地看著，自己也開始練習。他展現過人的天賦，於是父親也開始教他。不久之後，年幼的莫札特開始寫小型樂曲，並拿給父親看。它們寫得相當棒，於是他父親決定停止作曲，以專心教兒子。

❷ 在接下來的幾年，莫札特和他的父親及姊姊跑遍了歐洲各地，並以神童的身分為王子、國王與大主教等人表演。他們去了英國、義大利、法國和德國。無論去到哪裡，莫札特在音樂演奏與作曲方面的過人天賦都令人驚豔。他在十四歲時，寫了他的第一齣歌劇。在這些旅程中，他認識了許多著名的音樂家，自己也變得非常有名。全歐洲都在談論這位了不起的神童。

❸ 接下來幾年，莫札特試圖找一份固定的工作。這很困難，因為作曲家和音樂家的職缺少之又少。他在薩爾斯堡找到了他的第一份工作，但並不滿意，因為薪資非常低，而且大主教不喜歡歌劇。莫札特想寫的就是歌劇。他再次跑遍歐洲，這次是由他的母親陪同，以尋找更好的工作。他們很窮，他靠演奏會所賺得的小錢都得當成差旅費。當他們到了巴黎，他母親生了重病，接著突然過世。

❹ 1782年，莫札特跟老闆起了爭執，於是決定離開薩爾斯堡。他來到維也納，並擔任自由音樂家。他很快就因為寫歌劇和其他作品而變得大受歡迎、也獲得了名氣。他娶了音樂家康斯坦茨的女兒，他們共生了七個小孩，其中只有兩個活到長大成人。在這段期間，莫札特努力創作音樂，並靠演奏他的作品賺了不少錢。

❺ 1780年代接近尾聲時，莫札特開始出現財務困難。他再次跑遍歐洲，以尋找更好的工作，但卻沒能找到。他的音樂還是大受維也納民眾的歡迎。 1787年時，他寫下他最為人知的作品之一，名為〈小夜曲〉，並且大獲成功。

❻ 莫札特在1791年12月生了病，因為沒有錢就醫和吃藥，他的病情很快加劇。他太太盡了全力照顧他，他的朋友也幫助他在病榻上繼續作曲。在人生的最後一年，他病得很重，但寫出了他畢生最棒的作品。他在35歲辭世，葬在一個不起眼的墓裡，並因為付不起錢而沒有舉行葬禮。

閱讀理解

配合題，請判斷下列摘要各屬於文章的哪個段落，見範例。

Looking for a job	❸
Death	
Early life and family	
Vienna years	
Child prodigies	
Last years	

 重要詞彙

連連看，請為每個詞彙找出它的正確翻譯。

child prodigy •	• 成人時期
adulthood •	• 大主教
archbishop •	• 可獲得的
be employed by •	• 大熱門
big hit •	• 埋葬
bury •	• 神童
fall seriously ill •	• 作曲家
composer •	• 樂曲
composition •	• 演奏會
concert •	• 指揮
available •	• 受雇於
conduct •	• 老闆
employer •	• 生重病

▨ musical performance	•	•	財務困難
▨ financial difficulty	•	•	專心於
▨ freelance musician	•	•	自由音樂家
▨ opera	•	•	葬禮
▨ piano	•	•	音樂演奏
▨ funeral	•	•	歌劇
▨ piece	•	•	鋼琴
▨ survive	•	•	作品（一曲）
▨ professional musician	•	•	職位
▨ focus on	•	•	職業音樂家
▨ position	•	•	與⋯⋯起爭執
▨ quarrel with	•	•	固定工作
▨ regular job	•	•	存活
▨ talent	•	•	天賦
▨ unmarked grave	•	•	差旅費
▨ traveling expense	•	•	不起眼的墓

填 空

理解文章大意後，請用前項習題中的詞彙來完成句子，有些字須做適當變化。

▨ Mozart's father was a (01)＿＿＿＿＿ and (02)＿＿＿＿＿

(03)＿＿＿＿＿ by the (04)＿＿＿＿＿ of Salzburg.

▨ Mozart started playing the (05)＿＿＿＿＿ at the age of three and showed great (06)＿＿＿＿＿.

▨ After seeing his son's (07)＿＿＿＿＿, Mozart's father decided to

(08)＿＿＿＿＿ his son's musical education.

■ The Mozart family traveled around Europe performing as

(09) _____ .

■ Mozart played all kinds of (10) _____ , but he really wanted to write (11) _____ .

■ It was difficult for Mozart to find a (12) _____ , as there were no (13) _____ for musicians.

■ Because there were no jobs (14) _____ , Mozart traveled around Europe again, giving (15) _____ .

■ Although he made some money, he had to save it for (16) _____ .

■ His mother (17) _____ and then died.

■ Mozart (18) _____ with his (19) _____ , the Archbishop of Salzburg, and went to Vienna to become a (20) _____ , composing and performing his own (21) _____ .

■ He and his wife had seven children, but only two of them (22) _____ into (23) _____ .

■ One of his pieces was called *Eine kleine Nachtmusik* and it was a (24) _____ .

■ Mozart was buried in an (25) _____ and there was no (26) _____ .

你還可以學更多

a) 請利用網路查詢下列關鍵字，以了解更多關於 **Mozart** 的資訊：

- ✓ A picture of Mozart as a child
- ✓ Some pictures of Mozart as a man
- ✓ A picture of the Archbishop's palace in Salzburg
- ✓ *Eine kleine Nachtmusik*
- ✓ Mozart's father
- ✓ Mozart's wife

b) 請試著用英文討論下列話題：

1. 你想不想認識莫札特？為什麼？
2. 你覺得莫札特為什麼找不到工作？
3. 你喜不喜歡古典樂？為什麼？
4. 你想不想去歐洲旅遊？為什麼？
5. 你有沒有聽過莫札特的音樂？你會怎麼形容它？

解 答

 閱讀理解

Looking for a job	**3**
Death	**6**
Early life and family	**1**
Vienna years	**4**
Child prodigies	**2**
Last years	**5**

重要詞彙

adulthood	成人時期
archbishop	大主教
available	可獲得的
big hit	大熱門
bury	埋葬
child prodigy	神童
composer	作曲家
composition	樂曲
concert	演奏會
conduct	指揮
be employed by	受雇於
employer	老闆
fall seriously ill	生重病

financial difficulty	財務困難
focus on	專心於
freelance musician	自由音樂家
funeral	葬禮
musical performance	音樂演奏
opera	歌劇
piano	鋼琴
piece	作品（一曲）
position	職位
professional musician	職業音樂家
quarrel with	與……起爭執
regular job	固定工作
survive	存活
talent	天賦
traveling expense	差旅費
unmarked grave	不起眼的墓

 填 空

(01) professional musician

(02) composer

(03) employed

(04) Archbishop

(05) piano

(06) talent

(07) compositions

(08) focus on

(09) child prodigies

(10) musical performances

(11) operas

(12) regular job

(13) positions

(14) available

(15) concerts

(16) traveling expenses

(17) fell seriously ill

(18) quarreled

(19) employer

(20) freelance musician

(21) pieces

(22) survived

(23) adulthood

(24) big hit

(25) unmarked grave

(26) funeral

Unit 6

Ludwig van Beethoven
路德維希·凡·貝多芬

人物速覽

- 作曲家、音樂家、鋼琴家
- 1770 年生於德國波昂（Bonn, Germany），1827 年卒於奧地利維也納（Vienna, Austria）

❶ **Ludwig van Beethoven** was born in the town of Bonn[1] into a musical family. His father was a professional musician employed by the Elector of Bonn, the ruler of the town. Beethoven showed his talent from an early age, and his father, who was also his teacher, tried to exploit[2] his talent. His father, remembering Mozart's great success as a child prodigy, tried to promote Beethoven as a child prodigy. He lied about Beethoven's age at his son's first public concert.

❷ While he was a student, Beethoven traveled to Vienna to ask Mozart to become his teacher. No one knows if they actually met, but Beethoven was familiar with Mozart's music. While he was in Vienna, his mother died, and Beethoven had to return to Bonn to look after his younger brothers and his father, who was now an alcoholic[3] and violent man. Beethoven was a very good student and worked hard on his studies. His teachers thought he would become the new Mozart. One of his teachers was a famous composer called Haydn, who had been a friend of Mozart's.

❸ When Beethoven finished his studies, he moved to Vienna and tried to become a freelance musician. He focused on giving piano concerts and was very well known as a pianist. He started publishing his compositions around this time. He also traveled around Germany and became very famous. He even wrote some music for the king to play on his cello,[4] and

---

Ⓦ Ⓞ Ⓡ Ⓓ Ⓛ Ⓘ Ⓢ Ⓣ

1. Bonn [bɑn] *n.* 波昂（西德首都）
★ 2. exploit [ɪkˋsplɔɪt] *v.* 開發；開拓
★ 3. alcoholic [ˏælkəˋhɔlɪk] *adj.* 嗜酒如命的；有酒癮的
4. cello [ˋtʃɛlo] *n.* 大提琴

the king paid him with a boxful[5] of gold coins. His brother was his business manager, and helped him to make a good living by publishing and promoting his music.

❹ In 1796 Beethoven noticed that he was slowly going deaf and that he was suffering from tinnitus,[6] which is a kind of constant ringing noise in one's ears. This was terrible news for a musician, and he kept it secret from everyone around him for as long as he could. Even though he was losing his hearing, Beethoven swore to dedicate his life to his music. Eventually he became completely deaf. He still continued to compose, but had to stop playing music in public as he could not hear the other musicians.

❺ His most famous symphony,[7] his *Ninth*, was performed in 1824, and Beethoven himself conducted the orchestra[8] — without being able to hear it. At the end of the concert, it was said that someone had to turn him around so he could see the audience applauding[9] since he could not hear them.

❻ His last years were very unhappy. He became depressed and alcoholic, and had very little money. In addition to his deafness, he also had trouble with his stomach and was often in great pain. However, he

---

Ⓦ Ⓞ Ⓡ Ⓓ Ⓛ Ⓘ Ⓢ Ⓣ

5. boxful [`bɑks,fʊl] *n.* 一箱（之量）
6. tinnitus [tɪ`naɪtəs] *n.* 耳鳴
7. symphony [`sɪmfənɪ] *n.* 交響樂（曲）
★ 8. orchestra [`ɔrkɪstrə] *n.* 管弦樂團
★ 9. applaud [ə`plɔd] *v.* 鼓掌

had good friends who helped and supported him. He never gave up his dedication to his music, even though his music became more difficult and modern, and people did not want to hear it. He died in the middle of a thunderstorm. 20,000 people came to his funeral.

譯文

❶ 路德維希・凡・貝多芬出身於波昂鎮上的一個音樂家庭。父親是職業的音樂家暨作曲家，受雇於波昂的選侯，也就是該鎮的首長。貝多芬自小就展現他的天賦。他父親，也是他的老師，試圖開發他的天賦。念念不忘莫札特在神童時期的過人成就，他父親試圖把貝多芬包裝宣傳成神童。在他兒子的首場公開演奏會中，他謊報了貝多芬的年齡。

❷ 在學生時期，貝多芬跑到維也納請莫札特當他的老師。沒有人知道他們到底認不認識，但貝多芬對莫札特的音樂非常熟悉。他在維也納時，母親過世了，所以貝多芬必須回波昂照顧他的弟弟與父親。此時他父親是個酗酒又暴力的人。貝多芬是個非常優秀的學生，也很用功讀書。他的老師都認為他會成為新的莫札特。他有個老師是著名的作曲家，名叫海頓，是莫札特的朋友。

❸ 貝多芬完成學業後，他搬到了維也納，並嘗試成為自由音樂家。他專心舉行鋼琴演奏會，並成了非常知名的鋼琴家。大約在此期間，他開始發表他所作的曲子。他還跑遍了德國，並且變得非常有名。他甚至作了一些音樂讓國王用他的大提琴來演奏，而國王則賞了他一箱金幣。他弟弟是他的業務經理，靠著發表和推銷他的音樂幫助他過著不錯的日子。

❹ 1796年，貝多芬注意到他正慢慢喪失聽力，並受耳鳴所苦，也就是耳朵裡有一種持續的響聲。對音樂家來說，這是個可怕的消息。所以他對身邊的每個人都保密，能瞞多久就瞞多久。即使正在喪失聽力，貝多芬仍誓言要為他的

音樂投注畢生之力。最後，他變得全聾。他還是繼續作曲，但不得不停止公開演奏音樂，因為他聽不到其他音樂家的演奏。

❺ 他最有名的交響曲〈第九號交響曲〉在 1824 年演奏，貝多芬在聽不到的情況下，親自指揮管弦樂隊。在演奏會結束時，據說必須有人把他轉過身去，他才能看到鼓掌的觀眾，因為他聽不到掌聲。

❻ 他的晚年非常不快樂。他變得憂鬱又酗酒，而且積蓄少得可憐。除了耳聾外，他的胃也有毛病，常常痛得厲害。不過，他有好朋友來幫忙與資助他。儘管他的音樂變得比較難懂與現代，大家不想聽了，他也從來沒有放棄對音樂的付出。他在一場大雷雨當中過世，有兩萬人來參加他的葬禮。

閱讀理解

配合題，請判斷下列摘要各屬於文章的哪個段落，見範例。

His deafness	❹
Last years and death	
Success and fame	
Student years	
The Ninth Symphony	
Early life and family	

重要詞彙

連連看，請為每個詞彙找出它的正確翻譯。

▨ eventually	•	• 酗酒的
▨ audience	•	• 鼓掌
▨ applaud	•	• 觀眾
▨ cello	•	• 業務經理
▨ dedicate	•	• 大提琴
▨ alcoholic	•	• 持續的響聲
▨ depressed	•	• 付出
▨ exploit	•	• 憂鬱的
▨ be familiar with	•	• 最後
▨ constant ringing noise	•	• 開發
▨ give up	•	• 熟悉
▨ go deaf	•	• 放棄
▨ business manager	•	• 變聾

■ make a good living	•	•	金幣
■ in great pain	•	•	痛得厲害
■ gold coin	•	•	對……保密
■ keep it secret from	•	•	喪失他的聽力
■ lose his hearing	•	•	過著不錯的日子
■ modern	•	•	現代的
■ orchestra	•	•	管弦樂隊
■ publish	•	•	推銷
■ suffer from	•	•	發表
■ promote	•	•	受到……所苦
■ support	•	•	資助
■ swear to	•	•	誓言要……
■ violent	•	•	交響曲
■ symphony	•	•	可怕的消息
■ turn him around	•	•	大雷雨
■ terrible news	•	•	耳鳴
■ thunderstorm	•	•	把他轉過身
■ tinnitus	•	•	暴力的

 填 空

理解文章大意後，請用前項習題中的詞彙來完成句子，有些字須做適當變化。

■ Beethoven's father tried to **(01)**_____ his talent by

　　(02)_____ his son as a child prodigy. He was an

　　(03)_____ and a **(04)**_____ man.

■ The young Beethoven was **(05)**_____ Mozart's music.

■ He wrote some (06)_____ music for the king and the king paid him in (07)_____.

■ His brother was his (08)_____, helping him to (09)_____ and promote his music and (10)_____.

■ He noticed that he was (11)_____ and that he was (12)_____ from (13)_____. Tinnitus is a (14)_____ in your ears.

■ This was (15)_____ news, but he (16)_____ all his friends.

■ When he knew he was (17)_____, he (18)_____ (19)_____ his life to his music.

■ (20)_____ he went completely deaf and could not hear anything at all.

■ He conducted the (21)_____ for his *Ninth* (22)_____. At the end, they had to (23)_____ so he could see the (24)_____ (25)_____.

■ In his last years he was (26)_____ and (27)_____ due to his stomach.

■ His friends (28)_____ him, and he never (29)_____ composing music. His music became more (30)_____.

■ He died in the middle of a (31)_____.

你還可以學更多

a) 請利用網路查詢下列關鍵字，以了解更多關於 **Beethoven** 的資訊：

- ✓ A picture of Beethoven
- ✓ A picture of the house where Beethoven was born
- ✓ A picture of Haydn, Beethoven's teacher
- ✓ *The Ninth Symphony*
- ✓ Beethoven's father
- ✓ A picture of Beethoven's house in Vienna

b) 請試著用英文討論下列話題：

1. 你想不想認識貝多芬？為什麼？
2. 你覺得貝多芬的父親為什麼試圖啓發他的兒子？
3. 你比較喜歡貝多芬還是莫札特的音樂？為什麼？
4. 你想不想去參觀波昂的貝多芬博物館？為什麼？
5. 假如你要學習演奏某樣樂器，你會選哪一樣？

解 答

閱讀理解

His deafness	❹
Last years and death	❻
Success and fame	❸
Student years	❷
The Ninth Symphony	❺
Early life and family	❶

重要詞彙

alcoholic	酗酒的
applaud	鼓掌
audience	觀眾
business manager	業務經理
cello	大提琴
constant ringing noise	持續的響聲
dedicate	付出
depressed	憂鬱的
eventually	最後
exploit	開發
be familiar with	熟悉
give up	放棄
go deaf	變聾

gold coin	金幣
in great pain	痛得厲害
keep it secret from	對……保密
lose his hearing	喪失他的聽力
make a good living	過著不錯的日子
modern	現代的
orchestra	管弦樂隊
promote	推銷
publish	發表
suffer from	受到……所苦
support	資助
swear to	誓言要……
symphony	交響曲
terrible news	可怕的消息
thunderstorm	大雷雨
tinnitus	耳鳴
turn him around	把他轉過身
violent	暴力的

 填 空

(01) exploit

(02) promoting

(03) alcoholic

(04) violent

(05) familiar with

(06) cello

(07) gold coins

(08) business manager

(09) publish

(10) make a good living

(11) going deaf

(12) suffering

(13) tinnitus

(14) constant ringing noise

(15) terrible

(16) kept it secret from

(17) losing his hearing

(18) swore to

(19) dedicate

(20) Eventually

(21) orchestra

(22) *Symphony*

(23) turn him around

(24) audience

(25) applauding

(26) depressed

(27) in great pain

(28) supported

(29) gave up

(30) modern

(31) thunderstorm

Jessye Norman
潔西·諾曼

人物速覽

- 音樂家、歌劇演員
- 1945 年生於美國喬治亞州
  （Georgia, USA）
- 受邀在雷根和柯林頓總統的就職大典
  演唱
- 四度榮獲葛萊美獎

❶ Jessye Norman was born into a musical family. Her mother was an amateur[1] musician and she encouraged Jessye to start singing and learning piano when she was very young. From a young age she sang in church choirs.[2] At the age of nine, she heard opera for the first time and decided then and there[3] that she wanted to be an opera singer. At the age of 16, she entered a singing competition. She did not win it, but she was offered a scholarship[4] to study music by someone who heard her sing.

❷ After finishing her studies, Jessye went to Europe, where all young singers went to start their career. Her singing was so good and so unique that her first job was at the Deutsche Oper Berlin, one of the top opera houses in Germany. For the next seven years, she worked in all the major opera houses in Europe, singing all the major roles. She was especially in demand for her performances of queens, priestesses,[5] and other similarly noble[6] figures such as Aida, in the opera called *Aida* by Verdi. This was due to her great size and vocal range.

❸ From 1975 to 1980, Jessye did not perform in opera. Instead, she concentrated on her recording career, making recordings of many operas and lieder.[7] She also toured Europe giving song recitals[8] from her

---

Ⓦ Ⓞ Ⓡ Ⓓ Ⓛ Ⓘ Ⓢ Ⓣ

- ★ 1. amateur [ˈæməˌtʃʊr] *adj.* 業餘的
-   2. choir [kwaɪr] *n.* 唱詩班
-   3. then and there 【口語】當場；立即
- ★ 4. scholarship [ˈskɑləˌʃɪp] *n.* 獎學金
-   5. priestess [ˈpristɪs] *n.* 女祭司；女教士
- ★ 6. noble [ˈnobl̩] *adj.* 高貴的；貴族的
-   7. lieder [ˈlidə] *n.* 歌曲（lied 的複數型）
-   8. recital [rɪˈsaɪtl̩] *n.* 獨奏會；獨唱會

repertoire.[9] Her recordings won numerous[10] awards and she became very famous in Europe. In 1980 she returned to opera and made her North American opera debut.[11] She became one of the most popular classical singers of her time, and was invited to sing at the inaugurations[12] of Presidents Reagan and Clinton, a great honor. She was also invited to sing at the 60th birthday celebrations of Queen Elizabeth.

❹ Jessye Norman's voice has been described as being like liquid chocolate. She started her career as a dramatic[13] soprano,[14] which is the highest and strongest kind of voice for women. As she has become older, however, her voice has become lower, and she now sings mezzo[15] soprano roles, which are not so high. She can sing very slowly because she has very good breath control. She can also sing very loudly, even in works where she has to sing together with a big orchestra and choir. She is one of the most well-recognized classical musicians in the world, and one of the few African Americans in her profession.

❺ She has a very commanding[16] stage presence but is also well known for making jokes with the audience about her size. She likes to wear African style clothing and headscarves.[17] She is also famous for her

---

Ⓦ Ⓞ Ⓡ Ⓓ Ⓛ Ⓘ Ⓢ Ⓣ

9. repertoire [ˈrɛpɚˌtwɑr] *n.* 演唱目錄；全套作品
10. numerous [ˈnjumərəs] *adj.* 許多的
11. debut [dɪˋbju] *n.* 首次登台表演
12. inauguration [ɪnˌɔgjɚˋreʃən] *n.* 就職；就職典禮
13. dramatic [drəˋmætɪk] *adj.* 戲劇的
14. soprano [səˋpræno] *n.* 女高音
15. mezzo [ˈmɛdzo] *n.* 女中音

technical understanding of music and her great knowledge and scholarship.[18]

❻ In addition to her singing and performing career, Jessye Norman has been involved in numerous charitable[19] causes, including AIDS awareness, lupus,[20] homelessness, and charities[21] for African Americans.

譯文

❶ 潔西・諾曼出身於一個音樂家庭。母親是業餘音樂家，並且在她非常年輕的時候，就鼓勵潔西開始唱歌及學鋼琴。自小以來，她就在教會的唱詩班裡唱歌。9 歲時，她第一次聽到歌劇，當下就決定她要成為歌劇演員。16 歲時，她參加了歌唱比賽。她並沒有獲勝，但有個聽到她唱歌的人給了她獎學金去念音樂。

❷ 完成學業後，潔西去了歐洲，所有的年輕學生都是在那裡展開他們的生涯。她的歌唱得非常出色與獨特，所以在柏林德意志歌劇院找到了她的第一份工作，這是德國的一家頂尖歌劇院。在接下來的七年，她在歐洲各大歌劇院工作，並唱遍了各大角色。她最受歡迎的是飾演女王、女祭司和其他類似的權貴角色，像是威爾第名為《阿依達》這齣歌劇裡的阿依達。這是因為她的體型較大和音域寬廣。

16. commanding [kə`mændɪŋ] *adj.* 有威嚴的
17. headscarf [`hɛd͵skɑrf] *n.* 頭巾
18. scholarship [`skɑlə͵ʃɪp] *n.*（尤指人文科學的）學問；學識
19. charitable [`tʃærətəbḷ] *adj.* 慈善的
20. lupus [`lupəs] *n.* 狼瘡
21. charity [`tʃærətɪ] *n.* 慈善（的行為）

❸ 從1975年到1980年，潔西並沒有在歌劇中演出。取而代之，她全力投入了她的錄製生涯，錄製了許多歌劇和藝術歌曲。她還巡迴歐洲，並針對她的全套作品舉行歌曲獨唱會。她錄製的作品贏得了無數獎項，她在歐洲也享有盛名。1980年，她回到歌劇界，並在北美的歌劇中首度登台。她成了當時最受歡迎的古典歌手之一，並受邀在雷根和柯林頓總統的就職大典上演唱，可說是很大的榮耀。她也受邀在伊莉莎白女王六十大壽的慶典上演唱。

❹ 潔西·諾曼的聲音被形容為有如流動的巧克力。她的生涯一開始是擔任戲劇的女高音，也就是那種最高最強的女聲。但隨著年歲漸長，她的聲音變得比較低，現在她唱的都是沒那麼高的女中音角色。她可以唱得很緩，因為她的呼吸控制得非常好。她也可以唱得非常宏量，即使在跟大型交響樂隊及合唱團一起演唱的作品中也不例外。她是世界上最受推崇的古典音樂家之一，以及所屬行業中少數的非裔美國人。

❺ 她的舞台表現非常霸氣，同樣眾所皆知的是，她會拿自己的體型來跟觀眾開玩笑。她喜歡穿戴非洲式的服裝與方頭巾，而同樣出名的是她對於音樂的技術理解，以及她廣博的知識與學問。

❻ 除了歌唱與表演生涯外，潔西·諾曼還參與了許多慈善事業，包括愛滋病的宣導、狼瘡、無家可歸，以及對非裔美國人的救濟。

閱讀理解

配合題，請判斷下列摘要各屬於文章的哪個段落，見範例。

Middle years and fame	❸
Her charity work	
Her voice	
Her family and childhood	
Her performing presence	
Early years in Europe	

重要詞彙

連連看，請為每個詞彙找出它的正確翻譯。

▦ charity cause　　　　　　　　　•　　　　　　　• 獎學金

▦ in demand for　　　　　　　　　•　　　　　　　• 業餘音樂家

▦ lied　　　　　　　　　　　　　•　　　　　　　• 呼吸控制

▦ amateur musician　　　　　　　•　　　　　　　• 慈善活動

▦ breath control　　　　　　　　•　　　　　　　• 教會唱詩班

▦ church choir　　　　　　　　　•　　　　　　　• 古典的

▦ classical　　　　　　　　　　　•　　　　　　　• 霸氣的舞台表現

▦ commanding stage presence　•　　　　　　　• 戲劇女高音

▦ dramatic soprano　　　　　　　•　　　　　　　• 鼓勵

▦ headscarf　　　　　　　　　　•　　　　　　　• 方頭巾

▦ encourage　　　　　　　　　　•　　　　　　　• 有……的需要

▦ scholarship（可數名詞）　　　•　　　　　　　• 就職大典

▦ inauguration　　　　　　　　　•　　　　　　　• 藝術歌曲

▦ vocal range	•	• 液態巧克力
▦ major	•	• 主要的
▦ make a debut	•	• 首度登台
▦ technical understanding	•	• 女中音
▦ noble figure	•	• 權貴角色
▦ priestess	•	• 女祭司
▦ repertoire	•	• 獨唱會
▦ liquid chocolate	•	• 錄製生涯
▦ recital	•	• 全套作品；演唱目錄
▦ recording career	•	• 角色
▦ role	•	• 學問
▦ top opera house	•	• 歌唱比賽
▦ scholarship（不可數名詞）	•	• 技術理解
▦ singing competition	•	• 當場
▦ then and there	•	• 頂尖歌劇院
▦ tour	•	• 巡迴
▦ mezzo soprano	•	• 獨特的
▦ unique	•	• 音域

 填 空

理解文章大意後，請用前項習題中的詞彙來完成句子，有些字須做適當變化。

▦ Jessye's mother was an **(01)**＿＿＿＿＿＿ who encouraged her
daughter to sing in **(02)**＿＿＿＿＿＿.

▦ When she heard opera for the first time she decided **(03)**＿＿＿＿＿＿
to become an opera singer.

- Although she did not win the (04)_____ she was awarded a (05)_____ to study music.

- Her voice is (06)_____ and she has performed in all the (07)_____ in the world, in all the (08)_____ operatic (09)_____.

- She is in (10)_____ her performances of (11)_____ and (12)_____ because of her great (13)_____ range.

- In addition to performing opera, she also has a very successful (14)_____ and a very big (15)_____.

- She recorded (16)_____ and (17)_____ all over world performing lieder (18)_____.

- She made her North American (19)_____ in 1980.

- She is one of the most famous (20)_____ musicians in the world today.

- She sang at two presidential (21)_____.

- At the beginning of her career her voice was a (22)_____, but as she got older, she started to sing (23)_____.

- Her voice is like (24)_____, and she has very amazing (25)_____ control, and a very (26)_____, which makes her performances very exciting.

■ In addition to her great voice, she has great **(27)**＿＿＿＿＿＿ of the music.

■ She likes to wear **(28)**＿＿＿＿＿＿ and is involved in many **(29)**＿＿＿＿＿＿, helping other people.

 你還可以學更多

a) 請利用網路查詢下列關鍵字，以了解更多關於 **Jessye Norman** 的資訊：

> ✓ A picture of Jessye Norman
> ✓ A picture of her performing opera
> ✓ The opera called *Aida* by Verdi
> ✓ The Berlin opera house Deutsche Oper Berlin
> ✓ Lupus
> ✓ A video or audio recording of Jessye singing

b) 請試著用英文討論下列話題：

> 1. 你想不想認識潔西‧諾曼？為什麼？
> 2. 你覺得她為什麼喜歡穿非洲式的服裝？
> 3. 你喜不喜歡潔西的聲音？為什麼？
> 4. 你比較喜歡爵士歌曲、流行歌曲，還是古典歌曲？為什麼？
> 5. 你想不想去看歌劇表演？為什麼？

解 答

閱讀理解

Middle years and fame	❸
Her charity work	❻
Her voice	❹
Her family and childhood	❶
Her performing presence	❺
Early years in Europe	❷

 重要詞彙

scholarship（可數名詞）	獎學金
amateur musician	業餘音樂家
breath control	呼吸控制
charity cause	慈善活動
church choir	教會唱詩班
classical	古典的
commanding stage presence	霸氣的舞台表現
dramatic soprano	戲劇女高音
encourage	鼓勵
headscarf	方頭巾
in demand for	有……的需要
inauguration	就職大典
lied	藝術歌曲

liquid chocolate	液態巧克力
major	主要的
make a debut	首度登台
mezzo soprano	女中音
noble figure	權貴角色
priestess	女祭司
recital	獨唱會
recording career	錄製生涯
repertoire	全套作品；演唱目錄
role	角色
scholarship（不可數名詞）	學問
singing competition	歌唱比賽
technical understanding	技術理解
then and there	當場
top opera house	頂尖歌劇院
tour	巡迴
unique	獨特的
vocal range	音域

 填 空

(01) amateur musician

(02) church choirs

(03) then and there

(04) competition

(05) scholarship

(06) unique

(07) top opera houses

(08) major

(09) roles

(10) demand for

(11) priestesses

(12) noble figures

(13) vocal

(14) recording career

(15) repertoire

(16) lieder

(17) toured

(18) recitals

(19) debut

(20) classical

(21) inaugurations

(22) dramatic soprano

(23) mezzo soprano

(24) liquid chocolate

(25) breath

(26) commanding stage presence

(27) technical understanding

(28) headscarves

(29) charity causes

Unit 8

Kyung-Wha Chung
鄭京和

人物速覽

- 小提琴家、音樂家
- 1948 年生於南韓首爾
  （Seoul, South Korea）
- 曾獲留聲機大獎
  （Gramophone Award）

❶ Kyung-Wha Chung's mother was an amateur musician and she encouraged Kyung-Wha to start learning piano when she was very young. Kyung-Wha did not enjoy the piano and would often fall asleep during her lessons, but she was fascinated[1] by the violin when she first came across[2] it at seven years old. She began learning the instrument immediately, and by the age of nine had made such great progress with it that she was able to perform Mendelssohn's[3] *Violin Concerto*[4] with the Seoul[5] Philharmonic[6] Orchestra, the top orchestra in Korea.

❷ She became known as an astonishing[7] child prodigy together with her brothers and sisters, who were also very talented musicians. They toured Korea playing Western music together in the days when there were very few Asian musicians performing Western music. With her siblings,[8] and also on her own, Kyung-Wha won most of the Korean music competitions. However, their mother realized that opportunities for classical musicians in Korea were rare, and the family immigrated to America.

❸ Kyung-Wha wanted to study at Juilliard, a famous music school in New

---

Ⓦ Ⓞ Ⓡ Ⓓ Ⓛ Ⓘ Ⓢ Ⓣ

★ 1. fascinate [ˋfæsn̩ˌet] *v.* 使……著迷；使……迷惑
  2. come across 遇到
  3. Mendelssohn [ˋmɛndl̩ˌson] *n.* （德國作曲家）孟德爾頌
  4. concerto [kənˋtʃɛrto] *n.* 協奏曲
  5. Seoul [sol] *n.* （韓國首都）漢城
  6. philharmonic [ˌfɪləˋmɑnɪk] *n.* 交響樂團
★ 7. astonishing [əˋstɑnɪʃɪŋ] *adj.* 令人驚訝的
  8. sibling [ˋsɪblɪŋ] *n.* 兄弟姊妹

York, but she was too young to attend. Nevertheless, she auditioned,[9] and won a place and a scholarship. She found studying at the Juilliard very difficult. She could not speak English, and she was one of the youngest students there. She worked extremely hard, practicing for many hours every day, and slowly her technique began to mature.

❹ In 1967 she entered the Leventritt Competition, one of the greatest competitions for violin in the world. Her teacher and fellow students were against this, because they thought she had no chance of winning. Another famous young violinist from Israel[10] was also competing, and everyone thought he would win it. Kyung-Wha's mother decided to help her. She sold their home in Korea and bought her daughter a Stradivarius[11] violin. This violin is very rare and expensive and was made in the 1680s.

❺ Kyung-Wha Chung and her rival[12] played so well in the competition that the judges could not decide who was better. They asked the two violinists[13] to play again, but they still could not decide. Finally, the judges announced Kyung-Wha and the other violinist the joint[14] winners, the first time this had happened in the history of the competition.

❻ Her career took off in spite of the fact that there was a lot of prejudice[15] in the Western classical music world against Asian musicians. However,

---

Ⓦ Ⓞ Ⓡ Ⓓ Ⓛ Ⓘ Ⓢ Ⓣ

9. audition [ɔˋdɪʃən] v. 面試；試演；試聽
10. Israel [ˋɪzrɪəl] n. 以色列
11. Stradivarius [ˌstrædəˋvɛrɪəs] n. 史特拉第瓦里（義大利人 Stradivari 製造的小提琴等弦樂器）

her playing always won the respect of those who heard it. She is now one of the best violinists in the world, and she has done much to increase the standing[16] of Asian performers of Western classical music.

譯文

❶ 鄭京和的母親是業餘音樂家，在她非常年輕的時候，就鼓勵鄭京和開始學鋼琴。京和並不喜歡彈鋼琴，所以經常在學琴時打瞌睡。可是在七歲第一次看到小提琴時，她就迷上了它。她立刻開始學這樣樂器，到九歲時就有長足的進步，並有辦法跟南韓頂尖的管弦樂團「首爾愛樂管弦樂團」一同演奏孟德爾頌的〈小提琴協奏曲〉。

❷ 她跟她的兄弟姊妹都成了知名的驚人神童，他們也都是極具天分的音樂家。他們巡迴韓國一起演奏西方音樂，而在當時，演奏西方音樂的亞洲音樂家是少之又少。和她的兄弟姊妹一起，也靠著她自己，京和贏得了韓國大部分的音樂比賽。不過，他們的母親明白，古典音樂家在韓國沒什麼機會，於是一家人移民到了美國。

❸ 京和想要讀茱莉亞，它是紐約一所著名的音樂學校，但她因為太年輕而上不了。不過她還是去面試，並贏得了一席之地與獎學金。她發現，在茱莉亞念書困難重重。她不會說英語，並且是校內最年輕的學生之一。她十分用功，每天練習好幾個小時，她的技術也慢慢開始成熟。

★ 12. rival [ˋraɪvl] *n.* 競爭對手
   13. violinist [ˌvaɪəˋlɪnɪst] *n.* 小提琴手
   14. joint [ˋdʒɔɪnt] *adj.* 共同的；共有的
   15. prejudice [ˋprɛdʒədɪs] *n.* 偏見；歧視
   16. standing [ˋstændɪŋ] *n.* 地位

❹ 1967年時，她參加了列文崔特大賽，這是世界上數一數二的大型小提琴競賽。她的老師和同學對此並不支持，因為他們認為她沒有獲勝的機會。另一位來自以色列的知名年輕小提琴家也有參加比賽，大家都認為他會獲勝。京和的母親決定助她一臂之力。她賣掉了在韓國的房子，並買了一把史特拉第瓦里小提琴給她女兒。這把小提琴非常稀有與昂貴，製造於 1680 年代。

❺ 鄭京和與她的對手在比賽中都拉得相當好，評審無法決定誰更勝一籌。他們要兩位小提琴家再拉一次，但他們還是決定不了。最後評審宣布，京和與另一位小提琴家共同獲獎，這也是競賽史上第一次發生這種情形。

❻ 她的生涯就此展開，儘管西方的古典樂界對於亞洲的音樂家抱持著許許多多的偏見。不過，她的演出總是能贏得聽眾的尊敬。如今她是世界上最優秀的小提琴家之一，她也做了很多來提升亞洲演奏家在西方古典樂界的地位。

閱讀理解

請把下列摘要搭配上它所描述的段落,見範例。

Childhood and early studies	❶
The Leventritt competition	
Student in USA	
Top violinist	
Child prodigies	
Stradivarius violin	

重要詞彙

連連看,請把每個詞彙搭配上它的正確翻譯。

- rare •
- astonishingly •
- career •
- concerto •
- prejudice against •
- announce •
- be fascinated by •
- immigrate •
- audition •
- mature •
- music competition •
- progress •
- judge •

- 驚人地
- 試演
- 生涯
- 協奏曲
- 宣布
- 被⋯⋯迷上
- 移民
- 評審
- 成熟
- 音樂比賽
- 對⋯⋯的偏見
- 進步
- 稀有的

■ rival •		• 尊敬
■ be against •		• 對手
■ standing •		• 地位
■ talented •		• 史特拉第瓦里
■ take off •		• 展開
■ respect •		• 有天分的
■ technique •		• 技術
■ Stradivarius •		• 反對

 填 空

理解文章大意後，請用前項習題中的詞彙來完成句子，有些字須做適當變化。

■ As a child, Kyung-Wha was **(01)**＿＿＿＿＿＿ the violin.

■ She made such good **(02)**＿＿＿＿＿＿ in her studies that she performed a famous violin **(03)**＿＿＿＿＿＿ with the top orchestra in Korea at the age of nine.

■ She was **(04)**＿＿＿＿＿＿ **(05)**＿＿＿＿＿＿: everyone was surprised by her talent.

■ She won many **(06)**＿＿＿＿＿＿, but opportunities for classical musicians in Korea were very **(07)**＿＿＿＿＿＿.

■ Her mother decided to **(08)**＿＿＿＿＿＿ with the family to the USA.

■ She **(09)**＿＿＿＿＿＿ for the Juilliard school of music.

■ She worked so hard that her **(10)**＿＿＿＿＿＿ **(11)**＿＿＿＿＿＿

very quickly.

- She wanted to enter the competition, but her family and teachers (12)_____ it.

- Her mother sold their home and bought Kyung-Wha a (13)_____ violin.

- Kyung-Wha and her (14)_____ both played so well that the (15)_____ (16)_____ they were both winners.

- Her career (17)_____, and she soon gained the (18)_____ of audiences.

- Kyung-Wha Chung is a violinist of world-class (19)_____.

你還可以學更多

(a) 請利用網路查詢下列關鍵字，以了解更多關於 **Kyung-Wha Chung** 的資訊：

- ✓ A picture of Kyung-Wha Chung as a child
- ✓ A picture of Kyung-Wha Chung as an adult
- ✓ Mendelssohn's *Violin Concerto*
- ✓ The Juilliard School
- ✓ Kyung-Wha Chung's siblings
- ✓ Stradivarius violins

(b) 請試著用英文討論下列話題：

1. 你想不想認識鄭京和？為什麼？

2. 你覺得鄭京和的母親為什麼會賣掉房子來買史特拉第瓦里？

3. 你比較喜歡小提琴還是鋼琴？為什麼？

4. 你想不想參加音樂比賽？為什麼？

5. 你覺得亞洲音樂家演奏西方音樂能不能演奏得跟西方音樂家一樣好？

解 答

  閱讀理解

Childhood and early studies	❶
The Leventritt competition	❺
Student in USA	❸
Top violinist	❻
Child prodigies	❷
Stradivarius violin	❹

  重要詞彙

astonishingly	驚人地
audition	試演
career	生涯
concerto	協奏曲
announce	宣布
be fascinated by	被……迷上
immigrate	移民
judge	評審
mature	成熟
music competition	音樂比賽
prejudice against	對……的偏見
progress	進步
rare	稀有的

respect	尊敬
rival	對手
standing	地位
Stradivarius	史特拉第瓦里
take off	展開
talented	有天分的
technique	技術
be against	反對

 填 空

(01) fascinated by

(02) progress

(03) concerto

(04) astonishingly

(05) talented

(06) music competitions

(07) rare

(08) immigrate

(09) auditioned

(10) technique

(11) matured

(12) were against

(13) Stradivarius

(14) rival

(15) judges

(16) announced

(17) took off

(18) respect

(19) standing

Part 3

天馬行空的文學家

Toni Morrison

Dickens

J. K. Rowling

Dostoevsky

Charles Dickens
查爾斯 · 狄更斯

人物速覽

- 1812 年生於英國樸茨茅斯（Portsmouth, England），1870 年卒於英國羅契斯特（Rochester, England）
- 記者及編輯
- 社會改革人士及社會運動人士
- 小說家

❶ **Charles Dickens** was the second child in his family, and the first son. His father was a clerk[1] for the Royal Navy, and was not very good with money. Although the first ten years of Charles's life were very happy, his father eventually lost his job and the family moved to London, where they gradually became poorer and poorer. To help his family, Charles worked in a shoe polish[2] factory sticking[3] labels on bottles. It was very hard work in terrible conditions and the pay was bad. When he was 12, his father was arrested for debt and put in prison. Charles's family joined his father there, but Charles had to live by himself and work to give his family money while they were in prison.

❷ When the family was released from prison, Charles's mother wanted him to continue working in the factory. However, his father insisted that Charles go to school. Charles wanted to go to school because he knew that education was important if he wanted to have a good life. When he left school, he taught himself to write shorthand,[4] a kind of code for writing quickly. This was very useful in his early career. He worked as a journalist[5] and a legal clerk, writing and recording court cases and Parliamentary[6] debates. He soon gained a reputation as a good reporter.

❸ In 1836 he published his first non-fiction[7] book, a book of articles,

---

(W)(O)(R)(D) (L)(I)(S)(T)

1. clerk [klɜk] *n.* （政府機關的）書記；辦事員
2. polish [ˈpɑlɪʃ] *n.* 亮光劑；鞋油
3. stick [stɪk] *v.* 黏
4. shorthand [ˈʃɔrtˌhænd] *n.* 速記
5. journalist [ˈdʒɜnlɪst] *n.* 報章雜誌記者；新聞工作者
6. parliamentary [ˌpɑrləˈmɛntərɪ] *adj.* 國會的；議會的
7. non-fiction [ˌnɑnˈfɪkʃən] *n.* 非小說類的文學作品

which was very successful. He followed this by his second book, a novel called *Pickwick Papers*. This book made Dickens, at the age of 25, a famous and wealthy writer. *Pickwick* was hugely popular all over England and even in America. Dickens worked hard, and wrote many books in his early years. His many famous fictional[8] characters include Scrooge and Oliver Twist. Dickens was also a newspaper editor, and continued his work as a journalist.

❹ Dickens married Catherine Hogarth in 1836. They had ten children together. During the 1840s Dickens went to America with his family, and traveled widely in Europe, writing about his experiences. He loved to act in plays and had many friends who were actors. He once wrote a play and performed it at his house. The queen attended the performance.

❺ In addition to writing his famous novels, Dickens was actively involved in trying to reform[9] society. He wrote about education, single women, health and public sanitation,[10] and his efforts did a lot to help raise public awareness. He was very generous with his time and money and helped many good causes, including hospitals and shelters for women.

❻ Towards the end of his life, Dickens gave public readings of his books. These were well-received and huge crowds attended them. However, they

Ⓦ Ⓞ Ⓡ Ⓓ Ⓛ Ⓘ Ⓢ Ⓣ

8. fictional [ˈfɪkʃənl̩] *adj.* 小說的；虛構的
★ 9. reform [rɪˈfɔrm] *v.* 改革；改善
10. sanitation [ˌsænəˈteʃən] *n.* 衛生；衛生設施
11. tiring [ˈtaɪrɪŋ] *adj.* 令人疲倦的；費力的
12. exhaustion [ɪgˈzɔstʃən] *n.* 耗盡；極度疲憊
13. stroke [strok] *n.* （中風等的）發作

were tiring[11] for Dickens, and he started to get ill from exhaustion.[12] He died of a stroke[13] one afternoon at the age of 58 and was buried at Westminster Abbey in London, the highest honor for an English person.

譯文

❶ 查爾斯‧狄更斯是家中的第二個小孩及長子。父親是皇家海軍的書記，對錢財不太靈光。雖然查爾斯人生中的頭十年非常快樂，但他父親最後丟了飯碗，一家人搬到了倫敦，並且變得愈來愈窮。為了幫助家裡，查爾斯到一家鞋油工廠上班，貼標籤在瓶子上。這是非常辛苦的工作，環境惡劣、工資又微薄。當他 12 歲時，父親因為債務而被捕入獄。查爾斯的家人跟著父親一同入獄，但在他們坐牢時，查爾斯卻必須獨自生活，工作養家。

❷ 當一家人從牢裡被釋放，查爾斯的母親要他繼續到工廠上班。不過，他父親卻堅持要查爾斯去上學。查爾斯想要去上學，因為他知道，假如他想要過好日子，受教育就很重要。當他離開學校後，他靠著自修學會了速記，這是一種速寫的代碼。這在他的早期生涯中非常有用。他當過記者和法律書記，書寫並記錄訴訟案件和國會辯論。他很快就贏得了好記者的美名。

❸ 1836 年，他出版了他的第一本非小說著作，是一本文集，而且非常成功。他接著又出了第二本書，是一本叫做《匹克威克外傳》的小說。這本書使 25 歲的狄更斯成了知名與富有的作家。《匹克威克外傳》在全英國、甚至是美國都大受歡迎。狄更斯很勤奮，在早年時期寫了不少書。他有許多著名的虛構人物，包括斯科魯奇（《小氣財神》）和奧立佛‧崔斯特（《孤雛淚》）。狄更斯也是個報紙編輯，並持續擔任記者的工作。

❹ 狄更斯在 1836 年娶了凱瑟琳‧霍格斯，他們共生了十個孩子。在 1840 年代，狄更斯跟家人去了美國，跑遍了歐洲，並寫下了他的體驗。他很愛在戲

劇中演出，而且有許多朋友都是演員。他曾經寫了一齣戲，在自家表演。女王也來看了演出。

❺ 除了撰寫他著名的小說外，狄更斯也在試圖改革社會方面積極參與。他寫過關於教育、單身女性、健康與公共衛生等，他的努力對於提升民眾意識貢獻良多。他在時間與金錢上都非常大方，並幫忙推動了許多善事，包括醫院和女性庇護所。

❻ 在生命接近終點時，狄更斯針對他的著作舉行了公眾朗讀會。這些朗讀會大受歡迎，群眾也蜂擁而至。不過，它們卻累壞了狄更斯，他開始因為過度疲勞而病倒。有一天下午，他死於中風，得年 58 歲，葬於倫敦的西敏寺大教堂，這對英國人來說是最高榮譽。

閱讀理解

配合題，請判斷下列摘要各屬於文章的哪個段落，見範例。

Married life	❹
Childhood and early life	
Last years and death	
Education and early career	
Social campaigner	
Fame and fortune	

 重要詞彙

連連看，請為每個詞彙找出它的正確翻譯。

▨ clerk	•	• 演出
▨ act	•	• 因……被捕
▨ be arrested for	•	• 角色
▨ journalist	•	• 書記
▨ code	•	• 代碼
▨ debt	•	• 訴訟案件
▨ exhaustion	•	• 債務
▨ good cause	•	• 極度疲累
▨ court case	•	• 善事
▨ character	•	• 榮譽
▨ honor	•	• 堅持
▨ insist	•	• 文章
▨ article	•	• 報章雜誌記者；新聞工作者

▨ legal clerk	•	• 標籤
▨ newspaper editor	•	• 法律書記
▨ stroke	•	• 報紙編輯
▨ novel	•	• 小說
▨ shoe polish factory	•	• 國會辯論
▨ label	•	• 戲劇
▨ play	•	• 公眾朗讀會
▨ public reading	•	• 公共衛生
▨ Parliamentary debate	•	• 出版
▨ publish	•	• 改革
▨ reform	•	• 記者
▨ reporter	•	• 皇家海軍
▨ Royal Navy	•	• 庇護所
▨ shelter	•	• 鞋油工廠
▨ shorthand	•	• 速記
▨ society	•	• 社會
▨ public sanitation	•	• 中風

填　空

理解文章大意後，請用前項習題中的詞彙來完成句子，有些字須做適當變化。

■ Charles Dickens's father was a (01)＿＿＿＿＿＿ for the

(02)＿＿＿＿＿＿ .

■ When Charles was a boy, he worked in a (03)＿＿＿＿＿＿ , sticking

(04)＿＿＿＿＿＿ on bottles of shoe polish.

■ His father was (05)＿＿＿＿＿＿ for (06)＿＿＿＿＿＿ and put in

prison.

108

His father (07)_____ that Charles go to school.

Charles taught himself to write (08)_____, which is like a (09)_____ for writing very quickly.

He got a job as a (10)_____, and as a (11)_____ writing reports on (12)_____ and (13)_____.

He had a very good reputation as a (14)_____.

At the age of 24 he (15)_____ his first (16)_____ book of (17)_____. It made him famous.

He worked as a newspaper editor and created many famous (18)_____ (19)_____ in his (20)_____.

He liked to (21)_____ and perform (22)_____ in his house.

He tried to (23)_____ society, especially things like (24)_____ and education.

He gave generously to (25)_____, and established a (26)_____ for women.

Towards the end of his life he gave (27)_____ of his works, which were very popular.

He suffered from (28)_____ and died of a (29)_____.

He is buried in Westminster Abbey, a great (30)_____ for an English person.

你還可以學更多

a) 請利用網路查詢下列關鍵字，以了解更多關於 **Charles Dickens** 的資訊：

> ✓ A picture of Charles Dickens
>
> ✓ A picture of Oliver Twist
>
> ✓ A picture of Mr. Pickwick
>
> ✓ A picture of Scrooge
>
> ✓ Westminster Abbey
>
> ✓ The names of some of Dickens's novels

b) 請試著用英文討論下列話題：

> 1. 你想不想認識查爾斯‧狄更斯？為什麼？
>
> 2. 你覺得狄更斯是如何看待他的童年？
>
> 3. 你喜不喜歡讀小說？為什麼？
>
> 4. 你有沒有興趣讀一些查爾斯‧狄更斯的中譯著作？為什麼？
>
> 5. 你能不能想到一個能與狄更斯匹敵的中文作家？

解 答

  閱讀理解

Married life	❹
Childhood and early life	❶
Last years and death	❻
Education and early career	❷
Social campaigner	❺
Fame and fortune	❸

  重要詞彙

act	演出
be arrested for	因……被捕
character	角色
clerk	書記
code	代碼
court case	訴訟案件
debt	債務
exhaustion	極度疲累
good cause	善事
honor	榮譽
insist	堅持
article	文章
journalist	報章雜誌記者；新聞工作者

label	標籤
legal clerk	法律書記
newspaper editor	報紙編輯
novel	小說
Parliamentary debate	國會辯論
play	戲劇
public reading	公眾朗讀會
public sanitation	公共衛生
publish	出版
reform	改革
reporter	記者
Royal Navy	皇家海軍
shelter	庇護所
shoe polish factory	鞋油工廠
shorthand	速記
society	社會
stroke	中風

 填 空

(01) clerk **(02)** Royal Navy

(03) shoe polish factory **(04)** labels

(05) arrested **(06)** debt

(07) insisted **(08)** shorthand

(09) code **(10)** legal clerk

(11) journalist **(12)** court cases

(13) Parliamentary debates

(14) reporter

(15) published

(16) non-fiction

(17) articles

(18) fictional

(19) characters

(20) novels

(21) act

(22) plays

(23) reform

(24) public sanitation

(25) good causes

(26) shelter

(27) public readings

(28) exhaustion

(29) stroke

(30) honor

Unit 10

Fyodor Dostoevsky
費奧多・杜斯妥也夫斯基

人物速覽

- 小說家
- 1821年生於俄羅斯莫斯科 （Moscow, Russia），1881年卒於俄羅斯聖彼得堡（St. Petersburg, Russia）
- 政治犯

❶ **Fyodor Dostoevsky** was the second child in his family. His father was a violent alcoholic who used to beat his children and his servants. From an early age Dostoevsky loved to read. He was sent to school at a military academy[1] to learn how to be an officer in the Russian army. He was only interested in literature, however, and was not happy at school. As soon as he could, he left the army and became a writer. He worked first as a translator, translating books from French into Russian.[2] He also worked as a journalist. He published his first book, a novel called *Poor Folk*, in 1846. It was an immediate best- seller[3] and made Dostoevsky famous.

❷ At the time, Russia was a very backward[4] country. The tsar[5] was very autocratic[6] and there was no free speech and no free press.[7] Everything was censored.[8] Dostoevsky became involved in politics, which was very dangerous. He became part of a group that liked to get together and read political articles from Europe to each other. In 1849 Dostoevsky was arrested by the police for reading a banned[9] article. He was put on trial and sentenced to death. On the morning of December 22nd, he was taken outside with some of the other prisoners, blindfolded,[10] and placed

Ⓦ Ⓞ Ⓡ Ⓓ Ⓛ Ⓘ Ⓢ Ⓣ

1. academy [əˋkædəmɪ] *n.* 學校；學院
2. Russian [ˋrʌʃən] *n.* 俄語
3. best-seller [ˋbɛstˋsɛlə] *n.* 暢銷書
4. backward [ˋbækwəd] *adj.* 進步遲緩的；落後的
5. tsar [tsɑr] *n.* 舊時的俄國皇帝；沙皇
6. autocratic [ˏɔtəˋkrætɪk] *adj.* 獨裁的；專制的
7. press [prɛs] *n.* （報紙上的）評論；the press 則可用來指「出版物；新聞界」
8. censor [ˋsɛnsə] *v.* 審查
9. ban [bæn] *v.* 禁止
10. blindfold [ˋblaɪndˏfold] *v.* 蒙住（眼睛）

against a wall and a death sentence was read out to them. At the last moment, a messenger[11] came running from the tsar to say their punishment had been changed at the last minute. It was a mock[12] execution.[13]

❸ Dostoevsky spent the next four years in a prison camp[14] in the far east of Russia. He suffered terribly there, not only because of the cold and the work he had to do, but because there were no books and he was not allowed to write. After he was released, he was not allowed to return to St. Petersburg for another six years. He had to serve in the army and stay in exile.[15]

❹ When he returned to St. Petersburg, he started writing again. He wrote about his prison experiences, and that book became a best-seller. He spent the next twenty years writing novels and articles, and managing and editing newspapers. He became very famous in Russia during his lifetime, and was even friends with the new tsar.

❺ Dostoevsky was an epileptic.[16] He would suffer bad fits[17] and then be very weak for many days afterwards. He was also addicted to gambling.

ⓌⓄⓇⒹ ⓁⒾⓈⓉ

11. messenger [ˈmɛsn̩dʒɚ] n. 信差；使者
12. mock [mɑk] adj. 偽造的；假裝的
13. execution [ˌɛksɪˈkjuʃən] n. （判決的）執行
14. camp [kæmp] n. 營地；收容所
15. exile [ˈɛksaɪl] n. 放逐；流亡
16. epileptic [ˌɛpəˈlɛptɪk] n. 癲癇症患者
★ 17. fit [fɪt] n. （疾病的）發作；（陣發性的）痙攣
18. casino [kəˈsino] n. 賭場

He traveled to Europe many times, mainly to visit the casinos,[18] where he won, and then lost, lots of money. He was always in debt, and had to write fast and produce more books to pay off his debts.

❻ He is regarded as one of the greatest writers in the world. His books were usually about poor people, those who had no position in society. His most famous book is *Crime and Punishment*, which is about a murder. He describes the psychology of the murderer in great detail. Dostoevsky died of an epileptic fit in St. Petersburg. 40,000 people attended his funeral.

譯文

❶ 費奧多‧杜斯妥也夫斯基是家中的第二個小孩，父親是個有暴力傾向的酒鬼，動不動就毆打小孩和傭人。自小以來，杜斯妥也夫斯基就熱愛閱讀。他被送去軍校，學習怎麼在俄羅斯的軍隊裡當個軍官。不過，他只對文學有興趣，所以在學校待得並不開心。等到他有能力，他隨即離開軍隊而成為一位作家。他起先是當翻譯，把法文書譯成俄文。他也當過記者。他在1846年出版了他的第一本著作，是一部名為《窮人》的小說。它立刻就成了暢銷書，杜斯妥也夫斯基也因此成名。

❷ 當時的俄羅斯是個非常落後的國家。沙皇非常獨裁，既沒有言論自由，也沒有出版自由，什麼都要經過審查。杜斯妥也夫斯基捲入了政治，這是非常危險的事。他成了某個團體的一份子，這群人喜歡聚在一起、研讀從歐洲到彼此的政治文章。1849年，杜斯妥也夫斯基因為閱讀禁文而遭到警方逮捕。他被交付審判並處以死刑。在12月22日的早上，他跟其他一些囚犯被帶到戶外，蒙上眼睛、抵在牆上，並被宣告了死刑。在最後一刻，有位信差奉沙皇之命趕來，他們的刑罰在最後一刻改變了。這是一場假的處決。

❸ 在接下來的四年，杜斯妥也夫斯基都待在俄羅斯遠東地區的集中營裡。他在那裡飽受折磨，不僅是因為天寒以及他必須要做的工作，也是因為既沒書可看，又不准寫作。在他被釋放後，他接著有六年不准回到聖彼得堡。他必須在部隊服役，並持續流亡。

❹ 等他回到聖彼得堡，他再度開始寫作。他寫下了他的獄中經驗，而這本書也成了暢銷書。在接下來的二十年，他都在寫小說與文章，還有管理及編輯報紙。在他的有生之年，他在俄羅斯變得非常有名，甚至成了新沙皇的朋友。

❺ 杜斯妥也夫斯基是個癲癇症患者。他會因發作嚴重而苦不堪言，然後在接下來的許多天都非常虛弱。他還沉迷賭博。他多次前往歐洲，主要就是去賭場，在裡頭贏了又輸掉一大堆錢。他老是欠債，所以必須加快寫作，以便出更多的書來清償債務。

❻ 他被認為是世界上最偉大的作家之一。他的書通常都是描寫窮人，也就是在社會上沒有地位的人。他最有名的著作是《罪與罰》，講的是一樁謀殺案。他把凶手的心理狀態描寫得很詳細。杜斯妥也夫斯基在聖彼得堡因為癲癇症發作而過世，有四萬人參加了他的葬禮。

閱讀理解

配合題，請判斷下列摘要各屬於文章的哪個段落，見範例。

Reputation and death	❻
Prison and exile	
Epilepsy and gambling	
Childhood and early life	
Writing and fame	
His arrest and mock execution	

重要詞彙

連連看，請為每個詞彙找出它的正確翻譯。

- epileptic
- backward
- banned article
- best-seller
- blindfold
- casino
- censor
- be addicted to
- exile
- fit
- army
- free press
- beat

- 沉迷於
- 軍隊
- 落後的
- 禁文
- 毆打
- 暢銷書
- 蒙上眼睛
- 賭場
- 審查
- 癲癇症患者
- 流亡
- 發作
- 出版自由

▨ gamble	•	• 言論自由
▨ get together	•	• 賭博
▨ free speech	•	• 聚在一起
▨ literature	•	• 欠債的
▨ mock execution	•	• 文學
▨ murder	•	• 軍校
▨ in debt	•	• 假的處決
▨ murderer	•	• 謀殺
▨ tsar	•	• 凶手
▨ officer	•	• 軍官
▨ pay off his debts	•	• 還清他的債務
▨ prison camp	•	• 集中營
▨ death sentence	•	• 心理狀態
▨ psychology	•	• 刑罰
▨ translator	•	• 交付審判
▨ punishment	•	• 被認為是……
▨ put on trial	•	• 釋放
▨ be regarded as	•	• 死刑
▨ release	•	• 被處以死刑
▨ military academy	•	• 服役
▨ be sentenced to death	•	• 譯者
▨ serve	•	• 沙皇

 填 空

理解文章大意後，請用前項習題中的詞彙來完成句子，有些字須做適當變化。

▨ Dostoevsky's father used to **(01)**_____ him and his servants.

He went to school at a (02)_____ to become an (03)_____ in the Russian (04)_____.

He always loved (05)_____ and reading books. His first writing job involved being a (06)_____ of French and German books.

His first novel was a (07)_____.

Russia was a (08)_____ country. The (09)_____ did not allow (10)_____ or (11)_____. Everything was (12)_____.

Dostoevsky was part of a group that liked to (13)_____ to read political articles.

He was arrested for reading a (14)_____. He was (15)_____ and (16)_____.

He was blindfolded and given a (17)_____.

He spent four years in a (18)_____. When he was (19)_____ he had to (20)_____ in the army again, and stay in (21)_____ for another six years.

Dostoevsky was an (22)_____. He had bad (23)_____.

He was (24)_____ (25)_____ and traveled around Europe visiting (26)_____.

He was always (27)_____ and had to keep writing to (28)_____.

■ He is **(29)** _____ one of the greatest writers in the world.

■ His most famous book is about a **(30)** _____, and the

(31) _____ of the **(32)** _____.

 你還可以學更多

a) 請利用網路查詢下列關鍵字，以了解更多關於 **Fyodor Dostoevsky** 的資訊：

☑ A picture of Fyodor Dostoevsky

☑ A picture of Tsar Nicholas I

☑ A picture of a casino

☑ A picture of St. Petersburg

☑ Epilepsy

☑ The names of some of Dostoevsky's novels

b) 請試著用英文討論下列話題：

1. 你想不想認識費奧多‧杜斯妥也夫斯基？為什麼？

2. 你覺得杜斯妥也夫斯基對他的父親有什麼看法？

3. 你覺得杜斯妥也夫斯基對他的假處決有什麼看法？

4. 你有沒有興趣讀一些杜斯妥也夫斯基的中譯著作？為什麼？

5. 你知不知道還有哪些作家是因為他們的政治信仰而入獄？

解 答

閱讀理解

Reputation and death	❻
Prison and exile	❸
Epilepsy and gambling	❺
Childhood and early life	❶
Writing and fame	❹
His arrest and mock execution	❷

重要詞彙

be addicted to	沉迷於
army	軍隊
backward	落後的
banned article	禁文
beat	毆打
best-seller	暢銷書
blindfold	蒙上眼睛
casino	賭場
censor	審查
epileptic	癲癇症患者
exile	流亡
fit	發作
free press	出版自由

free speech	言論自由
gamble	賭博
get together	聚在一起
in debt	欠債的
literature	文學
military academy	軍校
mock execution	假的處決
murder	謀殺
murderer	凶手
officer	軍官
pay off his debts	還清他的債務
prison camp	集中營
psychology	心理狀態
punishment	刑罰
put on trial	交付審判
be regarded as	被認為是……
release	釋放
death sentence	死刑
be sentenced to death	被處以死刑
serve	服役
translator	譯者
tsar	沙皇

填 空

(01) beat

(02) military academy

(03) officer

(04) army

(05) literature

(06) translator

(07) best-seller

(08) backward

(09) tsar

(10) free speech

(11) free press

(12) censored

(13) get together

(14) banned article

(15) put on trial

(16) sentenced to death

(17) mock execution

(18) prison camp

(19) released

(20) serve

(21) exile

(22) epileptic

(23) fits

(24) addicted to

(25) gambling

(26) casinos

(27) in debt

(28) pay off his debts

(29) regarded as

(30) murder

(31) psychology

(32) murderer

Toni Morrison
托妮 · 莫里森

人物速覽

- 小說家
- 1931 年生於美國俄亥俄州
  （Ohio, USA）
- 1988 年普立茲獎得主
- 1993 年諾貝爾文學獎得主

❶ **Toni Morrison** was born into a working-class[1] African American family. From an early age she loved reading. When she was a little girl her father used to tell her stories that he made up — stories about the black community. Toni was puzzled[2] that in the books she enjoyed reading there were no black people even though there were lots of stories from the black community. She decided to become a writer.

❷ She studied English and literature in college, and after she graduated, she became a professor, teaching literature and writing. She married an architect and had two children, but the marriage did not last long. After her divorce she moved to New York, where she worked as an editor. During this time she started writing. Her first story was about a black girl who wants to have blue eyes.

❸ Her third novel was called *Song of Solomon*. It is the story of a black man and his family. It combines elements of history and magic. President Obama has said it is his favorite book of all time. The book became very popular and won the National Book Critics Circle Award, a major literary award in America. Her fifth novel, *Beloved*, was very controversial.[3] It is about the experience of black slaves in America and contains scenes of violence and sex. It won the Pulitzer Prize,[4] which is the top literary prize in America, and was made into a movie. The *New York Times Book*

Ⓦ Ⓞ Ⓡ Ⓓ Ⓛ Ⓘ Ⓢ Ⓣ

1. working-class [ˋwɜkɪŋ ˋklæs] *adj.* 勞工階級的
2. puzzle [ˋpʌz!] *v.* 使⋯⋯困惑
3. controversial [ˌkɑntrəˋvɜʃəl] *adj.* 引起爭議的
4. Pulitzer Prize [ˋpjulɪtsə ˋpraɪz] *n.* 普立茲獎

Review, an influential[5] literary magazine in America, said it was the best novel of the last 25 years.

❹ In 1993 Toni Morrison won the Nobel Prize for Literature. She is the first black woman to win it. She has also won numerous other awards for her writing. She has written children's books and made recordings of her books. One of her books has even been made into an opera. She also served as a professor of literature at Princeton University, one of the top universities in America. Her example has inspired many other black American women to tell their stories and to write books.

❺ Toni Morrison's novels are about race and about the effect of racism[6] on young children and women. They are also about the legacy[7] of slavery,[8] and how white Americans have not really acknowledged[9] the impact of slavery on American history. She also writes about the effects language has on the way people think about themselves.

❻ In 1993, shortly after winning the Nobel Prize, Toni's house burned to the ground. The fire destroyed all her notes, manuscripts,[10] papers, and her personal library. How the fire started is a mystery. Her son was living in the house at the time, but he was not hurt.

Ⓦ Ⓞ Ⓡ Ⓓ Ⓛ Ⓘ Ⓢ Ⓣ

★ 5. influential [ˌɪnfluˋɛnʃəl] *adj.* 有影響力的
6. racism [ˋresɪzəm] *n.* 種族歧視
7. legacy [ˋlɛgəsɪ] *n.* 繼承之物
★ 8. slavery [ˋslevərɪ] *n.* 奴隸的身分；奴隸制度
9. acknowledge [əkˋnɑlɪdʒ] *v.* 承認
10. manuscript [ˋmænjəˌskrɪpt] *n.* 原稿；手稿

譯文

❶ 托妮．莫里森出身於一個勞工階級的非裔美國家庭。自小以來，她就熱愛閱讀。當她是個小女孩時，父親經常編故事講給她聽，而且都是關於黑人社區的故事。托妮感到不解的是，她喜歡看的書裡都沒有提到黑人，即使有很多故事是出自黑人社區。於是她決定當個作家。

❷ 她在大學念的是英語及文學。畢業後，她成了一位教授，教的是文學及寫作。她嫁給一位建築師，生了兩個小孩，但這樁婚姻並沒有維持很久。離婚後，她搬到紐約，並當起了編輯。在這段期間，她開始寫作。她的第一則故事是寫一個黑人女孩想要擁有藍色的雙眼。

❸ 她的第三本小說《所羅門之歌》，寫的是一個黑人男子及其家庭的故事。其中融合了歷史與魔法元素。歐巴馬總統說這是他歷年來最喜歡的一本書。這本書變得大受歡迎，並贏得了全國書評圈獎，這是美國的一項文學大獎。她的第五本小說《寵兒》極具爭議性。它寫的是美國黑奴的體驗，包含了暴力與性的情節。它贏得了普立茲獎，也就是美國最重要的文學獎項，並拍成了電影。在美國頗具影響力的文學雜誌《紐約時報書評》說，它是過去 25 年來最棒的一本小說。

❹ 1993 年，托妮．莫里森贏得了諾貝爾文學獎。她是第一位得獎的黑人女性。她的作品還贏得了其他許許多多的獎項。她寫過童書，並把她的著作錄製成有聲書。她有一本書甚至改編成了歌劇。她還擔任過普林斯頓大學的文學教授，這是美國的一所頂尖大學。她的榜樣鼓舞了美國其他許多的黑人女性說出自己的故事，並撰寫成書。

❺ 托妮．莫里森的小說談到了種族，以及種族主義對於兒童和女性的影響。它也談到了蓄奴的傳統，以及美國白人根本沒有真正承認蓄奴對於美國歷史

的衝擊。她還寫到了語言對於人們是如何看待自己所造成的影響。

❻ 1993 年，在贏得諾貝爾獎不久後，托妮的住所付之一炬。祝融燒光了她所有的筆記、手稿、論文和私人藏書。這場火災是如何開始，成了一個謎。她兒子當時住在屋子裡，但並沒有受傷。

閱讀理解

配合題，請判斷下列摘要各屬於文章的哪個段落，見範例。

Two novels	❸
Childhood	
The fire	
Her ideas	
Early life and family	
Fame and recognition	

重要詞彙

連連看，請為每個詞彙找出它的正確翻譯。

- black community •
- legacy •
- burn to the ground •
- divorce •
- element •
- acknowledge •
- impact •
- influential •
- editor •
- literary award •
- literary magazine •
- combine •
- architect •

- 承認
- 建築師
- 黑人社區
- 付之一炬
- 融合
- 離婚
- 編輯
- 元素
- 衝擊
- 有影響力的
- 繼承之物
- 文學獎
- 文學雜誌

■ race •		• 文學大獎
■ manuscript •		• 被做成……
■ mystery •		• 手稿
■ numerous •		• 謎
■ paper •		• 筆記
■ slavery •		• 許許多多的
■ personal library •		• 論文
■ note •		• 私人藏書
■ puzzle •		• 感到不解
■ be made into •		• 種族
■ racism •		• 種族主義
■ literary prize •		• 情節
■ working-class •		• 不久後
■ scene •		• 蓄奴制度
■ shortly after •		• 奴隸
■ slave •		• 勞動階級

 填　空

理解文章大意後，請用前項習題中的詞彙來完成句子，有些字須做適當變化。

■ Toni Morrison was born into a **(01)**＿＿＿＿＿ family in the
(02)＿＿＿＿＿ .

■ She was **(03)**＿＿＿＿＿ why there were no black people in her
favorite books.

■ She married an **(04)**＿＿＿＿＿ and they had two children before
they **(05)**＿＿＿＿＿ .

■ She worked as an (06)_____ to support her family.

■ *Song of Solomon* (07)_____ (08)_____ of history and magic.

■ It won a major (09)_____.

■ *Beloved* is about (10)_____ in the US and has (11)_____ of sex and violence.

■ Morrison has won (12)_____ (13)_____.

■ An (14)_____ (15)_____ called her book *Beloved* the best novel of the last 25 years.

■ Her books have been (16)_____ movies and an opera.

■ Toni Morrison writes about (17)_____ and the (18)_____ of (19)_____ on children and women.

■ She believes that the (20)_____ of (21)_____ has not been (22)_____ by Americans.

■ (23)_____ winning the Nobel Prize, her house (24)_____.

■ The fire destroyed all her (25)_____ and (26)_____, (27)_____ and her (28)_____.

■ How the fire started is a (29)_____.

你還可以學更多

a) 請利用網路查詢下列關鍵字，以了解更多關於 **Toni Morrison** 的資訊：

- ✓ A picture of Toni Morrison
- ✓ The Nobel Prize for Literature
- ✓ *Song of Solomon*
- ✓ The *Beloved* movie
- ✓ The Pulitzer Prize
- ✓ The history of slavery in the USA

b) 請試著用英文討論下列話題：

1. 你想不想認識托妮‧莫里森？為什麼？
2. 台灣有種族主義嗎？
3. 你有沒有興趣讀一些托妮‧莫里森的中譯著作？為什麼？
4. 你對於美國的蓄奴歷史了解多少？

解 答

 閱讀理解

Two novels	❸
Childhood	❶
The fire	❻
Her ideas	❺
Early life and family	❷
Fame and recognition	❹

 重要詞彙

acknowledge	承認
architect	建築師
black community	黑人社區
burn to the ground	付之一炬
combine	融合
divorce	離婚
editor	編輯
element	元素
impact	衝擊
influential	有影響力的
legacy	繼承之物
literary award	文學獎
literary magazine	文學雜誌

literary prize	文學大獎
be made into	被做成……
manuscript	手稿
mystery	謎
note	筆記
numerous	許許多多的
paper	論文
personal library	私人藏書
puzzle	感到不解
race	種族
racism	種族主義
scene	情節
shortly after	不久後
slavery	蓄奴制度
slave	奴隸
working-class	勞動階級

 填 空

(01) working-class   **(02)** black community

(03) puzzled   **(04)** architect

(05) divorced   **(06)** editor

(07) combines   **(08)** elements

(09) literary award   **(10)** slaves

(11) scenes   **(12)** numerous

(13) literary prizes   **(14)** influential

(15) literary magazine

(16) made into

(17) race

(18) impact

(19) racism

(20) legacy

(21) slavery

(22) acknowledged

(23) Shortly after

(24) burned to the ground

(25) notes

(26) manuscripts

(27) papers

(28) personal library

(29) mystery

J. K. Rowling
J. K. 羅琳

人物速覽

- 小說家
- 1965 年生於英國格洛斯特
  （Gloucestershire, England）
- 《哈利波特》創作者
- 慈善家

❶ **J. K. Rowling** was born into a middle-class[1] English family, the older child and daughter. From an early age she loved to read and write stories for her little sister. She studied French at college and went to live for a year in France. When she came back, she trained to be an English language teacher before going to Portugal[2] to teach English. While in Portugal, she got married and had a daughter. However, after one year of marriage, she and her husband separated and J. K. moved back to England with her daughter.

❷ One day, J. K. was on a train journey when she suddenly had an idea for a book about a normal boy who attends a school for wizards.[3] As soon as she got home, she started writing the story. She worked on the story for many years, between jobs and between studying. She did most of the writing in cafés. She liked to work in cafés because they were warmer and she did not have much money to pay for heating[4] bills. She could only work when her daughter was asleep. While she was writing the book, her mother died of multiple[5] sclerosis.[6] This book eventually became *Harry Potter and the Philosopher's Stone*.

❸ In 1995, when the book was finished, she sent it to an agent, who liked it so much that he agreed to try to sell it for her. He sent the book to 12

Ⓦ Ⓞ Ⓡ Ⓓ Ⓛ Ⓘ Ⓢ Ⓣ

1. middle-class [ˈmɪdḷ ˈklæs] *adj.* 勞工階級的
2. Portugal [ˈpɔrtʃəgḷ] *n.* 葡萄牙
★ 3. wizard [ˈwɪzəd] *n.* 巫師
★ 4. heating [ˈhitɪŋ] *n.* 暖氣（裝置） *adj.* 加熱的
★ 5. multiple [ˈmʌltəpḷ] *adj.* 多重的；多數的
6. sclerosis [sklɪˈrosɪs] *n.* （動脈等的）硬化

publishers who all rejected it, saying it was not good. However, the eight-year-old daughter of a small London publishing house's chairman[7] read the first chapter of the manuscript[8] and liked it so much she told her father she wanted to read the whole thing. He thought that if his daughter liked it, other children would too. He decided to publish the book.

❹ The book was published in 1997, and it became an instant hit in both England and America. It won all the major literary prizes for children's literature in the UK. It was even popular with adults. The book was translated into 67 languages, and the film rights were sold to Hollywood. Over the next few years, J. K. wrote the whole Harry Potter series,[9] and a series of movies was made. Each book sold more copies than the one before it, and J. K. Rowling was suddenly famous all over the world.

❺ She was also suddenly very rich. Now, after the series has finished and all the movie and merchandising[10] rights have been sold, J. K. Rowling is one of the richest women in the world. She is the 144th richest person in England, and is the first person to become a billionaire[11] by writing books. She lives in Edinburgh[12] in Scotland.

Ⓦ Ⓞ Ⓡ Ⓓ Ⓛ Ⓘ Ⓢ Ⓣ

7. chairman [ˈtʃɛrmən] *n.* 總裁；主席；會長
8. manuscript [ˈmænjəˌskrɪpt] *n.* 原稿；手稿
★ 9. series [ˈsɪrɪz] *n.* 一系列；一連串
10. merchandising [ˈmɝtʃənˌdaɪzɪŋ] *n.* 商品的廣告推銷
11. billionaire [ˌbɪljənˈɛr] *n.* 億萬富翁
12. Edinburgh [ˈɛdn̩ˌbɝo] *n.* 愛丁堡
13. philanthropic [ˌfɪlənˈθrɑpɪk] *adj.* 慈善的；善心的

Part

3

❻ J. K. Rowling uses her money to help people all over the world. She is involved in many philanthropic[13] charities, especially multiple sclerosis, poverty in the third world and charities for single mothers and orphans.

譯文

❶ J. K. 羅琳出身於一個中產階級的英國家庭,是老大也是長女。自小以來,她就喜歡為她的小妹讀、寫故事。她在大學念的是法文,並到法國住了一年。在她回來後,她受訓成了一位英語老師,然後到葡萄牙教英文。在葡萄牙的時候,她結了婚並生了個女兒。但在婚後一年,她和丈夫分手,J. K. 也和女兒搬回了英國。

❷ 有一天,J. K. 在搭火車,她突然有了一本書的構想,是關於一個平凡男孩到巫師學校就讀。她一回到家,就立即開始寫故事。她利用工作、讀書空檔為這個故事努力了好幾年。她大部分都是在咖啡店寫作。她喜歡在咖啡店工作,因為那裡比較溫暖,而她也沒什麼錢可以付暖氣費。她只能在女兒睡著的時候工作。就在她寫這本書時,她母親因為多發性硬化症而過世。這本書最後成了《哈利波特:神秘的魔法石》。

❸ 1995年,在這本書完成時,她把它寄給一位經紀人。他愛不釋手,並答應設法幫她兜售。他把書寄給12家出版社,結果全數遭到拒絕,還說這本書不怎麼好。不過,倫敦一家小出版社老闆的八歲女兒看了第一章原稿,愛不釋手。她跟爸爸說,她想要讀全部。他想,假如他女兒喜歡的話,別的小孩也會喜歡才對。於是他決定出版這本書。

❹ 這本書在1997年出版,並立即在英美兩國暢銷。它贏得了英國各大兒童文學的文學大獎,甚至受到大人歡迎。這本書被譯成67種語言,拍片權也賣到了好萊塢。在接下來的幾年,J. K. 寫了全套的《哈利波特》系列,也被製作成一

系列的電影。每本書都是一本賣得比一本好，J. K. 羅琳在全世界一夕成名。

❺ 她還一夕爆富。在系列完結，所有的電影和商品銷售權也售出後，J. K. 羅琳如今是世界上最富有的女性之一。她是英國第 144 名的富豪，並且是靠寫書成為億萬富翁的第一人。她住在蘇格蘭的愛丁堡。

❻ J. K. 羅琳用她的錢幫助了世界各地的民眾。她投身許多慈善義舉，尤其是針對多發性硬化症、第三世界的貧困、以及單親媽媽和孤兒的慈善機構。

閱讀理解

配合題，請判斷下列摘要各屬於文章的哪個段落，見範例。

Fame	❹
Early life	
Her wealth	
Writing *Harry Potter*	
Her philanthropy	
Publishing *Harry Potter*	

重要詞彙

連連看，請為每個詞彙找出它的正確翻譯。

- chapter •
- film right •
- heating bill •
- reject •
- merchandising •
- billionaire •
- multiple sclerosis •
- orphan •
- philanthropic cause •
- poverty •
- children's literature •
- agent •
- publisher •

- • 經紀人
- • 億萬富翁
- • 章
- • 兒童文學
- • 拍片權
- • 暖氣費帳單
- • 商品的廣告推銷
- • 多發性硬化症
- • 孤兒
- • 慈善義舉
- • 貧困
- • 出版社
- • 拒絕

◼ series	•	• 分開	
◼ single mother	•	• 一系列	
◼ third world	•	• 單親媽媽	
◼ wizard	•	• 第三世界	
◼ separate	•	• 翻譯	
◼ translate	•	• 巫師	

 填 空

理解文章大意後，請用前項習題中的詞彙來完成句子，有些字須做適當變化。

◼ J. K. Rowling **(01)**＿＿＿＿＿＿ from her husband after only one year of marriage.

◼ The story of a boy at a school for **(02)**＿＿＿＿＿ came to her on a train journey.

◼ She wrote in cafés because she had no money to pay for **(03)**＿＿＿＿＿ .

◼ Her mother died of **(04)**＿＿＿＿＿ while she was writing *Harry Potter*.

◼ She found an **(05)**＿＿＿＿＿ who sent the book to lots of **(06)**＿＿＿＿＿ . 12 of them **(07)**＿＿＿＿＿ her book.

◼ The chairman's daughter read the first **(08)**＿＿＿＿＿ of the manuscript and wanted to read more.

◼ Although *Harry Potter* is sold as **(09)**＿＿＿＿＿ , many adults read it as well.

- The books have been (10)_____ into many different languages.

- The (11)_____ were sold to Hollywood.

- There is a book (12)_____ and a movie series, in addition to lots of HP merchandise.

- J. K. Rowling is a (13)_____, and is involved in many (14)_____ to help other people.

- She wants to help solve the problems of (15)_____ in the (16)_____, (17)_____ and their children, as well as (18)_____.

 你還可以學更多

a) 請利用網路查詢下列關鍵字，以了解更多關於 **J. K. Rowling** 的資訊：

✓ A picture of J. K. Rowling

✓ A picture of Harry Potter

✓ A scene from a Harry Potter movie

✓ Multiple sclerosis

✓ Some Harry Potter merchandise

✓ Edinburgh

b) 請試著用英文討論下列話題：

1. 你想不想認識 J. K. 羅琳？為什麼？

2. 你想成為世界上最有錢的人之一嗎？

3. 假如你跟 J. K. 羅琳一樣有錢，你會做什麼？

4. 你比較喜歡《哈利波特》的電影還是書？

5. 你最喜歡《哈利波特》電影或書的哪一部？你為什麼最喜歡它？

解 答

 閱讀理解

Fame	**4**
Early life	**1**
Her wealth	**5**
Writing *Harry Potter*	**2**
Her philanthropy	**6**
Publishing *Harry Potter*	**3**

 重要詞彙

agent	經紀人
billionaire	億萬富翁
chapter	章
children's literature	兒童文學
film right	拍片權
heating bill	暖氣費帳單
merchandising	商品的廣告推銷
multiple sclerosis	多發性硬化症
orphan	孤兒
philanthropic cause	慈善義舉
poverty	貧困
publisher	出版社
reject	拒絕

separate	分開
series	一系列
single mother	單親媽媽
third world	第三世界
translate	翻譯
wizard	巫師

 填 空

(01) separated

(02) wizards

(03) heating bills

(04) multiple sclerosis

(05) agent

(06) publishers

(07) rejected

(08) chapter

(09) children's literature

(10) translated

(11) film rights

(12) series

(13) billionaire

(14) philanthropic causes

(15) poverty

(16) third world

(17) single mothers

(18) orphans

Part 4

風格獨具的藝術家

Damien Hirst

Vincent van Gogh

Frida Kahlo

Zaha Hadid

Unit 13

Vincent van Gogh
文森‧梵谷

人物速覽

- 畫家
- 1853 年生於荷蘭（Holland），
  1890 年卒於法國南部
  （South of France）
- 深具影響力的藝術家

❶ **Vincent van Gogh** was born in Holland in 1853 to a middle-class family of art dealers[1] and ministers.[2] During his early life, Vincent had many different jobs. First, he worked in his uncle's art dealership,[3] buying and selling art. He lived for a time in London. Then he became a teacher, and after that, a bookseller. He tried to enter university to study theology,[4] but failed his entrance exam. In 1879 he worked as a Protestant[5] missionary[6] in a coal mining village in Belgium.[7] He lived very poorly and simply like the miners.[8] It was here that he started making his first drawings.

❷ His younger brother Theo encouraged his talent and persuaded him to seriously cultivate[9] his interest in art. Vincent enrolled[10] at the Royal Academy of Art in Brussels[11] and learned how to draw properly. For the next 10 years he lived in various cities in Holland, trying to make a living as an artist. He was desperately poor and often ill from hunger. A woman he was in love with committed suicide, and several other women he fell in

Ⓦ Ⓞ Ⓡ Ⓓ Ⓛ Ⓘ Ⓢ Ⓣ

1. dealer [ˈdilə] *n.* 商人
2. minister [ˈmɪnɪstə] *n.* 神職人員；牧師
3. dealership [ˈdiləˌʃɪp] *n.* 經銷權
4. theology [θiˈɑlədʒɪ] *n.* 神學
5. Protestant [ˈprɑtɪstənt] *adj.* 新教徒的；新教徒
6. missionary [ˈmɪʃənˌɛrɪ] *n.* 傳教士
7. Belgium [ˈbɛldʒɪəm] *n.* 比利時
8. miner [ˈmaɪnə] *n.* 礦工
9. cultivate [ˈkʌltəˌvet] *v.* 培養；啟發；教化
10. enroll [ɪnˈrol] *v.* 註冊；登記入會
11. Brussels [ˈbrʌslz] *n.* （比利時的首都）布魯塞爾

love with refused to marry him. From constant[12] hunger, poverty and loneliness, he started to show symptoms[13] of mental illness.

❸ Vincent moved to Paris with his brother Theo in 1886. At that time Paris was a center of modern art and Vincent met many artists who influenced his technique. He began to use bright colors, small dots,[14] and oil color. In two years he painted over 200 pictures, experimenting with different styles and trying to develop his exceptional[15] talent.

❹ In 1888, tired of Parisian[16] life but having made some money selling his paintings, he moved to a town called Arles, in the South of France. He persuaded his friend, another artist called Paul Gauguin, to come and live with him. At first this arrangement worked well. The two artists painted together, and talked about art. Then they began to quarrel, and Vincent, in fear that he would lose his friend, cut off his own ear. His mental health began to deteriorate.[17] He began to believe that he was being poisoned and refused to eat. He spent the next few years in various hospitals.

❺ The work he produced early in his life is very dark, with lots of browns and greys, featuring[18] local people and their lives. His mature art is full of bright colors and swirling[19] shapes, and portraits[20] of his friends. His most famous work is a still[21] life called *Sunflowers*.

Ⓦ Ⓞ Ⓡ Ⓓ Ⓛ Ⓘ Ⓢ Ⓣ

12. constant [`kɑnstənt] *adj.* 持續不斷的
★ 13. symptom [`sɪmptəm] *n.* 徵兆
14. dot [dɑt] *n.* 點
15. exceptional [ɪk`sɛpʃənḷ] *adj.* 出眾的；非凡的
16. Parisian [pə`rɪʒən] *adj.* 巴黎的；巴黎風格的
17. deteriorate [dɪ`tɪrɪə‚ret] *v.* 惡化；變壞

❻ In July 1890, just as his genius was being recognized, suffering from terrible depression²² due to his mental illness, Vincent walked into a cornfield²³ near his home and shot himself in the chest. He died two days later.

譯文

❶ 文森‧梵谷在1853年出生於荷蘭一個藝術品經銷商及神職人員的中產階級家庭。在他的早年期間，文森做過許多不同的工作。起先他在叔叔的藝術品經銷店工作，買賣藝術品。他在倫敦住過一段時間。後來他當了老師，之後是書商。他想要上大學讀神學，但沒通過入學考。1879年，他在比利時一個開採煤礦的村莊裡擔任新教的傳教士。他跟礦工一樣，過得非常清貧而簡單。也就是在這裡，他首度開始作畫。

❷ 他弟弟西奧啟發了他的天賦，並說服他要好好發展對藝術的興趣。文森到了布魯塞爾的皇家藝術學院註冊，學習要怎麼作畫才對。在接下來的10年，他住過荷蘭的各個城市，並試圖靠當藝術家來維生。他窮得不得了，並經常餓出病來。他所愛的一位女子自殺了，還有好幾位他所愛的女子拒絕嫁給他。在不斷的飢餓、貧窮與孤獨下，他開始出現精神病的症狀。

❸ 文森在1886年跟弟弟西奧搬到了巴黎。巴黎在當時是現代藝術的中心，文

18. feature [`fitʃə] v. 描寫……的特徵；使有……的特色
19. swirl [`swɜl] v. 旋轉；渦旋
★ 20. portrait [`portret] n. 肖像；畫像
21. still [stɪl] adj. 靜止的；安靜的
★ 22. depression [dɪ`prɛʃən] n. 憂鬱；沮喪
23. cornfield [`kɔrn,fild] n. 玉蜀黍田

森認識了許多藝術家，影響了他的技法。他開始採用明亮的色調、小圓點和油畫顏料。在兩年內，他畫了200多幅畫，實驗不同的畫風，並嘗試發揮他過人的天賦。

❹ 1888年，他厭倦了巴黎的生活，靠著賣畫賺得的一點錢，他搬到了法國南部一個叫做阿爾勒的鎮上。他說服他的朋友搬來跟他一起住，他也是一位藝術家，名叫保羅‧高更。起先這項安排頗為順利。兩位藝術家一起作畫、討論藝術。後來他們開始爭吵，文森害怕失去他的朋友，於是把自己的耳朵割了下來。他的心理健康開始惡化。他開始相信自己被人下了毒，拒絕進食。在接下來的幾年，他都待在不同的醫院裡。

❺ 他早年所畫的作品非常陰暗，用了大量的棕色與灰色，並以地方居民和他們的生活為主題。他的成熟畫作則充滿明亮的色調和漩渦式的圖形，以及朋友的肖像。他最有名的作品是一幅靜物畫，名叫〈向日葵〉。

❻ 1890年7月，正當他的天賦獲得肯定，並因精神病而為嚴重憂鬱症所苦，文森走進了他家附近的玉米田，朝著自己的胸口開槍，並在兩天後過世。

閱讀理解

配合題，請判斷下列摘要各屬於文章的哪個段落，見範例。

Paris	❸
Suicide	
South of France	
Early life	
His art	
Early career	

重要詞彙

連連看，請為每個詞彙找出它的正確翻譯。

▨ art dealership   •
▨ dot   •
▨ bookseller   •
▨ coal mining   •
▨ entrance exam   •
▨ cornfield   •
▨ art dealer   •
▨ cultivate   •
▨ deteriorate   •
▨ draw   •
▨ depression   •
▨ enroll   •
▨ drawing   •

• 藝術品經銷商
• 藝術品代理經銷權
• 書商
• 煤礦開採
• 玉米田
• 啟發；培養
• 憂鬱症
• 惡化
• 點
• 畫
• 圖畫
• 註冊
• 入學考

▨ genius	•	•	實驗
▨ feature	•	•	以……為主題
▨ mental health	•	•	天才
▨ theology	•	•	心理健康
▨ mental illness	•	•	精神病
▨ minister	•	•	礦工
▨ oil color	•	•	神職人員；牧師
▨ miner	•	•	油畫顏料
▨ painting	•	•	畫作
▨ experiment	•	•	肖像
▨ Protestant missionary	•	•	新教的傳教士
▨ portrait	•	•	爭吵
▨ quarrel	•	•	靜物
▨ still life	•	•	畫風
▨ swirling shape	•	•	漩渦狀
▨ symptom	•	•	症狀
▨ talent	•	•	天賦
▨ technique	•	•	技法
▨ style	•	•	神學

 填 空

理解文章大意後，請用前項習題中的詞彙來完成句子，有些字須做適當變化。

▨ Vincent came from a family of **(01)** _____ and **(02)** _____ .

▨ He worked in an **(03)** _____ and then as a **(04)** _____ .

- He wanted to study (05)_____, but he failed the (06)_____.

- He worked as a (07)_____ in a (08)_____ town.

- He made his first (09)_____ of the (10)_____ and other people from the area.

- His brother encouraged his (11)_____ and persuaded him to (12)_____ his art.

- He (13)_____ in a famous art school where he learned to (14)_____.

- In his early life he suffered extreme poverty and began to show (15)_____ of (16)_____.

- He worked hard to improve his (17)_____, using (18)_____ and (19)_____ in his (20)_____, and (21)_____ with different (22)_____.

- After a bad (23)_____ with his friend, his (24)_____ began to (25)_____.

- His work was full of (26)_____ shapes, (27)_____ local people and their lives.

- He liked to paint (28)_____ of his friends.

- He painted a famous (29)_____ of sunflowers.

■ Just as his (30)_____ was being recognized he suffered from

a very bad bout of (31)_____ and shot himself in a

(32)_____.

 你還可以學更多

a) 請利用網路查詢下列關鍵字，以了解更多關於 **Vincent van Gogh** 的資訊：

- ✓ A picture of Vincent van Gogh
- ✓ A painting by Vincent van Gogh
- ✓ A painting by his friend Gauguin
- ✓ Van Gogh's painting *Sunflowers*
- ✓ The Van Gogh Museum in Amsterdam
- ✓ Arles

b) 請試著用英文討論下列話題：

1. 你想不想認識文森·梵谷？為什麼？
2. 你想去巴黎旅遊嗎？
3. 你會不會畫畫？
4. 你比較喜歡文森的畫還是他朋友高更的畫？為什麼？
5. 你最喜歡文森·梵谷的哪一幅畫？你為什麼喜歡它？

解 答

 閱讀理解

Paris	❸
Suicide	❻
South of France	❹
Early life	❶
His art	❺
Early career	❷

 重要詞彙

art dealer	藝術品經銷商
art dealership	藝術品代理經銷權
bookseller	書商
coal mining	煤礦開採
cornfield	玉米田
cultivate	啟發；培養
depression	憂鬱症
deteriorate	惡化
dot	點
draw	畫
drawing	圖畫
enroll	註冊
entrance exam	入學考

experiment	實驗
feature	以……為主題
genius	天才
mental health	心理健康
mental illness	精神病
miner	礦工
minister	神職人員；牧師
oil color	油畫顏料
painting	畫作
portrait	肖像
Protestant missionary	新教的傳教士
quarrel	爭吵（可當動詞和名詞）
still life	靜物
style	畫風
swirling shape	漩渦狀
symptom	症狀
talent	天賦
technique	技法
theology	神學

 填　空

(01) art dealers　　　**(02)** ministers　　　**(03)** art dealership

(04) bookseller　　　**(05)** theology　　　**(06)** entrance exam

(07) Protestant missionary　　**(08)** coal mining　　**(09)** drawings

(10) miners

(11) talent

(12) cultivate

(13) enrolled

(14) draw

(15) symptoms

(16) mental illness

(17) technique

(18) dots

(19) oil colors

(20) paintings

(21) experimenting

(22) styles

(23) quarrel

(24) mental health

(25) deteriorate

(26) swirling

(27) featuring

(28) portraits

(29) still life

(30) genius

(31) depression

(32) cornfield

Frida Kahlo
芙烈達・卡羅

人物速覽

- 畫家
- 1907 年生於墨西哥科悠坎（Coyoac Coyoacán, Mexico），1954
  年卒於墨西哥科悠坎
- 深具影響力的墨西哥藝術家

❶ **Frida Kahlo** was born in Mexico in 1907. Her father was a German immigrant[1] and her mother was of predominantly[2] indigenous[3] Mexican descent.[4] These two influences had a big impact on Frida's life and art. She was the second youngest child in the family, and had no brothers, only sisters. During her childhood, the Mexican Revolution broke out. Her parents helped the revolutionaries.[5]

❷ When she was six years old, Frida got polio,[6] an illness which causes paralysis[7] of the limbs. Her right leg was always thinner than her left due to this illness. When she was 18 she was badly injured in a traffic accident. She broke her back, her collarbone,[8] several ribs,[9] her pelvis[10] and her right leg, which was broken in 11 places. She also injured her shoulder. An iron bar pierced[11] her stomach and her uterus.[12] She had 35 operations, and was unable to move for three months. For the rest of her life she was often in great pain.

Ⓦ Ⓞ Ⓡ Ⓓ Ⓛ Ⓘ Ⓢ Ⓣ

★ 1. immigrant [ˋɪməgrənt] *n.* （來自外國的）移民
2. predominantly [prɪˋdɑmənəntlɪ] *adv.* 主要地；佔優勢地
3. indigenous [ɪnˋdɪdʒənəs] *adj.* 原產的；固有的
4. descent [dɪˋsɛnt] *n.* 血統；家世；出身
5. revolutionary [ˌrɛvəˋluʃənˌɛrɪ] *n.* 革命者
6. polio [ˋpolɪˌo] *n.* 小兒痲痺症
7. paralysis [pəˋræləsɪs] *n.* 痲痺；癱瘓
8. collarbone [ˋkɑləˌbon] *n.* 鎖骨
9. rib [rɪb] *n.* 肋骨
10. pelvis [ˋpɛlvɪs] *n.* 骨盆
11. pierce [pɪrs] *v.* 刺穿
12. uterus [ˋjutərəs] *n.* 子宮

❸ During her recuperation,[13] Frida started to paint. She painted herself and her suffering and her pain. She was strongly influenced by indigenous Mexican art and by European surrealism.[14] Her paintings look like dreams, but she said she just painted her own reality. Many of her paintings are striking[15] images of her pain and suffering, and include images from traditional Mexican art.

❹ When she recovered from her injuries, she went to visit a famous Mexican artist called Diego Rivera. Rivera was a muralist,[16] and was already famous in America and Europe. He strongly encouraged her art. They fell in love and were married in 1929, even though Frida's mother was against the marriage. They had a tumultuous[17] marriage that involved affairs on both sides. At one point Frida found out that Diego was romantically involved with her sister. Although they eventually divorced, they got married again in 1940, and stayed married until Frida's death.

❺ Frida was an individualist.[18] She liked to wear traditional Mexican clothes and jewelry. She smoked and drank like a man, and she fell in love with both men and women. She was beautiful, and had a mustache[19] and a unibrow.[20] Both she and her husband were communists[21] and believed strongly in the greatness of Mexican culture.

Ⓦ Ⓞ Ⓡ Ⓓ Ⓛ Ⓘ Ⓢ Ⓣ

13. recuperation [rɪ͵kupəˋreʃən] *n.* 恢復
14. surrealism [səˋriəl͵ɪzəm] *n.* 超現實主義
15. striking [ˋstraɪkɪŋ] *adj.* 醒目的；給人印象深刻的
16. muralist [ˋmjʊrəlɪst] *n.* 壁畫家
17. tumultuous [tuˋmʌltʃʊəs] *adj.* 喧囂的；動搖的
18. individualist [͵ɪndəˋvɪdʒʊəlɪst] *n.* 個人主義者
★ 19. mustache [ˋmʌstæʃ] *n.* （蓄在上唇的）小鬍子

❻ During the final year of her life she was very ill. Her right leg had to be amputated[22] due to gangrene,[23] and she spent much of her time in bed. She wanted to die to end her suffering. She died of a pulmonary embolism,[24] although some people say she might have died of an overdose[25] of drugs. After her death, she was recognized as one of Mexico's greatest artists, and she is now more famous than her husband was.

譯文

❶ 芙烈達‧卡羅在 1907 年出生於墨西哥。父親是德國移民，母親則是道地土生土長的墨西哥後裔。這兩種影響對於芙烈達的人生及藝術有巨大的衝擊。她是家中第二小的孩子，沒有兄弟，只有姊妹。在她小時候，墨西哥革命爆發，她父母幫助了革命份子。

❷ 在六歲時，芙烈達得了小兒麻痺症，造成肢體癱瘓。由於得了這種病，她的右腿永遠都比左腿來得瘦。18 歲時，她在一場車禍中受了重傷。弄斷了她的背、鎖骨、幾根肋骨、骨盆和右腿，而且右腿斷了 11 處。她也傷到了肩膀。一根鐵條刺穿了她的胃和子宮。她動了 35 次手術，有三個月都動不了。在她接下來的人生，她經常感到劇痛。

---

20. unibrow [ˈjunɪˌbraʊ] *n.* 一字眉
★ 21. communist [ˈkɑmjuɪst] *n.* 共產主義者
22. amputate [ˈæmpjəˌtet] *v.* 切除
23. gangrene [ˈgæŋgrin] *n.* 壞疽
24. pulmonary embolism [ˈpʌlməˌnɛrɪ ˈɛmbəˌlɪzəm] *n.* 肺栓塞
25. overdose [ˈovɚˌdos] *n.* 過量的服用

❸ 在復元期間，芙烈達開始畫畫。她畫她自己，還有她的苦難與疼痛。她深受墨西哥的本土藝術以及歐洲的超現實主義所影響。她的畫看起來有如夢境，但她說她只是畫出自己的現實人生。她的許多畫作都是表現她痛苦和受苦的醒目圖像，也包含了墨西哥傳統藝術的圖像。

❹ 在受傷復元後，她去拜訪了墨西哥一位著名的藝術家，名叫迪雅哥・李維拉。李維拉是個壁畫家，在歐美已經很有名氣。他十分支持她的藝術。他們墜入愛河，並且在 1929 年結婚，儘管芙烈達的母親反對這樁婚事。他們的婚姻充滿波折，雙方都有外遇。芙烈達還一度發現，迪雅哥跟她的姊姊有感情牽扯。雖然他們最後離了婚，卻在 1940 年再度結婚，這段婚姻也一直維持到芙烈達過世為止。

❺ 芙烈達是個個人主義者。她喜歡穿戴傳統的墨西哥服裝與首飾。她像個男人一樣抽菸喝酒，並且跟男女都談過戀愛。她很漂亮，而且有八字鬍及一字眉。她和她先生都是共產主義份子，並對墨西哥文化的偉大懷抱著強烈的信仰。

❻ 在她人生的最後一年，她病得很重。她的右腿因為長出壞疽而必須切除，她有很長的時間都待在病榻上。她想要以死來結束她的苦難。她死於肺栓塞，雖然有些人說，她可能是死於用藥過量。在她死後，她被表揚為墨西哥最偉大的藝術家之一，如今她的名氣更高過了她先生。

閱讀理解

配合題，請判斷下列摘要各屬於文章的哪個段落，見範例。

Her character	❺
Childhood and family	
Her marriages	
Illness and accident	
Death	
Her paintings	

重要詞彙

連連看，請為每個詞彙找出它的正確翻譯。

indigenous •   • 切除

break out •   • 爆發

collarbone •   • 鎖骨

die of •   • 共產主義份子

gangrene •   • 死於……

image •   • 壞疽

amputate •   • 圖像

immigrant •   • 移民

communist •   • 本土的

be influenced by •   • 個人主義者

individualist •   • 受……影響

injure •   • 影響

influence •   • 受傷

limb	•	•	（四）肢
romantically involved	•	•	八字鬍
muralist	•	•	壁畫家
operation	•	•	手術
uterus	•	•	過量
paralysis	•	•	癱瘓
traffic accident	•	•	骨盆
pelvis	•	•	小兒痲痹症
surrealism	•	•	恢復
polio	•	•	革命
recuperation	•	•	肋骨
mustache	•	•	有感情牽扯的
revolution	•	•	醒目的
rib	•	•	超現實主義
overdose	•	•	車禍
striking	•	•	充滿波折的
tumultuous	•	•	子宮

 填 空

理解文章大意後，請用前項習題中的詞彙來完成句子，有些字須做適當變化。

■ European and Mexican (01)＿＿＿＿＿＿ had a big impact on her art.

■ The Mexican (02)＿＿＿＿＿＿ (03)＿＿＿＿＿＿ in 1910.

■ She contracted (04)＿＿＿＿＿＿ when she was child, which causes

(05)＿＿＿＿＿＿ of the (06)＿＿＿＿＿＿.

■ She was (07)_____ in a serious (08)_____ accident.

■ She broke her (09)_____ and her (10)_____ and her (11)_____ and injured her (12)_____.

■ She had 35 (13)_____.

■ She started painting during her (14)_____.

■ Her art was strongly (15)_____ (16)_____ Mexican art and by European (17)_____.

■ Her paintings are full of (18)_____ (19)_____.

■ Her husband was a famous (20)_____.

■ They were married twice and both marriages were (21)_____. They were both (22)_____ with other people.

■ Frida was an (23)_____, had one eyebrow and a (24)_____.

■ During her last year she had her right leg (25)_____ due to (26)_____.

■ Some say she (27)_____ a pulmonary embolism, others say she died of an (28)_____.

你還可以學更多

a) 請利用網路查詢下列關鍵字，以了解更多關於 **Frida Kahlo** 的資訊：

☑ A picture of Frida Kahlo

☑ A picture of Diego Rivera

☑ A painting by Frida Kahlo

☑ The Mexican Revolution

☑ Mexican art

☑ A mural by Diego Rivera

b) 請試著用英文討論下列話題：

1. 你想不想認識芙烈達？為什麼？

2. 你想去墨西哥旅遊嗎？

3. 你覺得芙烈達的性格轉變是車禍造成的嗎？

4. 你比較喜歡芙烈達‧卡羅的畫，還是她先生的壁畫？

5. 你知道其他還有什麼名人跟另一半結了兩次婚嗎？

解 答

 閱讀理解

Her character	❺
Childhood and family	❶
Her marriages	❹
Illness and accident	❷
Death	❻
Her paintings	❸

 重要詞彙

amputate	切除
break out	爆發
collarbone	鎖骨
communist	共產主義份子
die of	死於……
gangrene	壞疽
image	圖像
immigrant	移民
indigenous	本土的
individualist	個人主義者
be influenced by	受……影響
influence	影響
injure	受傷

limb	（四）肢
mustache	八字鬍
muralist	壁畫家
operation	手術
overdose	過量
paralysis	癱瘓
pelvis	骨盆
polio	小兒麻痺症
recuperation	恢復
revolution	革命
rib	肋骨
romantically involved	有感情牽扯的
striking	醒目的
surrealism	超現實主義
traffic accident	車禍
tumultuous	充滿波折的
uterus	子宮

填 空

(01) influences

(02) Revolution

(03) broke out

(04) polio

(05) paralysis

(06) limbs

(07) injured

(08) traffic

(09) collarbone

(10) ribs

(11) pelvis

(12) uterus

(13) operations

(14) recuperation

(15) influenced by

(16) indigenous

(17) surrealism

(18) striking

(19) images   **(20)** muralist   **(21)** tumultuous

(22) romantically involved   **(23)** individualist   **(24)** mustache

(25) amputated   **(26)** gangrene   **(27)** died of

(28) overdose

Unit 15

Zaha Hadid
札哈・哈蒂

人物速覽

- 建築師
- 1950 年生於伊拉克巴格達
  （Baghdad, Iraq）
- 2004 年普利茲克獎（Pritzker Prize）得主

❶ Zaha Hadid was born in Baghdad[1] in Iraq in 1950. Her father was an economist[2] who was actively involved in politics, and her family was one of the leading families of Iraq at the time. Zaha was educated in both Iraq and Switzerland, and eventually got a degree in mathematics from the American University in Beirut,[3] Lebanon.[4] After graduating, Zaha decided she wanted to study architecture, so she moved to London and enrolled in the Architectural[5] Association,[6] a very famous architecture school in London.

❷ At the school, she impressed[7] her teachers so much that when she graduated, she was offered a job there as a teacher. In the first part of her career, Zaha worked mainly as a professor of architecture in some of the most prestigious[8] architecture colleges around the world, including Harvard[9] and Yale.[10]

❸ Although she was well known as an architecture teacher, she did not get many of her projects built. Instead of making plans, she preferred to

Ⓦ Ⓞ Ⓡ Ⓓ Ⓛ Ⓘ Ⓢ Ⓣ

1. Baghdad [`bæɡdæd] *n.*（伊拉克首都）巴格達
2. economist [ɪ`kɑnəmɪst] *n.* 經濟學家
3. Beirut [`berut] *n.*（黎巴嫩首都）貝魯特
4. Lebanon [`lɛbənən] *n.* 黎巴嫩
5. architectural [ˌɑrkə`tɛktʃərəl] *adj.* 建築的
6. association [əˌsosɪ`eʃən] *n.* 團體；協會
7. impress [ɪm`prɛs] *v.* 給予印象；打動
8. prestigious [prɛs`tɪdʒəs] *adj.* 有聲望的
9. Harvard [`hɑrvəd] *n.* 哈佛大學
10. Yale [jel] *n.* 耶魯大學

do paintings of her ideas. She said that plans could not get across[11] the feel of her buildings. Hadid was one of the first architects to use computers to create models and designs for buildings. This allowed her to create shapes and spaces that no one had ever dreamed of before. Most engineers and clients said her buildings looked great at the drawing stage, but were impossible to build and were not useful. She won many architecture awards and became very well known, but still few of her projects were built.

❹ Her first project to get built was a fire station in Germany. Critics[12] and other architects admired it, but the people using the building hated it. They said it was not practical for its purpose, and they eventually moved out of the building and into another one. In 1994, Hadid won an international competition to build an opera house in Cardiff,[13] Wales.[14] Her design was very beautiful and attracted a lot of attention in the world of architecture. However, after an outcry[15] from Welsh[16] politicians and city government, the prize was taken away from her and given to someone else.

Ⓦ Ⓞ Ⓡ Ⓓ Ⓛ Ⓘ Ⓢ Ⓣ

11. get across *v.* 使想法傳達
★ 12. critic [ˋkrɪtɪk] *n.* 批抨家；評論家
13. Cardiff [ˋkɑrdɪf] *n.* 卡地夫
14. Wales [welz] *n.* 威爾斯
15. outcry [ˋaʊtˏkraɪ] *n.* 強烈的抗議；吶喊
16. Welsh [wɛlʃ] *adj.* 威爾斯的
17. base [bes] *v.* 以……為根據地
★ 18. commission [kəˋmɪʃən] *v.* 委託

❺ Slowly, Hadid's designs began to get used as clients and the public began to understand her work. She also began to understand how to construct buildings that people could use and that were practical. She designed a very famous car factory for BMW in Germany, in which the production line was covered in glass and looked like a snake. She designed a museum in America which was not like any other museum built before. In 2004 she won the Pritzker Architecture Prize, the world's most prestigious architecture prize. She was the first woman to win the prize.

❻ Zaha Hadid has also designed furniture, cars and jewelry. She is based[17] in London, where she has been commissioned[18] to build the swimming pool for the 2012 London Olympics. She is also building an opera house in China.

譯文

❶ 札哈‧哈蒂在1950年出生於伊拉克的巴格達。父親是個經濟學家,並積極參與政治,她的家族是伊拉克當時的主要家族之一。札哈在伊拉克和瑞士都受過教育,最後在黎巴嫩貝魯特的美利堅大學拿到數學學位。畢業後,札哈決定要念建築,於是她搬到倫敦,並報名了建築學院,這是倫敦非常著名的建築學校。

❷ 在學校期間,她讓老師留下了極為深刻的印象。所以在她畢業後,她在那裡獲得教職。在她第一部分的生涯中,札哈主要是在全世界一些最有名望的建築學院擔任建築學教授,包括哈佛和耶魯在內。

❸ 雖然她是個相當知名的建築學老師,但她所建造的案子並不多。相較於制訂計畫,她更喜歡把她的想法畫出來。她說,計畫沒辦法表現出她對於建築

的感覺。哈蒂是率先使用電腦來建立模型及設計建築的建築師之一，這使她得以打造出以往從來沒有人想過的外形與空間。大部分的工程師與客戶都說，她的建築在繪圖階段看起來很棒，但不可能蓋起來，而且不實用。她贏得許多建築獎項，並且變得非常有名，但她建造的案子還是很少。

❹ 她第一個建造的案子是德國的一個消防隊。評論家和其他建築師都很欣賞它，但使用這棟建築的人卻很討厭它。他們覺得以消防隊的目的來說並不實用，最後他們也從這棟建築搬到了另外一棟。1994年，哈蒂在一個國際競賽獲勝，並要到威爾斯的加地夫蓋一座歌劇院。她的設計非常出色，吸引了建築界的廣泛注意。但在威爾斯的政治人物及市政府強烈抗議下，這座獎在她的手中被奪走，並頒給了別人。

❺ 隨著客戶和大眾開始了解她的作品，哈蒂的設計逐漸獲得採用。她也開始了解到，要怎麼蓋出大家能用而且實用的建築。她在德國為BMW設計了非常著名的車廠，生產線由玻璃覆罩著，看起來有如一條蛇。她在美國設計了一座博物館，它跟以往所蓋的任何一座博物館都不一樣。2004年，她贏得了普利茲克建築獎，這是世界上最有聲望的建築大獎。她是第一位拿下這座獎的女性。

❻ 札哈．哈蒂也設計過家具、汽車和首飾。她目前住在倫敦，因為她受託為2012年倫敦奧運建造游泳池。而在中國，她也正在建蓋一座歌劇院。

閱讀理解

配合題，請判斷下列摘要各屬於文章的哪個段落，見範例。

Her working method and style	❸
Architecture training	
Some of her buildings	
The opera house prize	
Education and childhood	
Her current projects	

重要詞彙

連連看，請為每個詞彙找出它的正確翻譯。

- jewelry •
- car factory •
- engineer •
- commission •
- design •
- drawing stage •
- critic •
- fire station •
- furniture •
- attract a lot of attention •
- get a degree in •
- model •
- client •

- 引起廣泛注意
- 車廠
- 客戶
- 受託
- 評論家
- 設計
- 繪圖階段
- 工程師
- 消防隊
- 家具
- 拿到……的學位
- 珠寶
- 模型

■ project	•	• 搬出	
■ opera house	•	• 歌劇院	
■ production line	•	• 強烈抗議	
■ outcry	•	• 計畫	
■ plan	•	• 實用的	
■ move out	•	• 有聲望的	
■ practical	•	• 生產線	
■ prestigious	•	• 專案	

 ## 填 空

理解文章大意後，請用前項習題中的詞彙來完成句子，有些字須做適當變化。

■ Zaha Hadid **(01)**＿＿＿＿＿＿ mathematics.

■ She enrolled in a **(02)**＿＿＿＿＿＿ architecture school in London.

■ She was one of the first architects to use computers for her
(03)＿＿＿＿＿＿ at the **(04)**＿＿＿＿＿＿.

■ Although her **(05)**＿＿＿＿＿＿ and **(06)**＿＿＿＿＿＿ won many
awards, most **(07)**＿＿＿＿＿＿ and **(08)**＿＿＿＿＿＿ said her
(09)＿＿＿＿＿＿ were impossible to build.

■ She designed a **(10)**＿＿＿＿＿＿ which the **(11)**＿＿＿＿＿＿
admired but the users of the building didn't. Eventually, the firemen
(12)＿＿＿＿＿＿ of the building.

■ She won a major international design for the Cardiff **(13)**＿＿＿＿＿＿

which (14)_____, but after an (15)_____ from the people of the city, the prize was given to someone else.

■ She has learned how to make her ideas more (16)_____ for the people using her buildings.

■ She built a famous (17)_____ in Germany where the (18)_____ looks like a snake.

■ Zaha Hadid has designed (19)_____, (20)_____ and cars as well as buildings.

■ She has been (21)_____ to design the Olympic swimming pool for the London Olympics.

你還可以學更多

a) 請利用網路查詢下列關鍵字，以了解更多關於 Zaha Hadid 的資訊：

⊘ A picture of Zaha Hadid

⊘ Some pictures of the Fire Station in Weil-am-Rhein in Germany

⊘ Some pictures of the BMW building in Leipzig

⊘ Zaha Hadid's company

⊘ The Pritzker Prize

⊘ The London Olympics

b) 請試著用英文討論下列話題：

1. 你想不想認識札哈・哈蒂？為什麼？

2. 她建造的哪些建築是你想參觀的？

3. 你覺得建築物應該要重美觀還是重實用？

4. 你最愛的台灣建築是什麼？你為什麼喜歡它？

5. 你還認識其他哪些有名的建築師？你對他們有哪些了解？

解 答

 閱讀理解

Her working method and style	❸
Architecture training	❷
Some of her buildings	❺
The opera house prize	❹
Education and childhood	❶
Her current projects	❻

 重要詞彙

attract a lot of attention	引起廣泛注意
car factory	車廠
client	客戶
commission	受託
critic	評論家
design	設計
drawing stage	繪圖階段
engineer	工程師
fire station	消防隊
furniture	家具
get a degree in	拿到……的學位
jewelry	珠寶
model	模型

move out	搬出
opera house	歌劇院
outcry	強烈抗議
plan	計畫
practical	實用的
prestigious	有聲望的
production line	生產線
project	專案

 填 空

(01) got a degree in

(02) prestigious

(03) plans

(04) drawing stage

(05) models

(06) designs

(07) engineers

(08) clients

(09) projects

(10) fire station

(11) critics

(12) moved out

(13) opera house

(14) attracted a lot of attention

(15) outcry

(16) practical

(17) car factory

(18) production line

(19) furniture

(20) jewelry

(21) commissioned

Damien Hirst
達米恩 · 赫斯特

人物速覽

- 藝術家
- 1965 年生於英國布里斯托
  （Bristol, England）
- 1995年泰納獎（Turner Prize）
  得主
- 世界上最富有的藝術家

❶ **Damien Hirst** was born into a working-class family and had a difficult childhood. His father left the family when Damien was very young. Damien was always a naughty boy, stealing from shops and getting into trouble with the police. He showed only one talent at school, and that was for drawing. When he was 18 he went to an exhibition of contemporary[1] art at a famous gallery[2] in London. That visit changed his life. Damien decided he wanted to be an artist.

❷ He attended Goldsmiths University in London, a college famous for its modern art department. While he was a student, he worked in a mortuary[3] preparing bodies for funerals. While he was a student, Hirst became famous for his very different approach[4] to art. Instead of painting and drawing, Hirst was interested in conceptual[5] art, and liked to create installations[6] with long names.

❸ He organized an art show in his second year of college to show his own art and that of his friends. The exhibition was held in an abandoned[7] building in London's Docklands, a very unusual place for an art exhibition. After graduation, he continued to hold art shows in strange places with

---

Ⓦ Ⓞ Ⓡ Ⓓ Ⓛ Ⓘ Ⓢ Ⓣ

★ 1. contemporary [kən`tɛmpəˌrɛrɪ] *adj.* 當代的
★ 2. gallery [`gælərɪ] *n.* 畫廊
  3. mortuary [`mɔrtʃuˌɛrɪ] *n.* 太平間；停屍處
★ 4. approach [ə`protʃ] *n.* 方法
  5. conceptual [kən`sɛptʃuəl] *adj.* 概念的
  6. installation [ˌɪnstə`leʃən] *n.* 裝置（物）
★ 7. abandoned [ə`bændənd] *adj.* 被遺棄的
  8. millionaire [ˌmɪljən`ɛr] *n.* 百萬富翁

his friends. One of his shows was visited by a famous millionaire[8] called Charles Saatchi. Mr. Saatchi was so impressed with Damien's art that he decided to become his patron[9] and support the young artist in whatever he wanted to create.

❹ Hirst's art in this period was about death. His most famous work at this time was *The Physical Impossibility of Death in the Mind of Someone Living*. It was a dead shark floating in a tank[10] of formaldehyde,[11] a kind of liquid used for preserving[12] dead bodies. Saatchi bought the piece for £50,000. Another famous piece from this period was called *A Thousand Years*. It was a cow's head in a cage with maggots[13] feeding on the head. The maggots turned into flies and were then killed by electrocution.[14] When this was first shown to the public, many people vomited.[15] In 1995 he won the Turner Prize, the top prize for artists in the UK.

❺ Hirst is the richest and most famous British artist. He and his friends have made British art famous all over the world. He once sold a piece of art called *Lullaby Spring* for $19.2 million. Another of his works was sold for $100 million. As he became rich and famous, however, his art began to be copied and he has had to sue[16] other artists many times for stealing his ideas and making illegal copies of his work.

9. patron [ˋpetrən] *n.* 贊助者
10. tank [tæŋk] *n.* 水槽
11. formaldehyde [fɔrˋmældə͵haɪd] *n.* 甲醛；防腐劑
12. preserve [prɪˋzɝv] *v.* 保存；維持
13. maggot [ˋmægət] *n.* 蛆
14. electrocution [͵ɪlɛktrəˋkjuʃən] *n.* 觸電死亡；電刑
15. vomit [ˋvɑmɪt] *v.* 嘔吐
16. sue [su] *v.* 控告

❻ Hirst has created many different kinds of art, including music videos for famous pop groups, movies, paintings, and installations. He has also written a book about his life and written two hit pop songs. While some people think he is a genius of the modern art world, others hate his work. A famous critic has said that Hirst's work has no meaning apart from[17] its price. Regardless,[18] he has done much to popularize[19] modern art.

譯文

❶ 達米恩‧赫斯特出身於一個勞動階級家庭，並有個艱苦的童年。在達米恩非常小的時候，父親就離開了家。達米恩向來是個調皮的男孩，會去商店偷東西並招惹警察。他在學校時只展現出一項天賦，那就是畫畫。在 18 歲時，他去倫敦的著名畫廊看了一場當代藝術展。這次的參觀改變了他的人生。達米恩決定，他想要當個藝術家。

❷ 他到倫敦的金匠大學就讀，這所學院是以它的現代藝術系所而著稱。在學生時期，他到停屍間打工，為葬禮準備大體。在當學生時，赫斯特就變得很有名，因為他的藝術手法十分不同。除了畫畫和繪圖之外，赫斯特對觀念藝術也很有興趣，喜歡創作名字很長的裝置藝術。

❸ 他在大學二年級時辦了一場藝術展，展出自己和朋友的藝術品。這場展覽在倫敦碼頭區的廢棄大樓裡舉行。以藝術展覽來說，那是個非常特別的地方。畢業後，他跟朋友繼續在奇怪的地方舉辦藝術展。一位名叫查爾斯‧薩

17. apart from 除了……之外
18. regardless [rɪˋgɑrdlɪs] *adv.* 儘管如此；無論如何
19. popularize [ˋpɑpjələˏraɪz] *v.* 使……受歡迎；使……大眾化

奇的知名富豪去看了他的一場展出。薩奇先生相當欣賞達米恩的藝術，於是決定成為他的贊助人，支持這位年輕藝術家去創作他想要的東西。

❹ 在此時期，赫斯特的藝術是關於死亡。他在此時最有名的作品是《生者對死者無動於衷》，是一隻死掉的鯊魚浮在甲醛槽裡，這種液體是用來保存屍體。薩奇以五萬英鎊買下了這件作品。這段時期的另一件著名作品叫做作《一千年》，籠子裡有一個牛頭，頭上則有蛆在進食。蛆變成了蒼蠅，然後觸電而死。當它首度在大眾面前展示時，許多人為之作嘔。 1995 年，他贏得了泰納獎，是英國藝術家的最高獎項。

❺ 赫斯特是最富有與最出名的英國藝術家。他和他的朋友使英國藝術舉世聞名。他曾經以 1,920 萬美元賣出一件叫作《搖籃曲之春》的藝術品。他的另一件作品則賣了一億美元。但隨著他變得富有與出名，他的藝術開始被抄襲，他不得不多次控告其他藝術家剽竊他的創意，以及非法抄襲他的作品。

❻ 赫斯特創造了許多不同種類的藝術，包括著名流行團體的音樂錄影帶、電影、繪畫和裝置藝術。他還寫了一本書來談他的人生，並寫了兩首很紅的流行歌曲。有的人認為他是現代藝術界的天才，有的人則討厭他的作品。有位著名的評論家曾說，赫斯特的作品除了它的價碼外，毫無意義。儘管如此，他還是對現代藝術的普及貢獻良多。

閱讀理解

配合題,請判斷下列摘要各屬於文章的哪個段落,見範例。

College life	❷
Fame and fortune	
Childhood and early life	
His art	
His reputation	
Early career	

 重要詞彙

連連看,請為每個詞彙找出它的正確翻譯。

▨ mortuary • • 廢棄大樓

▨ approach to • • ……的方法

▨ art show • • 藝術展

▨ conceptual art • • 觀念藝術

▨ installation • • 當代藝術

▨ contemporary art • • 觸電死亡

▨ electrocution • • 展覽

▨ modern art • • 甲醛

▨ abandoned building • • 畫廊

▨ formaldehyde • • 非法抄襲

▨ gallery • • 裝置

▨ illegal copy • • 現代藝術

▨ exhibition • • 停屍間

maggot	•	•	蛆
vomit	•	•	音樂錄影帶
shark	•	•	贊助人
music video	•	•	鯊魚
sue	•	•	控告
talent	•	•	天賦
patron	•	•	作嘔

✏ 填 空

理解文章大意後，請用前項習題中的詞彙來完成句子，有些字須做適當變化。

■ Damien showed a (01)＿＿＿＿＿ for drawing from an early age.

■ He attended an (02)＿＿＿＿＿ of (03)＿＿＿＿＿ in a famous (04)＿＿＿＿＿ in London.

■ He preferred (05)＿＿＿＿＿ when he was in college.

■ He worked in a (06)＿＿＿＿＿ when he was a student.

■ His (07)＿＿＿＿＿ art was quite different. He was interested in (08)＿＿＿＿＿, and liked to make (09)＿＿＿＿＿ rather than pictures.

■ He held his first (10)＿＿＿＿＿ in an (11)＿＿＿＿＿ in London.

■ He found a millionaire who wanted to be his (12)＿＿＿＿＿.

■ His most famous piece of art was a (13)＿＿＿＿＿ in (14)＿＿＿＿＿.

■ Another famous piece of art by Hirst was a cow's head being eaten by (15)_____.

■ The maggots turned into flies which were then killed by (16)_____. Many people (17)_____ when they saw this piece.

■ Hirst has had to (18)_____ many people for making (19)_____ of his work.

■ He has also made (20)_____ for famous pop groups.

你還可以學更多

a) 請利用網路查詢下列關鍵字，以了解更多關於 **Damien Hirst** 的資訊：

☑ A picture of Damien Hirst

☑ A picture of the shark piece

☑ A picture of the cow's head piece

☑ A piece by Damien Hirst called Pharmacy

☑ The Turner Prize

☑ Damien Hirst's other art

b) 請試著用英文討論下列話題：

1. 你想不想認識達米恩‧赫斯特？為什麼？
2. 他有哪些藝術品是你想看的？
3. 你比較喜歡裝置類的觀念藝術，還是傳統的藝術？
4. 你覺得赫斯特是個偉大的藝術家，還是你同意評論家的看法？
5. 假如你看到牛頭被蛆啃食，你會想吐嗎？這為什麼會被視為藝術？

解 答

閱讀理解

College life	❷
Fame and fortune	❺
Childhood and early life	❶
His art	❹
His reputation	❻
Early career	❸

重要詞彙

abandoned building	廢棄大樓
approach to	……的方法
art show	藝術展
conceptual art	觀念藝術
contemporary art	當代藝術
electrocution	觸電死亡
exhibition	展覽
formaldehyde	甲醛
gallery	畫廊
illegal copy	非法抄襲
installation	裝置
modern art	現代藝術
mortuary	停屍間

maggot	蛆
music video	音樂錄影帶
patron	贊助人
shark	鯊魚
sue	控告
talent	天賦
vomit	作嘔

 填 空

(01) talent

(02) exhibition

(03) contemporary art

(04) gallery

(05) modern art

(06) mortuary

(07) approach to

(08) conceptual art

(09) installations

(10) art show

(11) abandoned building

(12) patron

(13) shark

(14) formaldehyde

(15) maggots

(16) electrocution

(17) vomited

(18) sue

(19) illegal copies

(20) music videos

Part 5

高瞻遠矚的科學家

Marie Curie

Alan Turing

Jane Goodall

Stephen Hawking

Unit 17

Marie Curie
瑪麗·居里

人物速覽

- 物理學家及化學家
- 1867 年生於波蘭華沙（Warsaw, Poland），1934 年卒於法國巴黎
- 1903 年諾貝爾物理獎（Nobel Prize in Physics）得主
- 1911 年諾貝爾化學獎（Nobel Prize in Chemistry）得主

❶ **Marie Curie** was born into a middle-class Polish[1] family. Both her parents were well-known teachers. Her father taught math and science, and her mother ran a school for young ladies. From an early age, Marie and her sisters showed talent in math and science. Her sister Bronislawa wanted to become a doctor, so Marie made a pact[2] with her. Marie would work and support her sister during her studies; when Bronislawa graduated, she in turn[3] would work and support Marie in her studies. Marie worked as a governess[4] for various different families and sent money to her sister, who was studying in Paris.

❷ In 1891, Marie went to Paris to study physics, chemistry and math at the Sorbonne, a famous university in Paris. She was very poor, despite her sister's help with money, and she studied hard during the day and tutored[5] at night. When she graduated, she wanted to return to Poland to work as a physicist,[6] but the university she applied to refused her application just because she was a woman. She decided to remain in Paris.

❸ Marie worked as a scientist on uranium.[7] It was already known that uranium was a source of energy called radioactivity.[8] Marie's discovery

---

Ⓦⓞⓡⓓ Ⓛⓘⓢⓣ

1. Polish [ˈpolɪʃ] *adj.* 波蘭的
2. pact [pækt] *n.* 協定；約定
3. in turn 依次地；依序地
4. governess [ˈgʌvənɪs] *n.* 女家庭教師
5. tutor [ˈtutɚ] *v.* 擔任家教
6. physicist [ˈfɪzəsɪst] *n.* 物理學家
7. uranium [juˈrenɪəm] *n.* 鈾
8. radioactivity [ˌredɪoækˈtɪvətɪ] *n.* 放射性

was that this energy came from the uranium atom,[9] and not from some chemical interaction[10] between uranium and its surroundings.[11] This was a very important discovery. During the process, she also discovered several other radioactive[12] substances[13] such as radium,[14] polonium,[15] and thorium.[16]

❹ In 1894, Marie met a French scientist called Pierre Curie. They fell in love and worked together. Pierre had his own scientific work, but he helped Marie with hers and insisted that she take all the credit for[17] it. Their work involved processing large amounts of a mineral[18] called pitchblende.[19] They did this hard work by hand, boiling it and stirring[20] it for hours, trying to find and isolate[21] the radioactive element. They did not know that this work was very dangerous to them both, because it exposed them to large amounts of radiation,[22] which is very harmful to the human body. Pierre was killed in a traffic accident in 1906. His death was a terrible shock to Marie.

❺ In 1903, Marie, Pierre and another scientist shared the Nobel Prize in Physics. She was the first woman to be awarded the prize. In 1911 she

---

Ⓦ Ⓞ Ⓡ Ⓓ Ⓛ Ⓘ Ⓢ Ⓣ

9. atom [ˋætəm] *n.* 原子
10. interaction [ˌɪntɚˋækʃən] *n.* 交互作用
11. surroundings [səˋraʊndɪŋz] *n.* 環境；四周
12. radioactive [ˌredɪoˋæktɪv] *adj.* 放射性的
★ 13. substance [ˋsʌbstəns] *n.* 物質
14. radium [ˋredɪəm] *n.* 鐳
15. polonium [pəˋlonɪəm] *n.* 釙
16. thorium [ˋθorɪəm] *n.* 釷
★ 17. take the credit for 因⋯⋯而獲得光榮；拿走⋯⋯的功勞

was awarded the Nobel Prize in Chemistry. She was the first person to be awarded the prize twice. The awards helped her to persuade the French government to fund her work. They opened an institute[23] of radium to study physics, chemistry and medicine. Marie was named the first director, an incredible[24] position for a woman to hold at the time.

❻ During her last years, despite her worldwide fame and success, Marie was lonely and depressed without her husband. She was also very ill. Years of exposure[25] to radiation had completely damaged her health. After her death she was buried next to her husband.

譯文

❶ 瑪麗‧居里出身於一個中產階級的波蘭家庭。父母都是知名的教師。父親教數學和自然科學,母親則辦了一所學校供年輕女子就讀。自小以來,瑪麗和她的姊妹就展現出數學和科學方面的天賦。姊姊博勞尼斯拉娃想要當醫生,於是瑪麗便跟她立下約定。在姊姊就學期間,瑪麗會工作養她;等博勞尼斯拉娃畢業後,再換她工作來支持瑪麗念書。瑪麗到各個不同的家庭擔任家庭教師,並把錢寄給在巴黎讀書的姊姊。

18. mineral [ˈmɪnərəl] *n.* 礦石
19. pitchblende [ˈpɪtʃˌblɛnd] *n.* 瀝青鈾礦(鈾和鐳的主要原礦)
20. stir [stɜ] *v.* 攪拌
★ 21. isolate [ˈaɪsḷˌet] *v.* 使……分離
★ 22. radiation [ˌredɪˈeʃən] *n.* 幅射
★ 23. institute [ˈɪnstəˌtut] *n.* 協會;研究所
24. incredible [ɪnˈkrɛdəbḷ] *adj.* 驚人的;難以置信的
★ 25. exposure [ɪkˈspoʒɚ] *n.* 暴露

❷ 1891 年，瑪麗前往巴黎的索邦攻讀物理、化學及數學，那是巴黎一所著名的大學。儘管姊姊幫忙出錢，她還是很窮。白天的時候，她用功讀書，晚上則去當家教。畢業後，她想要回波蘭當個物理學家，但她所申請的大學拒絕了她的申請，只因為她是個女人。於是她決定留在巴黎。

❸ 瑪麗當起了鈾方面的科學家。大家已經知道，鈾是所謂放射線這種能量的來源。瑪麗的發現則在於，這種能量是來自鈾的原子，而非來自鈾和周遭環境的一些化學交互作用。這是非常重要的發現。在此過程中，她還發現了其他數種放射性物質，像是鐳、釙和釷。

❹ 1894 年，瑪麗認識了名叫皮耶‧居里的法國科學家。他們墜入愛河，並一起工作。皮耶有自己的科學工作，但他協助瑪麗工作，並堅持由她享有一切的功勞。他們的工作牽涉到處理大量的一種礦物，所謂的瀝青鈾礦。他們徒手從事這些辛苦的工作，把它煮沸、攪拌好幾個鐘頭，以設法找出並隔離放射性元素。他們不曉得這些工作對他們兩個非常危險，因為這使他們暴露在大量的放射物中，對人體的傷害很大。皮耶在 1906 年死於車禍，他的死使瑪麗大受打擊。

❺ 1903 年，瑪麗、皮耶和另一位科學家共同得到了諾貝爾物理獎。她是第一位獲頒此獎的女性。1911 年，她獲頒諾貝爾化學獎。她是第一個二度獲獎的人。這些獎幫助她說服法國政府資助她的工作。他們設立了鐳研究所來研究物理、化學和醫學。瑪麗被任命為首任所長，對當時的女性來說這是個遙不可及的職位。

❻ 在她人生的最後幾年，儘管在全世界享有盛名與成就，失去丈夫卻使她感到孤獨和憂鬱。她也病得很重，長年暴露在放射物之中徹底拖垮了她的健康。她死後被葬在丈夫旁邊。

閱讀理解

配合題，請判斷下列摘要各屬於文章的哪個段落，見範例。

Student life	❷
The Nobel prizes	
Death	
Childhood and early life	
Her husband and marriage	
Her scientific discoveries	

 重要詞彙

連連看，請為每個詞彙找出它的正確翻譯。

- apply to   •
- physics   •
- mineral   •
- atom   •
- element   •
- application •
- expose   •
- governess   •
- institute   •
- chemistry   •
- interaction •
- isolate   •
- pact   •

- 申請（名詞）
- 申請（動詞）
- 原子
- 化學
- 元素
- 暴露
- 家庭教師
- 研究機構
- 交互作用
- 隔離
- 礦物
- 約定
- 物理

■ take all the credit for	•	• 處理
■ radiation	•	• 放射物
■ process	•	• 有幅射的
■ radioactivity	•	• 放射性
■ run a school	•	• 辦學校
■ uranium	•	• 物質
■ substance	•	• 享有……的所有功勞
■ tutor	•	• 當家教
■ radioactive	•	• 鈾

 填 空

理解文章大意後，請用前項習題中的詞彙來完成句子，有些字須做適當變化。

■ Marie's mother (01)_____ for young ladies, and her father
was a famous teacher.

■ She made a (02)_____ with her sister that they would support
each others' studies.

■ She worked as a (03)_____ in her early life.

■ She studied (04)_____ and (05)_____ at the
Sorbonne in Paris.

■ She (06)_____ a university in Poland to teach, but her
(07)_____ was refused because she was a woman.

■ She discovered that the (08)_____ of (09)_____ was
due to its (10)_____, and not due to the (11)_____ of

uranium and its surroundings, as was commonly believed.

■ She also discovered many other radioactive (12)_____.

■ Her husband insisted that Marie (13)_____ her discoveries.

■ Marie and her husband spent a lot of time (14)_____ large amounts of a (15)_____ called pitchblende.

■ They were able to (16)_____ the (17)_____ (18)_____ in pitchblende.

■ Their work (19)_____ them to very harmful levels of (20)_____.

■ Marie was named the first director of a scientific (21)_____ started by the French government.

 你還可以學更多

a) 請利用網路查詢下列關鍵字，以了解更多關於 **Marie Curie** 的資訊：

☑ A picture of Marie Curie

☑ A picture of Pierre Curie

☑ A picture of uranium

☑ A picture of someone with radiation poisoning

☑ Uranium

☑ Pitchblende

b) 請試著用英文討論下列話題：

1. 你想不想認識瑪麗‧居里？為什麼？
2. 因為性別而在申請大學職務時遭到拒絕，你覺得瑪麗有什麼感想？
3. 你覺得瑪麗‧居里的工作對科學的哪些方面很重要？
4. 你覺得瑪麗‧居里的工作對女權的哪些方面很重要？
5. 你覺得居里夫婦假如知道鐳的危險性，他們會停止研究它嗎？

解 答

 閱讀理解

Student life	❷
The Nobel prizes	❺
Death	❻
Childhood and early life	❶
Her husband and marriage	❹
Her scientific discoveries	❸

 重要詞彙

application	申請（名詞）
apply to	申請（動詞）
atom	原子
chemistry	化學
element	元素
expose	暴露
governess	家庭教師
institute	研究機構
interaction	交互作用
isolate	隔離
mineral	礦物
pact	約定
physics	物理

process	處理
radiation	放射物
radioactive	有輻射的
radioactivity	放射性
run a school	辦學校
substance	物質
take all the credit for	享有……的所有功勞
tutor	當家教
uranium	鈾

 填 空

(01) ran a school

(02) pact

(03) governess

(04) physics

(05) chemistry

(06) applied to

(07) application

(08) radioactivity

(09) uranium

(10) atom

(11) interaction

(12) substances

(13) take all the credit for

(14) processing

(15) mineral

(16) isolate

(17) radioactive

(18) element

(19) exposed

(20) radiation

(21) institute

Alan Turing
亞倫‧杜林

人物速覽

- 數學家
- 解碼專家
- 1912年生於英國倫敦，1954年卒於
  英國柴郡（Chesire, England）
- 現代電腦科學之父

❶ **Alan Turing** was born in London, but his parents spent a lot of time in India, where his father was working for the British government. Alan and his brother were brought up by friends of their parents and spent most of their childhood at expensive boarding[1] schools. From an early age, Alan showed great talent in math and science. He won a scholarship to Cambridge, and studied advanced[2] math there. His thesis[3] was so good that he was made a fellow[4] of King's College, Cambridge, a great and unusual honor for such a young student. He then went to America to do a Ph.D. at Princeton.

❷ It was in America that he became interested in cryptology,[5] which means the creation and breakage[6] of secret codes. When World War II broke out, Turing volunteered to work for the British government as a code breaker.[7] He and many other mathematicians[8] were sent to work at a secret location. Their job was to intercept[9] coded radio signals from the enemy and then decode[10] them. The work was difficult as the German codes, called Enigma,[11] were very advanced. Turing invented a machine that would break the codes. His work saved many thousands of English and American lives during the war.

─── Ⓦ Ⓞ Ⓡ Ⓓ Ⓛ Ⓘ Ⓢ Ⓣ ───────────

★ 1. boarding [ˋbordɪŋ] *n.* 寄宿；供膳宿
  2. advanced [ədˋvænst] *adj.* 高等的；進步的
  3. thesis [ˋθisɪs] *n.* 論文
  4. fellow [ˋfɛlo] *n.* （英國大學的）特別研究生
  5. cryptology [krɪpˋtɑlədʒɪ] *n.* 密碼術
  6. breakage [ˋbrekɪdʒ] *n.* 破解
  7. breaker [ˋbrekə] *n.* 破解者
  8. mathematician [ˌmæθəməˋtɪʃən] *n.* 數學家
  9. intercept [ˌɪntəˋsɛpt] *v.* 竊聽；攔截

❸ After the war, Turing continued to work for the government. He designed the world's first computer. He was appointed deputy[12] director of the new computing department at Manchester University, a famous university in the UK. While at Manchester, he worked on the problem of artificial[13] intelligence, designing machines that could think. He designed a famous test called the Turing Test. This test is still used today to measure[14] the intelligence of machines.

❹ Alan Turing was gay at a time when it was illegal to be gay. He had to keep this a secret from everyone he knew. In 1952, he made friends with a young man. The young man and his friend burgled[15] Turing's house while Turing was away. Turing called the police, and during the investigation the police found out about Turing and the young man's relationship. Turing was arrested for being gay.

❺ Because Turing's work had been so important for the government, he was given a choice. He could either go to prison for the crime of homosexuality,[16] or his arrest could stay secret but Turing would have to undergo[17] treatment[18] for his homosexuality. In those days homosexuality was regarded as an illness and there were various treatments available.

10. decode [diˋkod] *v.* 解碼
11. Enigma [ɪˋnɪgmə] *n.* 恩尼格瑪密碼
12. deputy [ˋdɛpjətɪ] *n.* 代理人；使節
★ 13. artificial [ˌɑrtəˋfɪʃəl] *adj.* 人工的；人造的
14. measure [ˋmɛʒə] *v.* 測量；評價
★ 15. burgle [ˋbɝgl] *v.* 行竊
16. homosexuality [ˌhoməsɛkʃuˋælətɪ] *n.* 同性戀
17. undergo [ˌʌndəˋgo] *v.* 接受；經歷
18. treatment [ˋtritmənt] *n.* 治療；處置

Turing chose the second option. He had chemical therapy,[19] which was very painful, humiliating[20] and had serious side effects.[21]

❻ Turing was found dead in his room in June 1954. A half eaten apple was found next to his bed. An autopsy[22] on his body found that he had died of cyanide[23] poisoning. It is still not known whether he was assassinated[24] because he was a security risk or whether he committed suicide. Since his death, Alan Turing has been recognized as the genius he was. The world's most auspicious[25] computing award is named the Turing Award in his honor.

譯文

❶ 亞倫‧杜林出生於倫敦，但他的父母在印度待了很長的時間，因為他父親在當地為英國政府工作。亞倫和他哥哥是由父母的友人代為撫養，他們的童年大部分都是在昂貴的寄宿學校中度過。亞倫自小就在數學及自然科學方面展現出很高的天賦。他拿到劍橋的獎學金，並到那裡攻讀高等數學。他的論文十分出色，使他成了劍橋國王學院的一員。對一個這麼年輕的學生來說，這是一項崇高而難得的榮譽。後來他又到美國的普林斯頓攻讀博士。

❷ 在美國期間，他開始對密碼學感到興趣，也就是編製與破解密碼。二次世

★ 19. therapy [ˈθɛrəpɪ] *n.* 療法
20. humiliating [hjuˈmɪlɪˌetɪŋ] *adj.* 屈辱的
21. side effect [ˈsaɪd ɪˈfɛkt] *n.* 副作用
22. autopsy [ˈɔtɑpsɪ] *n.* 驗屍
23. cyanide [ˈsaɪəˌnaɪd] *n.* 氰化物
24. assassinate [əˈsæsṇˌet] *v.* 暗殺；行刺
25. auspicious [ɔˈspɪʃəs] *adj.* 幸運的；吉利的

界大戰爆發時，杜林自願替英國政府擔任解碼員。他和其他許多數學家被派遣到祕密地點工作。他們的工作是攔截加密的無線電信號，然後加以破解。這項工作的困難之處在於，德國所謂「恩尼格瑪」的密碼非常先進。杜林發明了一台可以破解這些密碼的機器。在戰爭期間，他的工作拯救了成千上萬個英國人與美國人的性命。

❸ 到了戰後，杜林繼續替政府工作。他設計了世界上第一台電腦。他獲派擔任曼徹斯特大學新設運算系的副主任，這是英國一所著名的大學。在曼徹斯特時，他著手人工智慧的問題，設計懂得思考的機器。他設計了一項著名的測試，名為杜林測試。這項測試如今仍被用來測量機器的智力。

❹ 亞倫·杜林是個同性戀者，而在當時，同性戀並不合法。他必須保守這個秘密，不讓他所認識的每個人知道。1952年，他跟一位年輕男子交往。這位年輕男子趁杜林不在的時候，夥同友人到他家行竊。杜林向警方報了案，而在調查期間，警方發現了杜林和這位年輕男子的關係。杜林因同性戀而遭到逮捕。

❺ 由於杜林的工作對政府十分重要，因此他有個選擇。他可以因同性戀的罪名去坐牢；或者他被捕的事可以保密，但杜林必須去治療他的同性戀。在當時，同性戀被視為一種病，並且有不同的療法。杜林選擇了第二個。他接受了化療，非常痛苦與羞辱，而且有嚴重的副作用。

❻ 1954年6月，杜林被發現陳屍房內。在他的床邊發現一顆咬了一半的蘋果。勘驗他的屍體後發現，他是死於氰中毒。依然無法得知的是，他是因為屬於危安份子而遭人暗殺，還是自殺。自他死後，亞倫·杜林被公認為天才。世界上最崇高的運算獎也被命名為杜林獎，以向他致敬。

閱讀理解

配合題，請判斷下列摘要各屬於文章的哪個段落，見範例。

Code breaker	❷
His arrest	
His difficult choice	
Childhood and student life	
Death and reputation	
His contribution to math and computing	

 重要詞彙

連連看，請為每個詞彙找出它的正確翻譯。

- ▨ autopsy •
- ▨ bring up •
- ▨ enemy •
- ▨ burgle •
- ▨ chemical therapy •
- ▨ artificial intelligence •
- ▨ code breaker •
- ▨ cyanide poisoning •
- ▨ commit suicide •
- ▨ boarding school •
- ▨ cryptology •
- ▨ decode •

- • 人工智慧
- • 驗屍
- • 寄宿學校
- • 撫養
- • 行竊
- • 化療
- • 解碼員
- • 自殺
- • 密碼學
- • 氰中毒
- • 解碼
- • 敵人

▦ option	•	•	同性戀的
▦ homosexual	•	•	羞辱的
▦ intercept	•	•	不合法的
▦ illegal	•	•	攔截
▦ investigation	•	•	調查
▦ undergo treatment	•	•	選項
▦ secret location	•	•	無線電信號
▦ radio signal	•	•	密碼
▦ humiliating	•	•	秘密地點
▦ secret code	•	•	論文
▦ thesis	•	•	進行治療

填 空

理解文章大意後，請用前項習題中的詞彙來完成句子，有些字須做適當變化。

▦ Alan was (01)_____ by friends of his parents and at

(02)_____ in England.

▦ His (03)_____ at Cambridge was so good that he was made

a fellow.

▦ He became interested in (04)_____ while he was at

Princeton. He was an expert at making (05)_____, and an

expert (06)_____ as well.

▦ During the war he worked for the British government in a

(07)_____. His job was to (08)_____ coded

(09)_____ from the (10)_____ and then

(11) _____ them.

■ He was interested in the problem of (12) _____ .

■ Turing was gay at a time when it was (13) _____ to be gay.

■ His house was (14) _____ , and during the police

(15) _____ , the police discovered he was (16) _____ .

■ Turing chose to (17) _____ rather than go to prison.

■ This (18) _____ was difficult. He was given (19) _____ ,

which was (20) _____ and depressing.

■ After his death, an (21) _____ was performed. It was found he

died of (22) _____ .

■ It is still not known if he was assassinated or if he (23) _____ .

🌐 你還可以學更多

a) 請利用網路查詢下列關鍵字，以了解更多關於 **Alan Turing** 的資訊：

⊘ A picture of Alan Turing
⊘ A picture of a statue of Alan Turing
⊘ The Turing test
⊘ The A.M. Turing Award
⊘ The Enigma Code
⊘ Bletchley Park

b) 請試著用英文討論下列話題：

1. 你想不想認識亞倫‧杜林？為什麼？
2. 因為同性戀而遭到逮捕，你覺得杜林有什麼感想？
3. 你覺得他所得到的選擇公不公平？為什麼？
4. 他在戰時拯救了這麼多性命，你覺得政府有沒有公平地對待他？
   為什麼？
5. 杜林的工作在哪些方面對全世界來說很重要？

解 答

 閱讀理解

Code breaker	❷
His arrest	❹
His difficult choice	❺
Childhood and student life	❶
Death and reputation	❻
His contribution to math and computing	❸

 重要詞彙

artificial intelligence	人工智慧
autopsy	驗屍
boarding school	寄宿學校
bring up	撫養
burgle	行竊
chemical therapy	化療
code breaker	解碼員
commit suicide	自殺
cryptology	密碼學
cyanide poisoning	氰中毒
decode	解碼
enemy	敵人

homosexual	同性戀的
humiliating	羞辱的
illegal	不合法的
intercept	攔截
investigation	調查
option	選項
radio signal	無線電信號
secret code	密碼
secret location	祕密地點
thesis	論文
undergo treatment	進行治療

 填 空

(01) brought up

(02) boarding schools

(03) thesis

(04) cryptology

(05) secret codes

(06) code breaker

(07) secret location

(08) intercept

(09) radio signals

(10) enemy

(11) decode

(12) artificial intelligence

(13) illegal

(14) burgled

(15) investigation

(16) homosexual

(17) undergo treatment

(18) option

(19) chemical therapy

(20) humiliating

(21) autopsy

(22) cyanide poisoning

(23) committed suicide

Unit
19

Jane Goodall
珍‧古德

人物速覽

- 靈長類行為學家
- 動物權倡導人士
- 1934 年生於英國倫敦
- 聯合國和平大使

❶ When **Jane Goodall** was a little girl, her parents gave her a stuffed[1] toy chimpanzee.[2] She called the toy Jubilee. This was the start of her interest in animals, and especially her interest in chimpanzees and other kinds of primates.[3] Jane studied anthropology[4] at college, but was always interested in the social behavior of animals, especially primates.

❷ She got her first job helping a famous anthropologist[5] in Africa. She was assigned the task of studying chimpanzees. Up until that time, chimpanzees and other monkeys were regarded as being primitive[6] animals, which means that people believed primates did not have social relationships and did not communicate — believed, in other words, that primates were just dumb[7] animals.

❸ Jane discovered two important things about chimps.[8] She discovered first that they have a language; the sounds they make actually have meaning. She learned some of their words, and was able to communicate with the animals on a very basic level. From this she deduced[9] that chimps had a very basic level of cognition,[10] which means that they could

---

Ⓦ Ⓞ Ⓡ Ⓓ Ⓛ Ⓘ Ⓢ Ⓣ

1. stuffed [stʌft] *adj.* 填充的
2. chimpanzee [ˌtʃɪmpænˋzi] *n.* 黑猩猩
3. primate [ˋpraɪmɪt] *n.* 靈長類動物
4. anthropology [ˌænθrəˋpɑlədʒɪ] *n.* 人類學
5. anthropologist [ˌænθrəˋpɑlədʒɪst] *n.* 人類學家
★ 6. primitive [ˋprɪmətɪv] *adj.* 原始的
7. dumb [dʌm] *adj.* 【口語】愚蠢的
8. chimp [tʃɪmp] *n.* 【口語】chimpanzee 的省略
9. deduce [dɪˋdus] *v.* 推斷；推測
10. cognition [kɑgˋnɪʃən] *n.* 認知；認識力

think more or less like people by recognizing and solving problems. She also discovered that chimps have a social structure, and form families and social groups.

❹ The second thing she discovered was that chimps make and use tools. Before that time, it was widely believed that the difference between man and animals was that only man made and used tools. However, Jane noticed that the chimps would strip[11] leaves from trees, modify[12] the shape of the leaves, and then use the leaves to extract[13] ants from an anthill[14] in order to eat them. The chimps were making and using simple tools. This was a very important discovery and changed the way scientists think about animal behavior.

❺ Jane's work was very controversial.[15] Many scientists criticized her methods, saying they were not scientific. For example, her habit of naming the animals she was studying was regarded as unscientific, as well as her habit of talking to them in their own language. Another controversial thing she did was to support the work of zoos. She has

Ⓦ Ⓞ Ⓡ Ⓓ Ⓛ Ⓘ Ⓢ Ⓣ

11. strip [strɪp] v. 剝去
12. modify [ˋmɑdəˌfaɪ] v. 修正；改變
13. extract [ɪkˋstrækt] v. 取出
14. anthill [ˋæntˌhɪl] n. 蟻丘
15. controversial [ˌkɑntrəˋvɝʃəl] adj. 引起爭議的
16. poacher [ˋpotʃɚ] n. 偷獵者
17. controversy [ˋkɑntrəˌvɝsɪ] n. 爭議
18. activism [ˋæktɪvˌɪzəm] n. 實踐主義
19. UN [ˋjuˋɛn] n. 聯合國
★ 20. messenger [ˋmɛsṇdʒɚ] n. 信差；使者

often said that zoos are often better for the animals than the real environment, where animals are threatened by poachers[16] and hunters. In spite of these controversies,[17] Jane's work has done much to further our understanding of primate behavior.

❻ Jane became very interested in animal rights and activism.[18] Her work showed her that the difference between people and primates is not that great, so we should therefore treat animals better. In 1977, she founded the Jane Goodall Institute, which works to promote animal rights and environmental protection around the world. She has been honored in many countries and has received many awards for her work. In 2002, she was named a UN[19] Messenger[20] of Peace. Jane travels around the world all the time, teaching people about chimps and how to care for the environment.

譯文

❶ 珍‧古德是個小女孩的時候,父母給了她一個黑猩猩填充玩具。她把這個玩具叫做朱比利。這是她對動物感興趣的起點,尤其是對黑猩猩以及其他各種靈長類動物的興趣。珍在大學讀的是人類學,但她一直對動物的社會行為非常有興趣,尤其是靈長類動物。

❷ 她找到的第一份工作是在非洲幫忙一位知名的人類學家。她所獲派的任務是研究黑猩猩。在此之前,黑猩猩和其他猴子都被視為原始動物。這表示大家相信靈長類動物不具有社會關係,也不會溝通;換句話說,就是相信靈長類只是愚蠢的動物。

❸ 珍對於黑猩猩有兩項重要發現。她首先發現牠們有語言;牠們所發出的聲音其實有意義。她學了一些牠們的用字,並能跟這些動物作一些基本溝通。

她從這點推斷，黑猩猩具有非常基本程度的認知。這表示牠們或多或少能以人類的方式思考，察覺並解決問題。她還發現，黑猩猩具有社會結構，會組成家庭與社會團體。

❹ 她所發現的第二件事在於，黑猩猩會製作及使用工具。在此之前，一般普遍相信人跟動物的差別就在於，只有人類才會製作及使用工具。不過，珍注意到黑猩猩會折下樹上的葉子、調整葉子的形狀，然後用葉子挖出蟻丘裡的螞蟻，把它們吃掉。黑猩猩會製作及使用簡單的工具，這是非常重要的發現，也改變了科學家對動物行為的看法。

❺ 珍的工作極具爭議性。很多科學家批評她的方法，說它不科學。例如，她習慣替她所研究的動物取名字，就被認為不科學。還有，她習慣用牠們的語言來跟牠們說話。她所引發的另一個爭議之處在於，她支持動物園的作法。她常說，動物園通常比實際環境更適合動物，在實際環境中動物會受到盜獵者和獵人的威脅。儘管有這些爭議，珍的工作對於我們進一步了解靈長類動物行為還是貢獻良多。

❻ 珍對於動物權及實踐主義變得非常有興趣。她的工作向她證明了，人跟靈長類動物的差別並沒有那麼大，所以我們應該更好好對待動物。 1977年，她成立了珍古德協會，在全世界努力提倡動物權與環保。她在許多國家都受到推崇，並因為她的工作而獲得許多獎項。 2002年，她被任命為聯合國和平大使。珍一直在周遊世界，教導民眾認識黑猩猩及如何照顧環境。

閱讀理解

配合題，請判斷下列摘要各屬於文章的哪個段落，見範例。

Introduction to chimpanzees	❷
Controversies	
Chimp languag	
Animal rights	
Chimps and tools	
Childhood and student life	

重要詞彙

連連看，請為每個詞彙找出它的正確翻譯。

▨ communicate •	• 實踐主義
▨ animal right •	• 動物行為
▨ anthropologist •	• 動物權
▨ activism •	• 蟻丘
▨ anthill •	• 人類學家
▨ anthropology •	• 人類學
▨ assign •	• 螞蟻
▨ basic level •	• 分派
▨ ant •	• 基本程度
▨ chimpanzee •	• 黑猩猩
▨ criticize •	• 認知
▨ animal behavior •	• 溝通
▨ cognition •	• 批評

▨ dumb	•	• 推斷
▨ environmental protection	•	• 發現
▨ discovery	•	• 愚蠢的
▨ extract	•	• 環保
▨ form	•	• 取出
▨ habit	•	• 組成
▨ method	•	• 習慣
▨ deduce	•	• 獵人
▨ modify	•	• 方法
▨ poacher	•	• 修正
▨ primate behavior	•	• 盜獵者
▨ unscientific	•	• 靈長類動物的行為
▨ primate	•	• 靈長類動物
▨ scientific	•	• 原始的
▨ hunter	•	• 科學的
▨ scientist	•	• 科學家
▨ social behavior	•	• 社會行為
▨ threaten	•	• 社會團體
▨ social group	•	• 社會關係
▨ primitive	•	• 社會結構
▨ social relationship	•	• 剝去；折下
▨ task	•	• 填充玩具
▨ social structure	•	• 任務
▨ strip	•	• 威脅
▨ stuffed toy	•	• 不科學的

填 空

理解文章大意後，請用前項習題中的詞彙來完成句子，有些字須做適當變化。

▪ Jane's parents gave her a (01)_____ (02)_____ when she was a little girl. This started her interest in (03)_____.

▪ She studied (04)_____ in college. She was interested in the (05)_____ of animals.

▪ A famous (06)_____ (07)_____ her the task of studying chimps.

▪ At that time, most people thought chimps were (08)_____ animals, that they did not have (09)_____, and that they could not (10)_____ — that they were just (11)_____ animals.

▪ Jane discovered that chimps can communicate on a (12)_____, and that they form (13)_____ and (14)_____.

▪ She (15)_____ that they have (16)_____: that they can think.

▪ Her most important discovery about (17)_____ was that the chimps (18)_____ leaves from a tree and (19)_____ them to (20)_____ (21)_____ from an (22)_____.

▪ She was criticized by other (23)_____, who said that her (24)_____ were not (25)_____.

- Her (26) _____ of giving the animals names was regarded as

  (27) _____ .

- She knew that often wild animals were threatened by (28) _____

  and (29) _____ .

- She became interested in (30) _____ and (31) _____ .

- She now travels the world talking about (32) _____ .

你還可以學更多

a) 請利用網路查詢下列關鍵字，以了解更多關於 **Jane Goodall** 的資訊：

- ✓ A picture of Jane Goodall
- ✓ A picture of her toy chimp, Jubilee
- ✓ A picture of a real chimp
- ✓ The Jane Goodall Institute
- ✓ Primates
- ✓ An interview with Jane Goodall

b) 請試著用英文討論下列話題：

1. 你想不想認識珍・古德？為什麼？
2. 你想不想認識黑猩猩？為什麼？
3. 除了黑猩猩外，你還知道哪些靈長類動物？
4. 珍對黑猩猩的研究讓我們對人類有了哪些體認？
5. 你覺得動物待在動物園裡會過得更好、還是更糟？

解 答

 閱讀理解

Introduction to chimpanzees	❷
Controversies	❺
Chimp language	❸
Animal rights	❻
Chimps and tools	❹
Childhood and student life	❶

 重要詞彙

activism	實踐主義
animal behavior	動物行為
animal right	動物權
anthill	蟻丘
anthropologist	人類學家
anthropology	人類學
ant	螞蟻
assign	分派
basic level	基本程度
chimpanzee	黑猩猩
cognition	認知
communicate	溝通
criticize	批評

deduce	推斷
discovery	發現
dumb	愚蠢的
environmental protection	環保
extract	取出
form	組成
habit	習慣
hunter	獵人
method	方法
modify	修正
poacher	盜獵者
primate behavior	靈長類動物的行為
primate	靈長類動物
primitive	原始的
scientific	科學的
scientist	科學家
social behavior	社會行為
social group	社會團體
social relationship	社會關係
social structure	社會結構
strip	剝去；折下
stuffed toy	填充玩具
task	任務
threaten	威脅
unscientific	不科學的

填 空

(01) stuffed toy

(02) chimpanzee

(03) primates

(04) anthropology

(05) social behavior

(06) anthropologist

(07) assigned

(08) primitive

(09) social relationships

(10) communicate

(11) dumb

(12) basic level

(13) social structures

(14) social groups

(15) deduced

(16) cognition

(17) animal behavior

(18) stripped

(19) modified

(20) extract

(21) ants

(22) anthill

(23) scientists

(24) methods

(25) scientific

(26) habit

(27) unscientific

(28) poachers

(29) hunters

(30) animal rights

(31) activism

(32) environmental protection

Unit 20

Stephen Hawking
史蒂芬·霍金

人物速覽

- 理論物理學家
- 暢銷科學作家
- 1942年生於英國牛津
- 總統自由獎章（the Presidential Medal of Freedom）得主

❶ **Stephen Hawking**'s father was a professor at Oxford University in England, where he taught biology.[1] From an early age, Stephen was interested in math. He did not do very well at school and at college, and had strange study habits, preferring to think things through for himself rather than reading what other scholars had done and said. However, a few of his teachers realized that he had an exceptional[2] mind. At college he studied physics and astronomy,[3] and became interested in theoretical[4] physics.

❷ Theoretical physics is a very difficult subject, and not many people in the world understand it. Among his achievements[5] in this field, his work on black holes is his most famous. Black holes are areas of space where gravity[6] is so strong that it sucks[7] in everything nearby, including light. This means that black holes cannot be seen with the eye, but can only be inferred[8] theoretically, and by looking at the radiation they emit.[9] Black holes are also known as dead stars. Hawking furthered[10] our understanding of black holes and what they are.

Ⓦ Ⓞ Ⓡ Ⓓ Ⓛ Ⓘ Ⓢ Ⓣ

1. biology [baɪˋɑlədʒɪ] *n.* 生物學
★ 2. exceptional [ɪkˋsɛpʃənl̩] *adj.* 出眾的；優秀的
3. astronomy [əˋstrɑnəmɪ] *n.* 天文學
4. theoretical [ˌθiəˋrɛtɪkl̩] *adj.* 理論的；學理的
★ 5. achievement [əˋtʃivmənt] *n.* 成就
★ 6. gravity [ˋgrævətɪ] *n.* 重力；引力
★ 7. suck [sʌk] *v.* 吸
★ 8. infer [ɪnˋfɝ] *v.* 推論
9. emit [ɪˋmɪt] *v.* 放射；發出
10. further [ˋfɝðɚ] *v.* 促進；推展

❸ Stephen knew his work was very difficult to understand for non-specialists. However, he firmly believed that everyone should be able to understand his ideas. In 1988 he wrote a book called *A Brief History of Time* aimed at the lay[11] person. In it, he attempted to explain the basic concepts of theoretical physics and cosmology.[12] Surprisingly, the book became a huge best-seller. It was on the best-seller list for 4 years and has sold 9 million copies in many different languages. The book made Stephen Hawking rich and famous outside the small world of physics professors.

❹ When he was 21, Hawking was diagnosed[13] with a motor neuron disease.[14] His disease causes gradual paralysis[15] of his body. His doctors told him he only had two or three years to live. This made him very depressed, but he resolved to continue his work. His illness has gotten worse and worse. He is now completely paralyzed[16] and can only move his eyes and one of his cheeks. He cannot use his own voice or his hands.

❺ He uses a voice synthesizer[17] called a DECtalk. This machine was developed during the 1980s and is very difficult and time-consuming[18] to use. There are now more modern and easier machines for disabled[19]

Ⓦ Ⓞ Ⓡ Ⓓ Ⓛ Ⓘ Ⓢ Ⓣ

11. lay [le] *adj.* 外行的
12. cosmology [kɑz`mɑlədʒɪ] *n.* 宇宙論
13. diagnose [ˌdaɪəg`nos] *v.* 診斷
14. motor neuron disease [`motɚ `nʊrən dɪ`ziz] *n.* 運動神經元疾病
15. paralysis [pə`ræləsɪs] *n.* 痲痺；癱瘓
16. paralyze [`pærəˌlaɪz] *v.* 使……痲痺；使……癱瘓

people to use, but Stephen prefers to use this one, as he says he likes the sound of the artificial voice and has grown used to using it. What is interesting is that although Stephen is British, his voice has an American accent.[20]

❻ Stephen Hawking has been married twice. He married his first wife just after getting his diagnosis,[21] and they were married for 26 years. They had three children together. Hawking then married his nurse and they were married for 10 years. Hawking has received honors from many countries, and was one of the youngest people to be elected to the Royal Society, the top organization for scientists in the world.

譯文

❶ 史蒂芬的父親是英國牛津大學的教授，教的是生物學。自小以來，史蒂芬就對數學感興趣。他在求學及念大學時表現得不是頂好，而且有個奇怪的讀書習慣，寧可靠自己來想通事情，也不願意去看其他學者做過和說過什麼。不過，他的一些老師知道他有顆絕佳的頭腦。在大學時，他讀的是物理和天文學，並變得對理論物理感興趣。

❷ 理論物理是非常艱澀的學科，世界上沒多少人懂。以他在這個領域的成就

---

17. synthesizer [ˋsɪnθəˏsaɪzɚ] *n.* 合成器
18. time-consuming [ˋtaɪm kənˋsumɪŋ] *adj.* 耗時的
★ 19. disabled [dɪsˋebl̩d] *adj.* 殘廢的
★ 20. accent [ˋæksɛnt] *n.* 口音；腔調
21. diagnosis [ˏdaɪəgˋnosɪs] *n.* 診斷

而言，最有名的就是對於黑洞的研究。黑洞是引力極強的空間場域，會把周遭的一切都吸進來，包括光線在內。這表示黑洞無法用肉眼看到，而只能用理論來推斷，以及觀測它所發散出的輻射。黑洞也是所謂的死星。霍金使我們更加了解黑洞，以及它的本質。

❸ 史蒂芬知道，他的研究很難讓非專業人士了解。不過，他堅信人人都應該能了解他的想法。1988 年，他針對外行民眾寫了一本書叫做《時間簡史》。他在書中試圖解釋理論物理和宇宙論的基本觀念。出人意料的是，這本書變成了暢銷鉅著。在暢銷書排行榜上待了四年，並以許多不同的語言版本賣了900 萬冊。這本書讓史蒂芬．霍金在物理學教授的小圈圈外變得名利雙收。

❹ 在 21 歲時，霍金被診斷出一種運動神經元疾病。他的病會導致身體逐漸癱瘓。醫生告訴他，他只剩兩、三年可活。這使得他非常沮喪，但他決心繼續他的工作。他的病愈來愈嚴重。目前他已經完全癱瘓，只能動眼睛和一邊的臉頰。他沒辦法運用自己的聲音或雙手。

❺ 他使用了一種叫做 DECtalk 的語音合成器。這種機器是在 1980 年代開發而成，使用起來非常困難又耗時。目前有更現代與更簡便的機種可以讓失能人士使用，但史蒂芬寧可使用這種，因為他說他喜歡人工語音的聲音，而且也用得愈來愈習慣。有趣的地方在於，雖然史蒂芬是英國人，但他的語音卻是美國腔。

❻ 史蒂芬．霍金結過兩次婚。他跟第一任妻子是在診斷出得病不久後結婚，並維持了 26 年。他們共有三個小孩。後來霍金娶了他的護士，並維持了 10 年。霍金獲得過許多國家的榮譽，並且是入選皇家學會最年輕的人之一，這是全世界科學家的最高機構。

閱讀理解

配合題,請判斷下列摘要各屬於文章的哪個段落,見範例。

Black holes	❷
Childhood and student life	
His voice	
Family life and reputation	
Best-seller	
His illness	

重要詞彙

連連看,請為每個詞彙找出它的正確翻譯。

- achievement •
- disabled people •
- aim at •
- be diagnosed with •
- artificial voice •
- accent •
- attempt to •
- basic concept •
- black hole •
- cosmology •
- astronomy •
- biology •
- diagnosis •

- • 腔調
- • 成就
- • 針對
- • 人工語音
- • 天文學
- • 試圖
- • 基本觀念
- • 生物學
- • 黑洞
- • 宇宙論
- • 被診斷出
- • 診斷(名詞)
- • 失能人士

▨ emit	•	• 表現很好
▨ do well	•	• 散發
▨ exceptional	•	• 絕佳的
▨ field	•	• 領域
▨ theoretically	•	• 使我們更加了解……
▨ further our understanding of	•	• 逐漸的
▨ gradual	•	• 引力
▨ infer	•	• 推斷
▨ lay person	•	• 外行人
▨ motor neuron disease	•	• 運動神經元疾病
▨ gravity	•	• 非專業人士
▨ non-specialist	•	• 癱瘓
▨ paralyze	•	• 教授
▨ professor	•	• 決心……
▨ resolve to	•	• 空間
▨ space	•	• 讀書習慣
▨ study habit	•	• 吸進
▨ time-consuming	•	• 理論物理
▨ suck in	•	• 理論上地
▨ theoretical physics	•	• 把事情想通
▨ think things through	•	• 耗時的
▨ voice synthesizer	•	• 語音合成器

 填 空

理解文章大意後，請用前項習題中的詞彙來完成句子，有些字須做適當變化。

▨ Stephen's father was a **(01)** ＿＿＿＿＿＿ of **(02)** ＿＿＿＿＿＿ at

Oxford University in England.

■ Stephen did not (03)_____ at school. He had strange

(04)_____. He preferred to (05)_____ on his own.

■ His teachers recognized that he had an (06)_____ mind.

■ He studied (07)_____ and (08)_____ in college.

■ He has made many important (09)_____ in the

(10)_____ of theoretical physics.

■ (11)_____ are areas of (12)_____ where

(13)_____ is so strong that it even (14)_____ light.

They cannot be seen, but can be (15)_____ (16)_____.

■ Black holes (17)_____ radiation.

■ Hawking (18)_____ of black holes.

■ He wrote a book aimed at (19)_____. He wants the

(20)_____ to understand his ideas.

■ He (21)_____ to describe the (22)_____ of

(23)_____ in his book.

■ He was (24)_____ (25)_____. This illness causes

(26)_____ paralysis.

■ He (27)_____ continue his work after he received his

(28)_____.

■ He is now completely (29)_____ and can only communicate

with a (30)_____.

■ This voice synthesizer is very old and **(31)**_____ to use.

■ There are now more modern voice synthesizers for **(32)**_____ to use.

■ Hawking's **(33)**_____ has an American **(34)**_____ even though Hawking is British.

 你還可以學更多

a) 請利用網路查詢下列關鍵字，以了解更多關於 **Stephen Hawking** 的資訊：

- ✓ A picture of Stephen Hawking
- ✓ A picture of his bestselling book
- ✓ A picture of a black hole
- ✓ Stephen Hawking's voice
- ✓ Motor neuron disease
- ✓ The Royal Society

b) 請試著用英文討論下列話題：

1. 你想不想認識史蒂芬・霍金？為什麼？
2. 你覺得霍金對他的病有什麼感想？
3. 你喜不喜歡霍金的人工語音聲音？為什麼？
4. 你了解黑洞是什麼嗎？
5. 霍金的研究在哪些方面對人類很重要？

解答

閱讀理解

Black holes	❷
Childhood and student life	❶
His voice	❺
Family life and reputation	❻
Best-seller	❸
His illness	❹

重要詞彙

accent	腔調
achievement	成就
aim at	針對
artificial voice	人工語音
astronomy	天文學
attempt to	試圖
basic concept	基本觀念
biology	生物學
black hole	黑洞
cosmology	宇宙論
be diagnosed with	被診斷出
diagnosis	診斷（名詞）
disabled people	失能人士

do well	表現很好
emit	散發
exceptional	絕佳的
field	領域
further our understanding of	使我們更加了解……
gradual	逐漸的
gravity	引力
infer	推斷
lay person	外行人
motor neuron disease	運動神經元疾病
non-specialist	非專業人士
paralyze	癱瘓
professor	教授
resolve to	決心……
space	空間
study habit	讀書習慣
suck in	吸進
theoretical physics	理論物理
theoretically	理論上地
think things through	把事情想通
time-consuming	耗時的
voice synthesizer	語音合成器

填 空

(01) professor

(02) biology

(03) do well

(04) study habits

(05) think things through

(06) exceptional

(07) astronomy

(08) theoretical physics

(09) achievements

(10) field

(11) Black holes

(12) space

(13) gravity

(14) sucks in

(15) inferred

(16) theoretically

(17) emit

(18) furthered our understanding

(19) non-specialists

(20) lay person

(21) attempted

(22) basic concepts

(23) cosmology

(24) diagnosed with

(25) motor neurone disease

(26) gradual

(27) resolved to

(28) diagnosis

(29) paralyzed

(30) voice synthesizer

(31) time-consuming

(32) disabled people

(33) artificial voice

(34) accent

Part 6

獨領風騷的商場強人

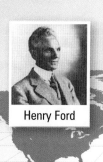

Henry Ford

Oprah Winfrey

Coco Chanel

Jerry Yang

Unit 21

Henry Ford
亨利・福特

人物速覽

- 發明家
- 企業改革者
- 1863 年生於美國密西根
  （Michigan, USA），1947 年卒於美
  國密西根
- 量產組裝線發明人

❶ **Henry Ford** was born to a poor farming family. His mother died when he was 13 years old. Henry's father wanted him to take over the farm, but Henry didn't want to be a farmer. He was interested in machines and wanted to work in the city. At the age of 16, he left the farm and went to work in a factory in Detroit.[1] While he was in Detroit, he invented a motor driven[2] bicycle with four wheels instead of two. He showed it to his boss, the famous inventor Thomas Edison. Edison was impressed and encouraged Ford to improve the machine. Ford decided to start his own company. After many stops and starts and changes of investors, the Ford Motor Company was started in 1903.

❷ At first, the Ford Motor company produced one product only: a car called the Model T. The Model T was very cheap to produce, and it was painted black as black was the cheapest color paint. It had three pedals[3] and no footbrake.[4] Although it was difficult to start, it was very easy to drive. It was extremely popular and by 1918 half of all the cars in America were Model Ts.

❸ Ford wanted to find a way to make his cars cheaper so that more people could afford them. After many experiments, he invented mass production.[5] In this method of manufacturing, instead of a few craftsmen[6]

Ⓦ Ⓞ Ⓡ Ⓓ Ⓛ Ⓘ Ⓢ Ⓣ

1. Detroit [dɪˋtrɔɪt] *n.* 底特律
2. motor driven [ˋmotɚ ͵drɪvən] *adj.* 馬達驅動的；電動的
3. pedal [ˋpɛdl] *n.* 踏板
4. footbrake [ˋfʊt͵brek] *n.* 腳剎車
5. mass production [ˋmæs prəˋdʌkʃən] *n.* 大量生產
6. craftsman [ˋkræfstmən] *n.* 工匠；技工

working on one car together until the car was completed, Ford used a lot of workers who only knew how to do one small job, which they just repeated. This meant that many cars could be produced at the same time. Production went even faster once an assembly line[7] was introduced to carry the car to each worker, rather than the workers walking to each car. Because mass production produced so many products at the same time, the unit cost of each product dropped.

❹ As well as this manufacturing innovation,[8] Ford also introduced two very important business innovations. The first was to pay his workers $5 per day. This was a very large sum of money in those days, and his factory attracted all the best workers, who stayed in the company for many years, giving their experience and loyalty[9] to the company, helping to reduce costs. Also, the high wages meant that many of the workers could afford to buy the cars themselves, and they did.

❺ The second important innovation was in the way the cars were sold. Ford established dealers[10] in every major city in America. He encouraged these dealers to start car clubs. He spent a lot of money on advertising, and made sure the local newspapers were always full of stories about the Model T. In 1930 he introduced a financing service,[11] lending money to low income people so that they could buy a Model T.

Ⓦ Ⓞ Ⓡ Ⓓ Ⓛ Ⓘ Ⓢ Ⓣ

★ 7. assembly line [ə`sɛmblɪ ˌlaɪn] *n.* 組裝生產線
  8. innovation [ˌɪnə`veʃən] *n.* 改革；革新
★ 9. loyalty [`lɔɪəltɪ] *n.* 忠誠
  10. dealer [`dilɚ] *n.* 商人；業者
  11. financing service [faɪ`nænsɪŋ `sɜvɪs] *n.* 融資服務

❻ Henry Ford's production and business methods were so successful that other car manufacturers soon appeared, all using the same systems and ideas that his company did. Soon, mass production was applied to other products apart from cars, and the modern consumer society was born.

譯文

❶ 亨利・福特出身於一個貧窮的農家。在他13歲時，母親就過世了。亨利的父親要他接管農場，但亨利並不想當農人。他對機械有興趣，並且想去城市工作。在16歲時，他離開了農場，到底特律的一家工廠上班。在底特律時，他發明了馬達傳動式的腳踏車，並以四輪取代兩輪。他把它拿給老闆看，也就是知名的發明家湯瑪斯・愛迪生。愛迪生很欣賞，並鼓勵福特改良這台機器。福特決定自己開公司。經過多次停停走走與投資人的更迭後，福特汽車公司在1903年建立。

❷ 一開始福特汽車公司只生產一種產品：一款名叫T型車的汽車。T型車的生產成本非常便宜，而且是漆成黑色，因為黑色是最廉價的色漆。它有三個踏板，沒有腳煞車。它雖然很難啟動，但卻非常好駕駛。它大受歡迎，所以到了1918年，美國有半數的汽車都是T型車。

❸ 福特想要找方法使他的汽車更便宜，好讓更多人買得起。在多次實驗後，他發明了量產。這種製造方法並不是由少數工匠一起做一輛車，直到車子做好為止。福特用了許多工人，他們只知道要怎麼持續重複做一小部分的工作。這表示許多車子可以在同一時間生產。等到引進了組裝線，使車子傳送到每個工人面前，而不必由工人走到每輛車前面，生產又變得更快了。由於量產是同時生產非常多的產品，所以每個產品的單位成本就降低了。

❹ 連同這項製造的創新，福特還引進了兩項非常重要的企業改革。第一項是每天付五美元給工人。這在當時是非常大的一筆錢，所以他的工廠吸引了所有最優秀的工人，他們在公司一待就是好多年，除了把本身的經驗與忠誠奉獻給公司，也有助於降低成本。此外，高薪也代表許多工人可以負擔得起買車，而他們也確實買了。

❺ 第二項重要改革是汽車的銷售方式。福特在美國各大城市建立了經銷商。他鼓勵這些經銷商成立汽車俱樂部。他花了很多錢打廣告，確保地方報紙永遠充滿著Ｔ型車的報導。1930年，他引進了融資服務，也就是借錢給低所得的民眾，使他們得以購買Ｔ型車。

❻ 亨利・福特的生產及營業之道十分成功，所以其他汽車製造商很快就出現了，而且全都採用跟他公司一樣的制度與概念。不久後，量產被應用到汽車之外的其他產品，現代消費社會也就此誕生。

閱讀理解

配合題，請判斷下列摘要各屬於文章的哪個段落，見範例。

High wages	❹
Early life and the Ford Motor Company	
Marketing and advertising	
The Model T	
Ford's impact on the world	
Mass production	

 重要詞彙

理解文章大意後，請用前項習題中的詞彙來完成句子，有些字須做適當變化。

■ establish • • 組裝線
■ business innovation • • 老闆
■ assembly line • • 企業改革
■ business method • • 經營之道
■ company • • 公司
■ craftsman • • 消費社會
■ dealer • • 工匠
■ boss • • 商人
■ footbrake • • 建立
■ experiment • • 實驗
■ factory • • 工廠
■ financing service • • 融資服務
■ consumer society • • 腳煞車

innovation	•	• 高薪
invent	•	• 使留下深刻印象
unit cost	•	• 創新
investor	•	• 發明
low income	•	• 投資人
impress	•	• 低所得
loyalty	•	• 忠誠
machine	•	• 機械
production	•	• 製造
manufacture	•	• 量產
motor driven	•	• 馬達傳動式的
high wage	•	• 踏板
worker	•	• 生產（動詞）
pedal	•	• 產品
produce	•	• 生產（名詞）
mass production	•	• 降低成本
product	•	• 接掌
reduce cost	•	• 單位成本
take over	•	• 工人

 填 空

理解文章大意後，請用前項習題中的詞彙來完成句子，有些字須做適當變化。

- Henry's father wanted him to (01)＿＿＿＿＿＿＿ the farm, but Henry was more interested in (02)＿＿＿＿＿＿＿.

- He worked in a (03)＿＿＿＿＿＿＿, where he (04)＿＿＿＿＿＿＿ a

(05) _____ four wheel bicycle.

- His boss was very (06) _____ with the machine.

- Henry started his own (07) _____ with some (08) _____.

- The company (09) _____ only one (10) _____: the Model T.

- The Model T had three (11) _____ but no (12) _____.

- Henry invented (13) _____ after many (14) _____. Instead of (15) _____ making one car together, he had many (16) _____ working on an (17) _____.

- His (18) _____ changed (19) _____ and made (20) _____ cheaper, because the (21) _____ of each product was lower.

- In addition to this manufacturing innovation in the way cars were made, Ford also introduced some (22) _____ in the way the cars were sold.

- The (23) _____ he paid his workers encouraged their (24) _____ and helped to (25) _____.

- He (26) _____ (27) _____ all over America to sell the cars, and also introduced a (28) _____ so that (29) _____ people could buy the car.

- Ford's (30) _____ started the modern (31) _____.

你還可以學更多

a) 請利用網路查詢下列關鍵字，以了解更多關於 **Henry Ford** 的資訊：

- ✓ A picture of Henry Ford
- ✓ A picture of his bestselling car, the Model T
- ✓ A picture of an assembly line
- ✓ Ford Motor Company
- ✓ Car clubs
- ✓ Thomas Edison

b) 請試著用英文討論下列話題：

1. 你想不想認識亨利・福特？為什麼？
2. 你想不想有一台 T 型車？為什麼？
3. 你喜不喜歡車子？為什麼？
4. 你知道車子是怎麼運作的嗎？
5. 你覺得世界上將來會出現哪些發明？

解 答

閱讀理解

High wages	❹
Early life and the Ford Motor Company	❶
Marketing and advertising	❺
The Model T	❷
Ford's impact on the world	❻
Mass production	❸

重要詞彙

assembly line	組裝線
boss	老闆
business innovation	企業改革
business method	經營之道
company	公司
consumer society	消費社會
craftsman	工匠
dealer	商人
establish	建立
experiment	實驗
factory	工廠
financing service	融資服務
footbrake	腳煞車

high wage	高薪
impress	使留下深刻印象
innovation	創新
invent	發明
investor	投資人
low income	低所得
loyalty	忠誠
machine	機械
manufacture	製造
mass production	量產
motor driven	馬達傳動式的
pedal	踏板
produce	生產（動詞）
product	產品
production	生產（名詞）
reduce cost	降低成本
take over	接掌
unit cost	單位成本
worker	工人

 填 空

(01) take over   **(02)** machines

(03) factory   **(04)** invented

(05) motor driven   **(06)** impressed

(07) company   **(08)** investors

(09) produced

(10) product

(11) pedals

(12) footbrake

(13) mass production

(14) experiments

(15) craftsmen

(16) workers

(17) assembly line

(18) innovations

(19) manufacturing

(20) production

(21) unit cost

(22) business innovations

(23) high wages

(24) loyalty

(25) reduce costs

(26) established

(27) dealers

(28) financing service

(29) low income

(30) business methods

(31) consumer society

Unit 22

Coco Chanel
可可 · 香奈兒

人物速覽

- 時裝設計師
- 1883 年生於法國索米爾（Saumur, France），1971 年卒於法國巴黎
- 女企業家

❶ **Coco Chanel** was born into a very poor French family. Her real name was Gabrielle, but her family called her 'Coco.' Her father was a traveling salesman and was often away. Her parents married after she was born. Her mother died when she was 12. Her father could not afford to keep a family, so Coco and her sisters were sent to an orphanage[1] where they were brought up by nuns. It was during her life in the orphanage that Coco learned how to sew clothes. When she was 18, she left the orphanage to make her own way in the world with her needle.

❷ Coco started designing hats as a hobby. In 1913, Coco opened her own shop selling hats, jackets and raincoats.[2] The business venture[3] was not a success, and soon closed, losing lots of money. But Coco was not deterred.[4] With the backing[5] of a rich lover, she managed to open another shop. Soon, some of the most famous actresses in France were wearing her hats.

❸ During the 1920s, Chanel revolutionized[6] fashion. Before that time, clothes for women were fussy,[7] with big, long skirts, lots of fabric[8] and corsets[9] and padding.[10] The clothes were difficult to put on and restricted

Ⓦⓞⓡⓓ Ⓛⓘⓢⓣ

★ 1. orphanage [ˈɔrfənɪdʒ] *n.* 孤兒；孤兒院
2. raincoat [ˈrenˌkot] *n.* 雨衣
3. venture [ˈvɛntʃɚ] *n.* 冒險的事業
4. deter [dɪˈtɝ] *v.* 阻止；阻礙
5. backing [ˈbækɪŋ] *n.* 支持；支援
6. revolutionize [ˌrɛvəˈluʃənˌaɪz] *v.* 徹底改革
7. fussy [ˈfʌsɪ] *adj.* 裝飾過頭的；過於講究細節的
8. fabric [ˈfæbrɪk] *n.* 布料
9. corset [ˈkɔrsɪt] *n.* 整形內衣
10. padding [ˈpædɪŋ] *n.* 襯墊；裝填

the movement of the wearer. Chanel designed a new look which included short skirts and pants for the first time in the history of women's fashion, no corsets, and short hair. Women who wore this new look were called 'flappers'[11] because of their wild dancing and independence. Chanel was inspired to create this look by the clothes men wore. She wanted to give women the same freedom of movement in their clothes that men had.

❹ In 1920, Chanel decided to make a perfume. She wanted something quite different from previous perfumes. She wanted something that did not smell like flowers, but that smelled unnatural. She asked a perfumer[12] to make her some samples. He presented her with nine small samples. She chose the 5th sample as her favorite, and called it Number 5. At that time it was the most expensive perfume in the world, and is still one of the most popular and famous.

❺ After World War II, the fashion industry was dominated[13] by other designers and Chanel was not popular. She designed a suit for women, which combined a heavy hard wearing fabric called 'tweed'[14] with style

---

Ⓦ Ⓞ Ⓡ Ⓓ Ⓛ Ⓘ Ⓢ Ⓣ

11. flapper [`flæpɚ] *n.* 搖擺女郎;摩登女郎
12. perfumer [pɚ`fjumɚ] *n.* 香水製造者
★ 13. dominate [`dɑməˌnet] *v.* 支配;控制
14. tweed [`twid] *n.* 粗呢
15. in return for 以⋯⋯回報;以⋯⋯交換
★ 16. license [`laɪsn̩s] *n.* 認可;授權;執照
17. controversial [ˌkɑntrə`vɝʃəl] *adj.* 有爭議的
18. figure [`fɪgjɚ] *n.* 人物
19. duke [djuk] *n.* 公爵
★ 20. liberate [`lɪbəˌret] *v.* 使⋯⋯獲自由;解放

and freedom. It was another revolution for fashion. She also used her business sense to look for new ways to expand her business. She decided to allow other designers to use her name in return for[15] a license[16] fee. In this way she started a trend which has become the main way the fashion industry operates today.

❻ Coco was always a controversial[17] figure.[18] She was independent and had lots of lovers, most of them very rich and influential. She knew many famous people, including dukes,[19] princesses, and movie stars, all of whom loved to wear her clothes and her perfume. Her impact on the 20th century is huge because she liberated[20] women's fashion and helped create the modern fashion industry.

譯文

❶ 可可‧香奈兒出身於一個非常貧窮的法國家庭。她的真名是嘉伯莉，但家人都叫她「可可」。她父親是個四處出差的推銷員，經常不在家。父母是在她出生後才結婚。在她12歲時，母親就過世了。父親負擔不起家裡的開銷，於是可可和妹妹被送去了孤兒院，由修女撫養長大。在孤兒院的生活期間，可可學會了怎麼縫衣服。等到18歲時，她離開了孤兒院，帶著縫衣針闖蕩天下。

❷ 可可開始把設計帽子當成嗜好。1913年，可可自己開店賣帽子、外套和雨衣。這次的創業並不成功，很快就收攤了，而且賠了很多錢。但可可並不氣餒。在有錢情人的資助下，她設法開了另一家店。不久後，法國有些最知名的女演員都戴起了她的帽子。

❸ 在1920年代，香奈兒顛覆了時尚。在此之前，女裝都是過度講究，裙子又大又長，布料很多，還有束腹和襯墊。這些衣服很難穿上去，也限制了穿著者的行動。香奈兒設計了新的樣貌，包括女性時裝史上首次出現的短裙和短

褲、沒了束腹，並搭配上短髮。以這種新樣貌來穿著的女性被稱為「搖擺女郎」，因為她們舞步狂野又獨立自主。香奈兒創造此種樣貌是受到男性服飾的啓發，她想要讓女性在服裝上跟男性享有同樣的自由。

❹ 1920 年，香奈兒決定做香水。她要的是跟過去截然不同的香水。她要的是聞起來不像花香、而是聞起來不自然的香水。她要一位香水業者做一些樣品給她。他給了她九種小樣品。她挑選了第五個樣品當作她的最愛，並把它稱為五號香水。當時它是世界上最貴的香水，迄今仍是最受歡迎與最有名的其中一款。

❺ 二次世界大戰後，時尚產業掌控在其他設計師手中，香奈兒並不受歡迎。她設計了一款女性套裝，並把所謂「粗花呢」的厚重耐磨布料跟時髦和自由結合在一起。這是時尚的另一項革命。她還運用了她的商業頭腦來尋找擴展事業的新方法。她決定讓其他設計師使用她的名稱，以換取權利金。她以這種方式開啓了一股潮流，並成了現今時裝業的主要經營方式。

❻ 可可一直是個具爭議性的人物。她很獨立，情人很多，而且大部分都是非常有錢又有影響力。她認識很多名人，包括公爵、公主和電影明星，他們全都愛穿她的衣服和用她的香水。她對於 20 世紀影響深遠，因為她解放了女性的時尚，並幫忙打造了現代時裝產業。

閱讀理解

配合題，請判斷下列摘要各屬於文章的哪個段落，見範例。

Hats	❷
Reputation and influence	
Chanel Number 5	
The Chanel suit	
Childhood and early life	
The flappers	

重要詞彙

連連看，請為每個詞彙找出它的正確翻譯。

- figure •
- fashion industry •
- backing •
- business venture •
- corset •
- designer •
- afford •
- business sense •
- design •
- be dominated by •
- expand her business •
- deter •
- fabric •

- • 負擔得起
- • 支持
- • 商業敏感度
- • 創業
- • 束腹
- • 設計師
- • 設計
- • 阻礙
- • 被⋯⋯支配
- • 擴展她的事業
- • 布料
- • 時裝產業
- • 人物

■ hardwearing	•	•	過度講究的
■ wearer	•	•	耐磨的
■ hobby	•	•	嗜好
■ in return for	•	•	換取……
■ jacket	•	•	受……啟發
■ liberate	•	•	外套
■ license fee	•	•	解放
■ be inspired by	•	•	權利金
■ needle	•	•	縫衣針
■ nun	•	•	修女
■ operate	•	•	經營
■ padding	•	•	孤兒院
■ perfume	•	•	襯墊
■ fussy	•	•	香水
■ perfumer	•	•	香水業者
■ style	•	•	雨衣
■ raincoat	•	•	限制
■ suit	•	•	徹底改革
■ restrict	•	•	樣品
■ orphanage	•	•	縫
■ revolutionize	•	•	裙子
■ sample	•	•	風格；流行款式
■ sew	•	•	套裝
■ skirt	•	•	巡迴推銷員
■ traveling salesman	•	•	潮流
■ trend	•	•	穿著者

填 空

理解文章大意後，請用前項習題中的詞彙來完成句子，有些字須做適當變化。

- Chanel's father was a (01)_____ who could not (02)_____ to keep a family.

- Coco and her sisters were brought up by (03)_____ in an (04)_____ .

- The nuns taught Coco how to (05)_____ . She was very skillful with her (06)_____ .

- She started (07)_____ hats as a (08)_____ .

- Her first shop sold hats, (09)_____ and (10)_____ . It was not a successful (11)_____ .

- Chanel was not (12)_____ , and with new (13)_____ from another rich friend, she opened another shop.

- Her designs (14)_____ fashion.

- In the early 20th century, women's clothes were (15)_____ , with long (16)_____ , lots of (17)_____ , and (18)_____ and (19)_____ . The clothes (20)_____ the movement of the (21)_____ .

- The 'flapper' look was (22)_____ men's clothes.

- Chanel wanted to create a (23)_____ . She asked a

(24) _____ to make some (25) _____ for her.

■ After the War, the fashion industry was (26) _____ other

(27) _____.

■ Chanel designed a (28) _____ made of (29) _____

fabric, but which still had great (30) _____.

■ Chanel had very good (31) _____ and was able to

(32) _____ by allowing other designers to use her name

(33) _____ a (34) _____.

■ She started a (35) _____ which still (36) _____ today in

the fashion industry.

■ Chanel was a controversial (37) _____, a truly (38) _____

woman.

🌀 你還可以學更多

a) 請利用網路查詢下列關鍵字，以了解更多關於 **Coco Chanel** 的資訊：

☑ A picture of Coco Chanel

☑ A picture of a flapper

☑ A picture of a Chanel suit

☑ The House of Chanel

☑ Chanel Number 5

☑ How perfumes are made

b) 請試著用英文討論下列話題：

1. 你想不想認識可可・香奈兒？為什麼？
2. 你喜不喜歡搖擺女郎的打扮？為什麼？
3. 你喜不喜歡香奈兒套裝？為什麼？
4. 你最愛的香水是什麼？你為什麼喜歡它？
5. 你所偏好的設計師是哪位？你為什麼喜歡他的衣服？

解 答

 閱讀理解

Hats	❷
Reputation and influence	❻
Chanel Number 5	❹
The Chanel suit	❺
Childhood and early life	❶
The flappers	❸

 重要詞彙

afford	負擔得起
backing	支持
business sense	商業敏感度
business venture	創業
corset	束腹
designer	設計師
design	設計
deter	阻礙
be dominated by	被……支配
expand her business	擴展她的事業
fabric	布料
fashion industry	時裝產業
figure	人物

fussy	過度講究的
hardwearing	耐磨的
hobby	嗜好
in return for	換取……
be inspired by	受……啓發
jacket	外套
liberate	解放
license fee	權利金
needle	縫衣針
nun	修女
operate	經營
orphanage	孤兒院
padding	襯墊
perfume	香水
perfumer	香水業者
raincoat	雨衣
restrict	限制
revolutionize	徹底改革
sample	樣品
sew	縫
skirt	裙子
style	風格；流行款式
suit	套裝
traveling salesman	巡迴推銷員
trend	潮流
wearer	穿著者

 填 空

(01) traveling salesman

(02) afford

(03) nuns

(04) orphanage

(05) sew

(06) needle

(07) designing

(08) hobby

(09) jackets

(10) raincoats

(11) business venture

(12) deterred

(13) backing

(14) revolutionized

(15) fussy

(16) skirts

(17) fabric

(18) corsets

(19) padding

(20) restricted

(21) wearer

(22) inspired by

(23) perfume

(24) perfumer

(25) samples

(26) dominated by

(27) designers

(28) suit

(29) hardwearing

(30) style

(31) business sense

(32) expand her business

(33) in return for

(34) license fee

(35) trend

(36) operates

(37) figure

(38) liberated

Unit 23

Oprah Winfrey
歐普拉 · 溫佛瑞

人物速覽

- 談話型節目主持人
- 1954 年生於美國密西西比
  （Mississippi, USA）
- 電視製作人
- 20 世紀最富有的非裔美國女性

❶ **Oprah**'s mother was only a teenager when Oprah was born. Oprah was brought up by her grandmother, who was very poor and very strict. She taught Oprah to read from the Bible. Other members of her family abused[1] her. Although her life was very hard, she was very good in school and was popular with teachers and students. She became pregnant at 14 and gave birth to a baby boy who died in infancy.[2]

❷ From an early age, Oprah was interested in drama.[3] She won a state-wide[4] competition for recitation,[5] and got a scholarship to Tennessee[6] State University. While she was there she started working for a black radio station reading the news. She was quickly noticed for her dramatic[7] and emotional reading. She started working for a TV station, where she was the first black female news anchor[8] and the youngest TV anchor.

❸ Oprah's success in TV was noticed by the big media channels and she was invited to go to Chicago to take over a talk show that had bad ratings.[9] After a few months, Oprah turned the talk show into the most popular TV show in the Chicago area. She was soon syndicated[10] and was broadcasting[11] her show, now called *The Oprah Winfrey Show*, all

---

Ⓦ Ⓞ Ⓡ Ⓓ Ⓛ Ⓘ Ⓢ Ⓣ

★ 1. abuse [ə`bjuz] *v.* 虐待
  2. infancy [`ɪnfənsɪ] *n.* 嬰兒期；年幼時期
  3. drama [`drɑmə] *n.* 戲劇
  4. state-wide [`stet͵waɪd] *adj.* 全州的
  5. recitation [͵rɛsə`teʃən] *n.* 背誦；朗誦
  6. Tennessee [͵tɛnə`si] *n.* 田納西州
★ 7. dramatic [drə`mætɪk] *adj.* 戲劇化的
  8. anchor [`æŋkɚ] *n.* 主播；主持人
  9. rating [`retɪŋ] *n.* 收視率；收聽率

over America. She is very good at getting people to feel comfortable and talk openly about themselves on TV. She interviewed Michael Jackson for her show in 1993, and a hundred million people watched. It was the most watched TV interview in TV history.

❹ In addition to her TV show, Oprah also owns and publishes two lifestyle[12] magazines. One of these magazines was the most successful start-up[13] in the magazine industry, and has a circulation[14] of more than 2 million readers. Oprah has also written numerous books, usually co-authored[15] with others, and they have all been best-sellers. Oprah started a book club on her TV show in 1996, where she introduced new books and classics to her audiences and encouraged them to read. The book club is very influential and helps to sell thousands of copies.

❺ Oprah is also a very good movie actress. She appeared in a movie called *The Color Purple* and was nominated[16] for an Oscar for her acting in it. In 1998, she produced and starred[17] in a movie of a famous book called *Beloved*, written by Nobel Prize winner Toni Morrison. The movie was not a commercial[18] success, but the critics said it was an excellent movie.

---

10. syndicate [ˈsɪndɪˌket] *v.* 使……加入聯合組織
11. broadcast [ˈbrɔdˌkæst] *v.* 廣播；播送
12. lifestyle [ˈlaɪfˌstaɪl] *n.* 生活方式；生活風格
13. start-up [ˈstɑrtˌʌp] *n.* 開始
★ 14. circulation [ˌsɜkjəˈleʃən] *n.* 發行量；流通
15. co-author [koˈɔθɚ] *v.* 合著；共同執筆
16. nominate [ˈnɑməˌnet] *v.* 提名
17. star [stɑr] *v.* 主演
18. commercial [kəˈmɝʃəl] *adj.* 商業上的

❻ Oprah lives on a big ranch[19] in California, but she has homes all over the world. Her TV show is syndicated to over 40 countries worldwide, and in America over 30 million people watch her show every week. Oprah is the founder of Oprah's Angel Network, a charity aimed at helping the less fortunate. Oprah is famous for her philanthropy,[20] giving away millions of dollars every year to various good causes. She is widely called the most influential woman in America.

譯文

❶ 在生歐普拉的時候，歐普拉的母親只是個青少年。歐普拉由祖母撫養長大，而她非常貧窮，又非常嚴格。她教導歐普拉讀聖經。其他的家人則虐待歐普拉。雖然歐普拉的生活艱困，但她非常會念書，受到師生歡迎。她在 14 歲時懷了身孕，並生了個男寶寶，但在襁褓中就夭折了。

❷ 歐普拉自小就對戲劇感興趣。她贏過全州的朗誦比賽，並取得田納西州州立大學的獎學金。她在那裡時，開始替一家黑人廣播電台工作並播報新聞。她戲劇化而感性的播報方式使她很快就受到注意。她開始替一家電視台工作，並且是該台第一位女性的黑人新聞主播，以及最年輕的電視主持人。

❸ 歐普拉在電視上的成功受到了大型媒體頻道的注意，她受邀到芝加哥接下一個收視率很差的談話型節目。過了幾個月，歐普拉把那個談話型節目變成了芝加哥地區最受歡迎的電視節目。她很快就上了聯播，並對全美播放她的節目，現在叫做《歐普拉秀》。她擅長讓人覺得自在並公開在電視上談論自

Ⓦ Ⓞ Ⓡ Ⓓ Ⓛ Ⓘ Ⓢ Ⓣ

19. ranch [ræntʃ] *n.* 農場；牧場
20. philanthropy [fə`lænθrəpɪ] *n.* 慈善行為；博愛

己。她在1993年為她的節目訪問了麥可‧傑克森，結果有上億人收看。這是電視史上最多人收看的電視訪問。

❹ 除了電視節目，歐普拉還擁有並出版了兩種生活雜誌。其中一種是雜誌業中最成功的後起之秀，並擁有兩百多萬個讀者的發行量。歐普拉也寫了很多書，通常是跟別人合著，而且全部是暢銷書。1996年，歐普拉在她的電視節目創立了一個讀書會，由她向觀眾介紹新書和經典著作，鼓勵他們閱讀。這個讀書會深具影響力，並幫忙賣出了成千上萬本書。

❺ 歐普拉也是個非常優秀的電影演員。她演過一部叫做《紫色姊妹花》的電影，並靠著她在劇中的演出獲得了奧斯卡獎的提名。1998年，她製作並主演了一部電影。它是由一本叫做《寵兒》的名著改編而成，作者是諾貝爾獎得主托妮‧莫里森。這部電影並不賣座，但評論家說，它是一部出色的電影。

❻ 歐普拉住在加州的一座大農場裡，但她在世界各地都有住所。她的電視節目對全世界40多個國家聯播，在美國每週有超過3,000萬人收看她的節目。歐普拉是「歐普拉天使網路」的創辦人，這項慈善事業是以幫助不幸的人為目的。歐普拉的善行很有名，她每年都會捐出數百萬美元去做各種善事。她被廣稱為全美最具影響力的女性。

配合題，請判斷下列摘要各屬於文章的哪個段落，見範例。

TV	❸
Life and influence	
Childhood	
Publishing	
Movies	
Early career	

 重要詞彙

連連看，請為每個詞彙找出它的正確翻譯。

- interview •
- book club •
- broadcast •
- charity •
- classic •
- co-author •
- abuse •
- dramatic •
- emotional •
- founder •
- circulation •
- lifestyle magazine •
- commercial success •

- 虐待
- 讀書會
- 播放
- 慈善事業
- 發行量
- 經典著作
- 合寫
- 商業上的成功
- 戲劇化的
- 感性的
- 創辦人
- 訪問
- 生活雜誌

▨ recitation	•	• 雜誌業
▨ worldwide	•	• 媒體頻道
▨ news	•	• 新聞
▨ news anchor	•	• 新聞主播
▨ nominate for	•	• 提名……
▨ Oscar	•	• 奧斯卡獎
▨ philanthropy	•	• 善行
▨ radio station	•	• 廣播電台
▨ TV station	•	• 收視率
▨ magazine industry	•	• 朗誦
▨ rating	•	• 主演……
▨ turn sth. into sth.	•	• 開始;新秀
▨ start-up	•	• 使……加入聯合組織
▨ media channel	•	• 談話型節目
▨ syndicate	•	• 把某物變成某物
▨ talk show	•	• 電視主持人
▨ star in	•	• 電視台
▨ TV anchor	•	• 全世界的

 填 空

理解文章大意後,請用前項習題中的詞彙來完成句子,有些字須做適當變化。

■ She won a competition for dramatic **(01)**＿＿＿＿＿.

■ She got a job in a **(02)**＿＿＿＿＿ reading the **(03)**＿＿＿＿＿.

■ She was noticed for her **(04)**＿＿＿＿＿ and **(05)**＿＿＿＿＿ reading of the news.

■ She started working for a (06)_____, where she was the youngest (07)_____ and the first black female (08)_____.

■ The big (09)_____ noticed her talent and asked her to take over a (10)_____ that had poor (11)_____.

■ She soon (12)_____ a huge success, and the show was (13)_____. It was soon (14)_____ all over America.

■ She has a warm and personal (15)_____ style.

■ She also owns and produces two (16)_____. One of these magazines was the most successful (17)_____ in the (18)_____. It has a (19)_____ of 2 million readers.

■ She has also (20)_____ many bestselling books.

■ Her (21)_____ promotes new books and (22)_____.

■ She was (23)_____ an (24)_____ for her acting performance in the movie *The Color Purple*.

■ She also produced and (25)_____ a movie of Toni Morrison's book *Beloved*. The movie was not a (26)_____.

■ Oprah's shows are broadcasted (27)_____.

■ She is the (28)_____ of a (29)_____ called Oprah's Angels Network, and is well known for her (30)_____, giving away millions of dollars every year.

你還可以學更多

a) 請利用網路查詢下列關鍵字，以了解更多關於 **Oprah Winfrey** 的資訊：

> ⊘ A picture of Oprah Winfrey
>
> ⊘ *The Oprah Winfrey Show*
>
> ⊘ Oprah's interview with Michael Jackson
>
> ⊘ *The Color Purple* and *Beloved*
>
> ⊘ Oprah's book club
>
> ⊘ Oprah's Angels Network

b) 請試著用英文討論下列話題：

> 1. 你想不想認識歐普拉・溫佛瑞？為什麼？
> 2. 你想不想上她的節目？為什麼？
> 3. 你想不想在傳播媒體工作？為什麼？
> 4. 你最喜歡的電視節目是什麼？你為什麼喜歡它？
> 5. 你認為歐普拉為什麼會這麼成功？

解 答

 閱讀理解

TV	❸
Life and influence	❻
Childhood	❶
Publishing	❹
Movies	❺
Early career	❷

 重要詞彙

abuse	虐待
book club	讀書會
broadcast	播放
charity	慈善事業
circulation	發行量
classic	經典著作
co-author	合寫
commercial success	商業上的成功
dramatic	戲劇化的
emotional	感性的
founder	創辦人
interview	訪問
lifestyle magazine	生活雜誌

magazine industry	雜誌業
media channel	媒體頻道
news	新聞
news anchor	新聞主播
nominate for	提名……
Oscar	奧斯卡獎
philanthropy	善行
radio station	廣播電台
rating	收視率
recitation	朗誦
star in	主演……
start-up	開始；新秀
syndicate	使……加入聯合組織
talk show	談話型節目
turn sth. into sth.	把某物變成某物
TV anchor	電視主持人
TV station	電視台
worldwide	全世界的

 填 空

(01) recitation
(02) radio station
(03) news

(04) emotional
(05) dramatic
(06) TV station

(07) TV anchor
(08) news anchor
(09) media channels

(10) talk show
(11) ratings
(12) turned it into

(13) syndicated
(14) broadcasting
(15) interview

(16) lifestyle magazines

(17) start-up

(18) magazine industry

(19) circulation

(20) co-authored

(21) book club

(22) classics

(23) nominated for

(24) Oscar

(25) starred in

(26) commercial success

(27) worldwide

(28) founder

(29) charity

(30) philanthropy

Jerry Yang
楊致遠

人物速覽

- 網路企業家
- 1968 年生於台灣台北
- 雅虎執行長暨共同創辦人
- 億萬富豪

❶ **Jerry**'s father died when he was two years old. When he was 8 years old, his mother decided to immigrate[1] to America with Jerry and his younger brother. Jerry could not speak any English, except for one word: 'shoe.' He learned English very quickly, however. He studied electrical engineering at Stanford University in California.

❷ While he was at Stanford studying for his Ph.D., the internet was in its early days. In 1996, Jerry started a webpage[2] which just provided links[3] to cool sites[4] on the net. He called it Jerry's Guide to the World Wide Web. He made friends with a guy called David Filo, who wrote some of the code that their guide used. Their webpage of links soon became very popular with other students.

❸ In the early days of the internet, many companies were starting up very quickly, and lots of new businesses were being created. It was the age of the dotcom[5] company. Jerry and David realized their webpage had great business potential when a venture capitalist[6] offered to give them $2 million in capital to turn their webpage into a company. They renamed[7] it Yahoo after a character in a book. In 1996 they decided to have an IPO,[8]

Ⓦ Ⓞ Ⓡ Ⓓ Ⓛ Ⓘ Ⓢ Ⓣ

1. immigrate [ˈɪməˌgret] *v.* （自外國）移入
2. webpage [ˈwɛbˌpedʒ] *n.* 網頁
3. link [lɪŋk] *n.* 連結
4. site [saɪt] *n.* （網）站
5. dotcom [ˈdɑtˌkʌm] *n.* 達康（即為 .com，泛指網路公司）
★ 6. capitalist [ˈkæpətlɪst] *n.* 資本家
7. rename [riˈnem] *v.* 重新命名
8. IPO 公司股票首度在股市公開買賣（Initial Public Offering 的縮寫）
9. share [ʃɛr] *n.* 股份

and sold shares[9] in their company on the stock exchange.[10] They raised $33.8 million dollars by this method, and Yahoo became one of the most successful companies in the new dotcom age.

❹ In the late 90s, Yahoo diversified[11] into a web portal.[12] It began buying other smaller internet companies and using their programs and codes to expand its own services. It added an email service, a games service, a messenger service like MSN, internet shopping, a news service and a search function. During this period, Yahoo shares in America and Japan broke new records for share prices.

❺ In 2005, Yahoo ran into[13] controversy[14] in China when they gave the Chinese government the contact details of some Chinese journalists who were using Yahoo to communicate with each other and talk about the government. The dissidents[15] were arrested, tortured[16] and imprisoned.[17] Jerry Yang and his partner Filo were heavily criticized for this decision. Their critics say they broke international law, and violated[18] the human rights of their users. Jerry Yang apologized to the families of the dissidents.

★ 10. stock exchange [ˈstɑk ɪksˈtʃendʒ] n. 股票交易所
　　11. diversify [daɪˈvɜsəˌfaɪ] v. 多樣化；多角化
★ 12. web portal [ˈwɛb ˈportl] n. 入口網站
　　13. run into 陷入（狀態）
　　14. controversy [ˈkɑntrəˌvɜsɪ] n. 爭論；爭議
　　15. dissident [ˈdɪsədənt] n. 持不同意見者；反對組織者
　　16. torture [ˈtɔrtʃə] v. 折磨；拷問
　　17. imprison [ɪmˈprɪzn̩] v. 關入監牢；監禁
★ 18. violate [ˈvaɪəˌlet] v. 違背；違反

❻ Jerry married a Japanese woman whom he met at Stanford. He now lives in California. The Yahoo board[19] of directors asked him to resign[20] as CEO because of the China incident and because he was not aggressive[21] enough in dealing with competition from Google and Microsoft. He still serves on the board, but has no decision-making powers. He is estimated to be worth around $2.3 billion.

譯文

❶ 楊致遠在兩歲時，父親就過世了。八歲時，母親決定帶著他跟弟弟移民到美國。致遠一句英語都不會說，除了一個字：「鞋」。不過他學英文學得非常快。在加州的史丹福大學，他念的是電子工程。

❷ 他在史丹福念博士時，網際網路正處於草創時期。 1996 年，致遠架設了一個網頁，提供連結到網路上很酷的網站。他把它稱為「致遠的全球資訊網指南」。他跟一個叫做大衛‧費羅的傢伙結為朋友，費羅寫了一些程式碼來供他們的指南使用。他們的連結網頁很快就受到其他學生的歡迎。

❸ 在網際網路的草創時期，有許多公司興起得非常快，有很多新事業也被創造出來。那是網路公司的年代。致遠和大衛發現，他們的網頁極具商業潛力，因為有創投業者願意給他們兩百萬美元的資金來把他們的網頁變成一家公司。他們以一本書中的人物為名，把它更名為雅虎。 1996 年，他們決定首

───── Ⓦ Ⓞ Ⓓ Ⓛ Ⓘ Ⓢ Ⓣ ─────

19. board [bord] *n.* 董事會
★ 20. resign [rɪˋzaɪn] *v.* 辭職
★ 21. aggressive [əˋgrɛsɪv] *adj.* 積極的

次公開發行公司股票，並在證交所出售公司的股份。他們靠這種方式募集到
3,380萬美元，雅虎也成了新網路時代最成功的公司之一。

❹ 到了90年代末期，雅虎擴大為入口網站。它開始收購其他比較小的網路公
司，並用它們的程式與程式碼來拓展服務。它增加了電子郵件服務、遊戲服
務、類似MSN的即時訊息服務、網路購物、新聞服務和搜尋功能。在這段期
間，雅虎的股票在美國和日本都創下了股價的新記錄。

❺ 2005年，雅虎在中國引發了爭議，因為它把某些中國記者的詳細聯絡資料
交給了中國政府，而他們都是用雅虎來互相聯絡及談論政府。這些異議人士
遭到逮捕、拷問和監禁。因為這個決定，楊致遠和他的合夥人費羅飽受批
評。批評他們的人說，他們違反了國際法，也侵犯了用戶的人權。楊致遠則
向異議人士的家人致歉。

❻ 致遠娶了一位他在史福丹認識的日本女子。目前他住在加州。雅虎的董事
會要求他辭去執行長一職，這既是因為中國的事件，也是因為他在應付谷歌
和微軟的競爭上不夠積極。他目前仍然在董事會任職，但沒有決策權。他的
身價據估大約有23億美元。

閱讀理解

配合題，請判斷下列摘要各屬於文章的哪個段落，見範例。

Jerry's web page	❷
Yahoo in China	
Early days of Yahoo	
Reputation and worth	
Childhood	
Yahoo	

 重要詞彙

連連看，請為每個詞彙找出它的正確翻譯。

- aggressive •
- board of directors •
- dissident •
- business potential •
- code •
- apologize to •
- character •
- competition •
- capital •
- contact details •
- break new records •
- controversy •
- decision-making power •
- dotcom •

- 積極的
- 向⋯⋯致歉
- 董事會
- 創下新記錄
- 商業潛力
- 資金
- 人物
- 代碼
- 競爭
- 詳細聯絡資料
- 爭議
- 決策權
- 異議人士
- 網路公司

■ resign	•	• 多角化
■ electrical engineering	•	• 電子工程
■ email	•	• 電子郵件
■ diversify	•	• 據估計
■ human right	•	• 遊戲
■ be estimated to	•	• 指南
■ share	•	• 人權
■ guide	•	• 監禁
■ webpage	•	• 事件
■ imprison	•	• 國際法
■ incident	•	• 首度公開發行
■ international law	•	• 連結
■ IPO	•	• 即時通
■ link	•	• 程式
■ messenger	•	• 籌措資金
■ program	•	• 陷入
■ raise capital	•	• 辭職
■ game	•	• 搜尋功能
■ web portal	•	• 服務
■ run into	•	• 股價
■ search function	•	• 股份
■ service	•	• 證交所
■ share price	•	• ……的年代
■ worth	•	• 拷問
■ stock exchange	•	• 創投業者
■ the age of	•	• 違背
■ torture	•	• 網頁
■ venture capitalist	•	• 入口網站
■ violate	•	• 價值

填 空

理解文章大意後，請用前項習題中的詞彙來完成句子，有些字須做適當變化。

■ Jerry studied (01)_____ at college.

■ He designed a (02)_____ which was a (03)_____ with
(04)_____ to other pages on the web. His friend wrote the
(05)_____ .

■ It was (06)_____ the (07)_____ company, and lots of
companies were starting up.

■ When a (08)_____ offered them some (09)_____ ,
Jerry and David realized their idea had great (10)_____ .

■ Yahoo was named after a (11)_____ in a book.

■ At the (12)_____ , they sold (13)_____ on the
(14)_____ and raised even more (15)_____ . The
company became very rich.

■ They (16)_____ and started offering lots of different services
and (17)_____ , including a (18)_____ ,
(19)_____ , (20)_____ and (21)_____ .

■ Their share prices were so high that they (22)_____ .

■ The company (23)_____ trouble in China when it caused a
(24)_____ . It gave the Chinese government the
(25)_____ of some (26)_____ who were using Yahoo
to communicate.

■ The dissidents were arrested, (27)_____ and

(28)_____. Yahoo was accused of breaking (29)_____

and their critics said they had (30)_____ the

(31)_____ of their users.

■ Jerry (32)_____ the families of the dissidents.

■ Jerry was asked to (33)_____ from the (34)_____

because of the China (35)_____, and because he was not

(36)_____ enough in dealing with (37)_____.

■ He is still on the board, but has no (38)_____, so he has no

control.

■ He is (39)_____ be (40)_____ $2.3 billion.

你還可以學更多

a) 請利用網路查詢下列關鍵字，以了解更多關於 Jerry Yang 的資訊：

⊘ A picture of Jerry Yang

⊘ A picture of David Filo

⊘ The history of Yahoo

⊘ The full range of Yahoo's services

⊘ Yahoo's share price

⊘ Yahoo main page

b) 請試著用英文討論下列話題：

1. 你想不想認識楊致遠？為什麼？
2. 你比較喜歡雅虎即時通還是 MSN？為什麼？
3. 你有使用其他哪些網路服務？
4. 你想不想替雅虎工作？為什麼？
5. 你對於雅虎的中國事件有什麼看法？

解 答

 閱讀理解

Jerry's web page	❷
Yahoo in China	❺
Early days of Yahoo	❸
Reputation and worth	❻
Childhood	❶
Yahoo	❹

重要詞彙

aggressive	積極的
apologize to	向……致歉
board of directors	董事會
break new records	創下新記錄
business potential	商業潛力
capital	資金
character	人物
code	代碼
competition	競爭
contact details	詳細聯絡資料
controversy	爭議
decision-making power	決策權
dissident	異議人士

dotcom	網路公司
diversify	多角化
electrical engineering	電子工程
email	電子郵件
be estimated to	據估計
game	遊戲
guide	指南
human right	人權
imprison	監禁
incident	事件
international law	國際法
IPO	首度公開發行
link	連結
messenger	即時通
program	程式
raise capital	籌措資金
run into	陷入
resign	辭職
search function	搜尋功能
service	服務
share price	股價
share	股份
stock exchange	證交所
the age of	……的年代
torture	拷問

venture capitalist	創投業者
violate	違背
webpage	網頁
web portal	入口網站
worth	價值

 填 空

(01) electrical engineering **(02)** webpage **(03)** guide

(04) links **(05)** code **(06)** the age of

(07) dotcom **(08)** venture capitalist **(09)** capital

(10) business potential **(11)** character **(12)** IPO

(13) shares **(14)** stock exchange **(15)** capital

(16) diversified **(17)** programs **(18)** web portal

(19) games **(20)** messenger **(21)** search function

(22) broke new records **(23)** ran into **(24)** controversy

(25) contact details **(26)** dissidents **(27)** tortured

(28) imprisoned **(29)** international law **(30)** violated

(31) human rights **(32)** apologized to **(33)** resign

(34) board of directors **(35)** incident **(36)** aggressive

(37) competition **(38)** decision-making powers

(39) estimated to **(40)** worth

Part 7

超越巔峰的運動家

Michelle Kwan

Amelia Earhart

Tiger Woods

Jesse Owens

Unit 25

Amelia Earhart
愛蜜莉亞・埃爾哈特

人物速覽

- 女飛行員
- 1897 年生於美國堪薩斯（Kansas, USA），1937 年失蹤
- 第一位獨自飛越大西洋的女性
- 第一位獲頒十字飛行榮譽勳章（Distinguished Flying Cross）的女性

❶ **Amelia** was born into a rich and influential Kansas family. Her grandfather was a banker and her father was a lawyer. As a young child she was a tomboy,[1] playing rough[2] and adventurous[3] games with her younger sister. She was educated by a governess[4] at home until she was 12, when she went to school for the first time. At school she was interested in science. From an early age she showed great interest in books and reading. She had a happy childhood until her father became an alcoholic and lost his job.

❷ In 1918 there was a great flu epidemic,[5] and Amelia volunteered as a nurse. During her time as a nurse, she caught the flu herself and became very ill with inflamed[6] and infected[7] sinuses.[8] She had a number of operations to drain[9] her sinuses, but they were never really successful. She was to suffer from sinus problems all her life, affecting her balance and giving her bad headaches. During her convalescence,[10] which lasted almost a year, she developed an interest in machines.

❸ In 1920 Amelia and her father went to visit an air show, where her father

Ⓦ Ⓞ Ⓡ Ⓓ Ⓛ Ⓘ Ⓢ Ⓣ

1. tomboy [ˈtɑmˌbɔɪ] *n.* 行為像男生的女孩
★ 2. rough [rʌf] *adj.* 粗魯的；粗野的
3. adventurous [ədˈvɛntʃərəs] *adj.* 有冒險性的
4. governess [ˈgʌvənɪs] *n.* 女家庭教師
5. epidemic [ˌɛpəˈdɛmɪk] *n.* 流行；傳染病的發生
6. inflamed [ɪnˈflemd] *adj.* 發炎的；紅腫的
★ 7. infected [ɪnˈfɛktɪd] *adj.* 感染的
8. sinus [ˈsaɪnəs] *n.* 靜脈竇
★ 9. drain [dren] *v.* 使……流出；使……枯竭
10. convalescence [ˌkɑnvəˈlɛsn̩s] *n.* 復原期間；療養期間

paid $10 for Amelia to have a 10-minute ride in an airplane. It changed Amelia's life, and she knew she had to fly. The aviation[11] industry was in its very early days, and airplanes and flight were new and exciting. There were very few female flyers.[12] Amelia worked hard, taking all kinds of jobs to pay for her flying lessons. She eventually saved up enough money to buy her own biplane.[13] She got her pilot's license in 1923.

❹ Amelia set many records when she got her pilot's license. She took her plane to 14,000 feet, the highest any woman had flown before. She was the first woman to reach a speed of 100 kilometers per hour in an airplane. She flew the Atlantic[14] in 1928 as part of a team, and then flew it again by herself in 1932. The flight lasted 15 hours, and during this time, Amelia could not sleep. She was the first woman to fly the Atlantic, and the first person to fly it twice. She was also the first woman to fly non-stop[15] from coast[16] to coast across the United States.

❺ Amelia was a celebrity.[17] She was a woman in the new world of flying. She wrote many books about her experiences as a pilot and went on lecture tours across America where many people came to hear her talk about her experiences. She designed and sold her own clothes and luggage for flyers. She was involved in starting many airlines that are still going today.

(W) (O) (R) (D)　(L) (I) (S) (T)

11. aviation [ˌevɪˋeʃən] *n.* 航空；飛行
12. flyer [ˋflaɪɚ] *n.* 飛行員
13. biplane [ˋbaɪˌplen] *n.* 雙翼飛機
14. the Atlantic [ðə ətˋlæntɪk] *n.* 大西洋
15. non-stop [nɑnˋstɑp] *adv.* 直達；不休息地
16. coast [kost] *n.* 海岸；沿岸

❻ In 1937 Amelia set out[18] to fly around the world along the equator.[19] Her co-pilot[20] was a man called Fred Noonan. The flight was difficult and dangerous because in those days airplanes could not carry much fuel and there were not many places to land to refuel.[21] While they were flying across the Pacific Ocean, they lost radio contact and were never heard or seen again.

譯文

❶ 愛蜜莉亞出身於一個富裕且具有影響力的堪薩斯家庭。祖父是個銀行家，父親則是個律師。在兒童時期，她是個男孩子氣的野丫頭，跟妹妹玩的遊戲都是既粗野又危險。她在家裡跟著一位家庭教師上課，直到 12 歲才第一次上學。在學校時，她對自然科學感興趣。她自小就對書本及閱讀展現出高度的興趣。她有個快樂的童年，直到她父親變成了酒鬼並失去工作為止。

❷ 1918 年出現了重大的流感疫情，愛蜜莉亞自願擔任護士。在擔任護士時，她自己也得了流感，而且病情變得非常嚴重，竇道發炎又感染。她開了幾次刀來抽乾竇液，但從來沒有真的成功過。她一輩子都受到竇的毛病所苦，既影響了她的平衡，也使她頭痛欲裂。在持續將近一年的療養期間，她培養出了對機械的興趣。

17. celebrity [səˋlɛbrətɪ] *n.* 名人
18. set out 出發
19. the equator [ðə ɪˋkwetə] *n.* 赤道
20. co-pilot [ˋkoˌpaɪlət] *n.* 副駕駛員
21. refuel [riˋfjuəl] *v.* 再……供給燃料；加油

❸ 1920年，愛蜜莉亞和父親去看了一場飛行表演。她父親花了10美元讓愛蜜莉亞在飛機上坐了10分鐘。這改變了愛蜜莉亞的一生，她知道自己一定要飛。航空業才剛起步，飛機和飛行都是既新鮮又刺激。女性飛行員少之又少。愛蜜莉亞很拚命，接下了各式各樣的工作，賺錢去上她的飛行課。終於，她存夠了錢可以買自己的雙翼飛機。她在1923年拿到了機師執照。

❹ 拿到機師執照後，愛蜜莉亞創下許多紀錄。她把飛機開到1萬 4,000 英尺高，是以往所有女性中飛得最高的。她也是第一位讓飛機的速度達到每小時100公里的女性。她在1928年以機隊成員的形式飛越了大西洋，後來在1932年又單獨飛了一次。這趟飛行花了15個小時，而且在這段期間，愛蜜莉亞都不能睡覺。她是第一位飛越大西洋的女性，以及第一個飛了兩次的人。她也是第一位橫跨美國兩岸飛行而不休息的女性。

❺ 愛蜜莉亞是個名人。她是飛行這個新世界中的女性。她寫了許多書來談她當機師的經驗，並且巡迴全美演講，許多人來聽她暢談自己的經驗。她設計了飛行員的服裝與行李箱來販售。她幫忙創立過多家航空公司，而且至今仍在營運。

❻ 1937年，愛蜜莉亞開始沿著赤道飛行全世界。她的副機師是位名叫弗瑞德．努南的男性。這趟飛行既困難又危險，因為在這段期間，飛機載不了多少燃料，也沒有多少地方可以降落加油。在飛越太平洋時，他們失去了無線電聯繫，從此再也沒有人聽過或看過他們。

閱讀理解

配合題，請判斷下列摘要各屬於文章的哪個段落，見範例。

Flying lessons	❸
Childhood	
Missing	
Celebrity and reputation	
The flu epidemic	
Her achievements	

重要詞彙

連連看，請為每個詞彙找出它的正確翻譯。

▨ from coast to coast •	• 冒險的
▨ air show •	• 影響
▨ dangerous •	• 飛行表演
▨ airline •	• 航空公司
▨ aviation industry •	• 航空業
▨ balance •	• 平衡
▨ adventurous •	• 銀行家
▨ banker •	• 雙翼飛機
▨ biplane •	• 名人
▨ celebrity •	• 橫跨兩岸地
▨ affect •	• 復原
▨ convalescence •	• 副機師
▨ co-pilot •	• 危險的

■ flight	•	• 培養
■ flu epidemic	•	• 抽乾
■ speed	•	• 赤道
■ flyer	•	• 飛行
■ develop	•	• 流感疫情
■ fuel	•	• 飛行員
■ infected sinus	•	• 燃料
■ land	•	• 竇道感染
■ drain	•	• 降落
■ lawyer	•	• 律師
■ lecture tour	•	• 巡迴演講
■ non-stop	•	• 不休息地
■ pilot	•	• 機師
■ tomboy	•	• 機師執照
■ pilot's license	•	• 無線電聯繫
■ equator	•	• 加油
■ volunteer	•	• 粗魯的
■ radio contact	•	• 出發
■ refuel	•	• 速度
■ rough	•	• 男孩子氣的女生
■ set out	•	• 自願

 填　空

理解文章大意後，請用前項習題中的詞彙來完成句子，有些字須做適當變化。

■ Amelia's father was a (01)＿＿＿＿＿＿, and her grandfather was a
(02)＿＿＿＿＿.

■ She was a (03)＿＿＿＿＿＿ when she was a child, and liked playing
(04)＿＿＿＿＿＿ and (05)＿＿＿＿＿＿ games.

■ During the (06)＿＿＿＿＿＿ of 1918 she (07)＿＿＿＿＿＿ as a
nurse. She caught the flu and suffered from (08)＿＿＿＿＿＿.

■ She had several operations to (09)＿＿＿＿＿＿ her sinuses, but
they gave her headaches and problems all her life, (10)＿＿＿＿＿＿
her (11)＿＿＿＿＿＿.

■ During her (12)＿＿＿＿＿＿ she (13)＿＿＿＿＿＿ an interest in
machines.

■ Her father took her to an (14)＿＿＿＿＿＿. In those days the
(15)＿＿＿＿＿＿ was just beginning. It was the early days of
(16)＿＿＿＿＿＿ and there were very few female (17)＿＿＿＿＿＿.

■ Amelia bought a (18)＿＿＿＿＿＿ when she got her (19)＿＿＿＿＿＿.

■ She set many new records, including records for height and
(20)＿＿＿＿＿＿.

■ She was the first woman to fly (21)＿＿＿＿＿＿ from
(22)＿＿＿＿＿＿ across the United States.

■ Amelia was a (23)＿＿＿＿＿＿ and a famous female (24)＿＿＿＿＿＿.

■ She traveled around America giving (25)＿＿＿＿＿＿, and she
wrote many books.

■ She also helped to set up many (26)＿＿＿＿＿＿ which are still
operating today.

■ In 1937 she (27)_____ to fly around the world along the

(28)_____. She had a (29)_____ with her. The flight

was very (30)_____, as there was often nowhere to

(31)_____ and (32)_____.

■ They lost (33)_____ and were never heard or seen again.

 你還可以學更多

a) 請利用網路查詢下列關鍵字，以了解更多關於 **Amelia Earhart** 的資訊：

⊘ A picture of Amelia Earhart as an adult

⊘ A picture of a biplane

⊘ The history of flight

⊘ All of Amelia Earhart's records

⊘ Amelia Earhart Birthplace Museum

⊘ How flying works

b) 請試著用英文討論下列話題：

1. 你想不想認識愛蜜莉亞‧埃爾哈特？為什麼？
2. 你想不想當個機師？為什麼？
3. 你認為獨自長途飛行是什麼感覺？
4. 你比較喜歡搭乘小飛機還是很大的飛機？為什麼？
5. 你搭過最久的飛機是多久？

解 答

閱讀理解

Flying lessons	❸
Childhood	❶
Missing	❻
Celebrity and reputation	❺
The flu epidemic	❷
Her achievements	❹

重要詞彙

adventurous	冒險的
affect	影響
air show	飛行表演
airline	航空公司
aviation industry	航空業
balance	平衡
banker	銀行家
biplane	雙翼飛機
celebrity	名人
from coast to coast	橫跨兩岸地
convalescence	復原
co-pilot	副機師
dangerous	危險的

develop	培養
drain	抽乾
equator	赤道
flight	飛行
flu epidemic	流感疫情
flyer	飛行員
fuel	燃料
infected sinus	竇道感染
land	降落
lawyer	律師
lecture tour	巡迴演講
non-stop	不休息地
pilot	機師
pilot's license	機師執照
radio contact	無線電聯繫
refuel	加油
rough	粗魯的
set out	出發
speed	速度
tomboy	男孩子氣的女生
volunteer	自願

 填 空

(01) lawyer **(02)** banker **(03)** tomboy

(04) rough **(05)** adventurous **(06)** flu epidemic

(07) volunteered	**(08)** infected sinuses	**(09)** drain
(10) affecting	**(11)** balance	**(12)** convalescence
(13) developed	**(14)** air show	**(15)** aviation industry
(16) flight	**(17)** flyers	**(18)** biplane
(19) pilot's license	**(20)** speed	**(21)** non-stop
(22) coast to coast	**(23)** celebrity	**(24)** pilot
(25) lecture tours	**(26)** airlines	**(27)** set out
(28) equator	**(29)** co-pilot	**(30)** dangerous
(31) land	**(32)** refuel	**(33)** radio contact

Unit
26

Jesse Owens
傑西・歐文斯

人物速覽

- 田徑運動員
- 1913 年生於美國阿拉巴馬（Alabama, USA），1980 年卒於美國亞歷桑納（Arizona, USA）
- 四面奧運金牌得主
- 總統自由獎章（Presidential Medal of Freedom）得主

❶ Jesse was born into a very poor black family from a poor neighborhood in a poor state. During his childhood, he had to work to earn his own pocket money. While he was running from his jobs to his school, he noticed that he was faster than other boys, and that he enjoyed running. At school, his coach encouraged him, seeing that Jesse had talent. After high school he attended Ohio[1] State University. He could not get a scholarship because he was black, so he continued to work and study at the same time. While at college he won lots of medals[2] for sporting events and broke many records.

❷ Even though he was winning lots of medals for his college, and was well known as an athlete,[3] he still could not eat with the other white athletes. At that time in America, black and white people were not allowed to eat in the same restaurants, stay in the same hotels, or even ride on the same buses. They had to use separate doors to enter theaters and drink from different water fountains.[4] This policy was called racial segregation.[5]

❸ In 1936 Jesse joined the US team for the Berlin Olympics. This was very controversial because at that time Germany was governed by Hitler and the Nazis.[6] Hitler believed that black people were inferior[7] to white

Ⓦ Ⓞ Ⓡ Ⓓ Ⓛ Ⓘ Ⓢ Ⓣ

1. Ohio [oˋhaɪo] *n.* 俄亥俄州
★ 2. medal [ˋmɛdl̩] *n.* 獎章；獎牌
★ 3. athlete [ˋæθlɪt] *n.* 運動員
4. water fountain [ˋwɔtɚ ˋfauntn̩] *n.* 飲水機
5. segregation [ˌsɛgrɪˋgeʃən] *n.* 隔離
6. the Nazis [ðə ˋnɑtsɪz] *n.* 納粹（黨）
★ 7. inferior [ɪnˋfɪrɪɚ] *adj.* 下等的；劣等的

people. When Jesse won his first medal, Hitler was polite, but not very friendly. By the time Jesse won his fourth medal, Hitler was furious[8] that a black American had beaten the white German sportsmen. Jesse became famous all over the world. The records he set at the 1936 Olympics were not broken until 1984. He was asked by the founder of Adidas to wear their shoes during the Olympics. Jesse became the first black sportsman to endorse[9] sportswear[10] products.

4 After the Olympics, Jesse returned to America. He wanted to take advantage of his new fame by earning a living as a professional sportsman. However, because of racial segregation, things did not work out very well for him. The President of the US would not meet him to honor his Olympic achievement although he met other white Olympic athletes. He was not able to find work as a sportsman because he was black. He ran a dry cleaning business, and then worked in a gas station. He went bankrupt when the American government sued him for non-payment[11] of taxes.

5 During his last years, things got better for Jesse. After racial segregation ended, he was appointed[12] a goodwill[13] ambassador[14] and

---

(W) (O) (R) (D) (L) (I) (S) (T)

8. furious [ˈfjʊrɪəs] *adj.* 狂怒的
9. endorse [ɪnˈdors] *v.* 代言；推薦商品
10. sportswear [ˈsportsˌwɛr] *n.* 運動服裝
11. non-payment [nɑnˈpemənt] *n.* 未付
12. appoint [əˈpɔɪnt] *v.* 指派；任命
13. goodwill [ˈɡʊdˈwɪl] *n.* 友好；親善
14. ambassador [æmˈbæsədə] *n.* 大使
15. committee [kəˈmɪtɪ] *n.* 委員會

traveled around the world advising companies on their racial policies and helping the Olympic Committee[15] with its work in organizing the next Olympics. He always insisted that the Olympics were above politics and war.

❻ Jesse married his childhood sweetheart. They were married for 44 years, and had three daughters together. Jesse died of lung cancer. His great achievements in sports were finally recognized and honored all over the world. A movie was made of his life called *The Jesse Owens Story*.

譯文

❶ 傑西出身於一個非常貧窮的黑人家庭，位在一個窮州的貧民區。在他小時候，他必須靠打工來賺自己的零用錢。從工作的地方跑去學校時，他注意到自己比其他的男孩跑得快，而且他喜歡跑步。在學校期間，他的教練很鼓勵他，因為他看出傑西有天分。念完高中後，他上了俄亥俄州州立大學。他因為是黑人而拿不到獎學金，所以繼續半工半讀。在大學期間，他在運動賽事中贏得許多獎牌，並打破了多項紀錄。

❷ 即使他為自己的大學贏得了許多獎牌，並且是相當知名的運動員，但他還是不能跟其他的白人運動員同桌吃飯。在當時的美國，黑人和白人不准在同一間餐廳吃飯、住同一間旅館，甚至是搭同一輛巴士。他們必須走不同的門進戲院，並用不同的飲水機喝水。這項政策被稱為種族隔離。

❸ 1936年，傑西加入美國隊前往柏林奧運。這極具爭議性，因為當時德國是由希特勒及納粹所統治。希特勒相信，黑人不如白人。當傑西贏得第一面獎牌時，希特勒還算客氣，但不怎麼友善。等到傑西贏得第四面獎牌時，希特勒大發雷霆，因為美國黑人打敗了德國的白人運動選手。傑西變得舉世聞

名。他在1936年的奧運所創下的紀錄直到1984年才被打破。他還應愛迪達創辦人的邀請，在奧運期間穿上他們的球鞋。傑西成了第一位替運動服產品代言的運動選手。

❹ 在奧運會後，傑西回到了美國。他想要利用他的新名聲當個職業運動選手，並以此為生。不過，由於種族隔離的緣故，事情進展得不太順利。美國總統並沒有接見他，推崇他在奧運會上的成就，但卻接見了其他白人的奧運運動員。他找不到運動選手的工作，因為他是個黑人。他經營了乾洗業，後來又去加油站工作。當美國政府控告他未繳稅時，他破產了。

❺ 在他人生的最後幾年，傑西的日子變得比較好過。在種族隔離結束後，他被任命為親善大使，周遊世界指導公司的種族政策，並協助奧委會籌辦後續的奧運會。他一直堅決地認為，奧運是超脫於政治與戰爭。

❻ 傑西娶了他的青梅竹馬。他們的婚姻維持了44年，一共生了三個女兒。傑西死於肺癌。他在運動方面的偉大成就終於獲得了全世界的肯定與推崇。他的生平被拍成電影，片名是《傑西歐文斯的故事》。

閱讀理解

配合題，請判斷下列摘要各屬於文章的哪個段落，見範例。

Berlin Olympics	❸
School and college	
Goodwill ambassador	
Family and death	
Racial segregation	
After the Olympics	

重要詞彙

連連看，請為每個詞彙找出它的正確翻譯。

▪ coach ·   · 運動員

▪ athlete ·   · 青梅竹馬；小時候的情人

▪ pocket money ·   · 教練

▪ dry cleaning business · · 乾洗業

▪ childhood sweetheart · · 代言

▪ endorse ·   · 加油站

▪ goodwill ambassador · · 親善大使

▪ inferior to ·   · 劣於……

▪ policy ·   · 肺癌

▪ gas station ·   · 獎牌

▪ lung cancer ·   · 未繳稅款

▪ medal ·   · 零用錢

▪ non-payment of taxes · · 政策

■ win	•	• 種族政策
■ racial segregation	•	• 種族隔離
■ go bankrupt	•	• 創下紀錄
■ sporting event	•	• 運動賽事
■ racial policy	•	• 運動選手
■ sportsman	•	• 運動服產品
■ sportswear product	•	• 利用
■ set a record	•	• 破產
■ take advantage of	•	• 贏得

填 空

理解文章大意後，請用前項習題中的詞彙來完成句子，有些字須做適當變化。

■ Jesse had to work to earn his own (01)_____ when he was a child.

■ His sports (02)_____ saw that he had talent.

■ While he was at college he participated in many (03)_____ and (04)_____ many (05)_____.

■ He was not allowed to eat with the other (06)_____ because of the (07)_____ of (08)_____, which kept white and black people separate.

■ Hitler believed that black people were (09)_____ white people.

■ Jesse (10)_____ for the number of medals won by one person.

■ He was asked by Adidas to **(11)**_____ their **(12)**_____.

■ He wanted to **(13)**_____ his fame and reputation, but he didn't have any luck.

■ He had a **(14)**_____, and worked for a while in a **(15)**_____.

■ Eventually he **(16)**_____ and was in trouble for **(17)**_____.

■ He eventually became a **(18)**_____ for the United States.

■ He advised companies on their **(19)**_____.

■ He married his **(20)**_____ and they had three children.

■ Jesse Owen died of **(21)**_____.

🌐 你還可以學更多

a) 請利用網路查詢下列關鍵字，以了解更多關於 **Jesse Owens** 的資訊：

- ✓ A picture of Jesse Owens
- ✓ A picture of Jesse Owens at the Berlin Olympics
- ✓ The International Olympic Committee
- ✓ A movie of Jesse at the Berlin Olympics
- ✓ Goodwill ambassadors

b) 請試著用英文討論下列話題：

1. 你想不想認識傑西‧歐文斯？為什麼？
2. 你想不想當個職業運動員？為什麼？
3. 你能跑得多快？
4. 你最喜歡的運動是什麼？
5. 你覺得現在的社會還存在著種族歧視嗎？

解 答

閱讀理解

Berlin Olympics	❸
School and college	❶
Goodwill ambassador	❺
Family and death	❻
Racial segregation	❷
After the Olympics	❹

重要詞彙

athlete	運動員
childhood sweetheart	青梅竹馬；小時候的情人
coach	教練
dry cleaning business	乾洗業
endorse	代言
gas station	加油站
goodwill ambassador	親善大使
inferior to	劣於……
lung cancer	肺癌
medal	獎牌
non-payment of taxes	未繳稅款
pocket money	零用錢
policy	政策

racial policy	種族政策
racial segregation	種族隔離
set a record	創下紀錄
sporting event	運動賽事
sportsman	運動選手
sportswear product	運動服產品
take advantage of	利用
go bankrupt	破產
win	贏得

 填 空

(01) pocket money

(02) coach

(03) sporting events

(04) won

(05) medals

(06) athletes

(07) policy

(08) racial segregation

(09) inferior to

(10) set a record

(11) endorse

(12) sportswear products

(13) take advantage of

(14) dry cleaning business

(15) gas station

(16) went bankrupt

(17) non-payment of taxes

(18) goodwill ambassador

(19) racial policies

(20) childhood sweetheart

(21) lung cancer

Unit 27

Michelle Kwan
關穎珊

人物速覽

- 花式溜冰選手
- 1980 年生於美國加州
- 兩面奧運獎牌得主，五屆世界冠軍
- 美國歷史上獲獎最多的花式溜冰選手

❶ **Michelle** was born into a Chinese immigrant[1] family. Her parents were both from Hong Kong, and she was brought up speaking English, Cantonese[2] and Mandarin. She first stepped on the ice when she was five years old, and immediately fell in love with skating. She trained very hard with her sister, skating in the early morning before school, and then after school in the evening as well. At the age of 13 she left school and was taught at home so that she could dedicate[3] more time to her skating.

❷ She started skating in competitions from a young age. She won the 1994 World Junior Figure Skating Championships.[4] At the age of 13 she went to Norway[5] as part of the US team for the 1994 Winter Olympics, but did not compete. During her early career she experienced many problems. She was not growing fast enough, and her body did not have enough strength. She signed a contract with a sportswear company to endorse its skates,[6] but the boots gave her problems. She had foot fractures[7] and problems with her toes. In spite of this, she still continued to practice and work on her skating. She won the Olympic silver medal[8] in 1998.

Ⓦ Ⓞ Ⓡ Ⓓ Ⓛ Ⓘ Ⓢ Ⓣ

1. immigrant [ˋɪməgrənt] *adj.* 自國外移入的
2. Cantonese [͵kæntənˋniz] *n.* 廣東話
3. dedicate [ˋdɛdə͵ket] *v.* 奉獻；致力於
4. championship [ˋtʃæmpɪən͵ʃɪp] *n.* 冠軍賽；冠軍地位
5. Norway [ˋnɔrwe] *n.* 挪威
★ 6. skate [sket] *n.* 冰鞋；冰刀
7. fracture [ˋfræktʃɚ] *n.* 破裂；裂縫
★ 8. silver medal [ˋsɪlvɚ ˋmɛdl] *n.* 銀牌

❸ In 2001, Michelle decided to change her coach. There were many rumors about this, but Michelle just said she wanted to take responsibility for her own skating. She completed the 2001-2002 season with no coach, which had never been done before. That season she won the US Championships for the fourth time, receiving a total of nine 6s from all the judges. She was all set to win the Olympics that year. However, the strain[9] of the competition and her lack of a coach gave Michelle some problems, and she fell over during her performance. In spite of this, the judges still thought her skating was excellent, and she was awarded the bronze medal.[10]

❹ In 2006 she qualified[11] for the Olympics again. She was nearing the end of her professional career and wanted to try one last time for the gold medal.[12] However, that year she was troubled with a hip[13] injury which effected her dancing. In spite of her strong desire to compete, she had to withdraw[14] from the contest. In spite of her many titles,[15] Michelle has never won the Olympic gold medal.

❺ Michelle is known for her ability to combine technical merit[16] with artistic feeling. She is especially famous for a move called the "change-of-

---

9. strain [stren] *n.* 緊張；壓力
★ 10. bronze medal [ˋbrɑnz ˋmɛdl] *n.* 銅牌
★ 11. qualify [ˋkwɑləˌfaɪ] *v.* 獲得資格
★ 12. gold medal [ˋgold ˋmɛdl] *n.* 金牌
13. hip [hɪp] *n.* 臀部（連接腿和軀幹的突起部分）
★ 14. withdraw [wɪðˋdrɔ] *v.* 退出；抽回
15. title [ˋtaɪtl] *n.* 頭銜；【運動】優勝；冠軍；錦標
16. merit [ˋmɛrɪt] *n.* 優點；長處；價值

edge spiral,"[17] in which the skater[18] moves on one leg with the other leg stretched[19] out behind, making a spiral on the ice. She chooses her music carefully, and dances to it with great feeling and sincerity.[20] At the 1998 US Championships, her skating was so beautiful that she moved one of the judges to tears.

❻ Michelle was named Public Diplomacy[21] Ambassador[22] by President Bush, and she continues to hold this position under President Obama. She has traveled to China many times as ambassador, and has been an inspiration[23] to many Chinese Americans.

譯文

❶ 關穎珊出生於一個華裔移民家庭。父母都是來自香港,所以她是說英語、廣東話和普通話長大的。她在五歲時第一次踏到冰上,並且立刻就愛上了溜冰。她跟姊姊訓練得非常辛苦,一大早上學前就要溜,傍晚放學後也要溜。到了 13 歲時,她輟學在家受教,如此才能投入更多的時間在溜冰上。

❷ 從幼年的時候,她就開始參加溜冰比賽。她贏得了 1994 年世界青少年花式溜冰錦標賽。到了 13 歲時,她入選美國代表隊到挪威參加 1994 年的冬季奧

Ⓦ Ⓞ Ⓡ Ⓓ Ⓛ Ⓘ Ⓢ Ⓣ

17. spiral [ˋspaɪrəl] *n.* 旋轉
★ 18. skater [ˋsketɚ] *n.* 溜冰者
★ 19. stretch [strɛtʃ] *v.* 伸展;拉長
20. sincerity [sɪnˋsɛrətɪ] *n.* 誠懇;真實
21. diplomacy [dɪˋploməsɪ] *n.* 外交
★ 22. ambassador [æmˋbæsədɚ] *n.* 大使;使節
★ 23. inspiration [ˌɪnspəˋreʃən] *n.* 激勵;啟發

運，但並沒有下場比賽。在早期生涯中，她遇到許多問題。她發育得不夠快，所以身體的力量不足。她跟一家運動服裝公司簽約代言溜冰鞋，但鞋子卻造成了她的問題。她的腳部骨折，腳趾也出了問題。儘管如此，她還是繼續練習及努力溜冰。她贏得了1998年的奧運銀牌。

❸ 到了2001年，穎珊決定更換教練。這件事引發了許多謠傳，但穎珊只表示說，她想要為自己的溜冰事業負責。她不靠教練完成了2001到2002年的賽季，這是前所未見的事。該季她第四度贏得了美錦賽，而且所有的裁判總共給了她九個六分。她做好了萬全的準備要贏得當年的奧運。不過，緊繃的比賽跟缺少教練卻對穎珊造成一些問題，她在表演當中摔了一跤。儘管如此，裁評還是認為她溜得很棒，她也拿到了銅牌。

❹ 2006年，她再度入選奧運。她正接近職業生涯的尾聲，所以想要為金牌做最後一次嘗試。不過，那年她受到臀傷的困擾，影響了她的舞步。儘管她的求勝慾望強烈，卻不得不退出比賽。儘管擁有多項優勝，但穎珊從來沒有贏過奧運金牌。

❺ 穎珊是以能將技術性與藝術表現融為一體而聞名。她尤其有名的是一個叫做「變刃迴旋」的動作，也就是溜冰選手用單腳移動，另一隻腳則往後延伸，以便在冰上迴旋。她的音樂選得很謹慎，跳舞時也充滿了感情與真誠。在1998年的美錦賽上，她溜得非常優美，因而讓一位裁判感動到掉下淚來。

❻ 穎珊被布希總統任命為公共外交大使，而且在歐巴馬總統就任後繼續擔任這個職位。她多次以大使的身分前往中國，並鼓舞了許多華裔美國人。

閱讀理解

配合題,請判斷下列摘要各屬於文章的哪個段落,見範例。

2001 Olympics	❸
Public diplomacy ambassador	
2006 Olympics	
Childhood and education	
Her style	
Early career	

 重要詞彙

連連看,請為每個詞彙找出它的正確翻譯。

- compete •
- contest •
- public diplomacy ambassador •
- fall over •
- artistic feeling •
- in tears •
- figure skating •
- fracture •
- hip injury •
- bronze medal •
- hold this position •
- inspiration •
- move •

- • 藝術感
- • 銅牌
- • 競爭;爭奪
- • 比賽
- • 摔跤
- • 花式溜冰
- • 骨折
- • 臀傷
- • 擔任這個職位
- • 掉淚的
- • 鼓舞
- • 動作
- • 公共外交大使

rumor	•	•	有……的資格
season	•	•	謠傳
silver medal	•	•	賽季
skater	•	•	簽約
sincerity	•	•	銀牌
skate	•	•	真心
sign a contract	•	•	溜冰選手
spiral	•	•	溜冰鞋
take responsibility for	•	•	溜冰
sportswear company	•	•	迴旋
skating	•	•	運動服裝公司
strain	•	•	緊繃
technical merit	•	•	延伸；伸展
title	•	•	負責……
be troubled with	•	•	技術性
qualify for	•	•	錦標；優勝
be all set to	•	•	受到困擾
withdraw	•	•	做好萬全準備……
stretch out	•	•	退出

 填 空

理解文章大意後，請用前項習題中的詞彙來完成句子，有些字須做適當變化。

■ Michelle started **(01)**＿＿＿＿＿＿＿ when she was five and she has
won many awards for her **(02)**＿＿＿＿＿＿.

■ She went to the Winter Olympics in 1994, but did not **(03)**＿＿＿＿＿＿.

■ She (04)_____ with a (05)_____ to endorse their

(06)_____, but the boots gave her problems.

■ She suffered from foot (07)_____.

■ There were many (08)_____ about the reasons why Michelle

stopped working with her coach, but Michelle said she wanted to

(09)_____ her own skating.

■ In that (10)_____, she (11)_____ win the Olympic

medal, but the (12)_____ was too much for her and she

(13)_____.

■ She was awarded the (14)_____ in the 1998 Olympics, and

the (15)_____ in the 2002 Olympics.

■ She (16)_____ the 2006 Olympics, but she was

(17)_____ a (18)_____ that year and was not able to

skate due to the pain. She had to (19)_____ from the

(20)_____.

■ She has won more (21)_____ for her skating than any other

skater in America.

■ She is known for her (22)_____ and her (23)_____,

which often makes those who are watching her cry.

■ She is known for her (24)_____ called the "change-of-edge

spiral," in which the (25)_____ makes a (26)_____ on

the ice with one leg (27)_____ behind her.

■ She danced with such (28)_____ that even the judge was

(29)_____ .

■ Michelle is a (30)_____ and travels to China to build

relationships between the US and China. She is an (31)_____

to many young Chinese Americans.

 你還可以學更多

a) 請利用網路查詢下列關鍵字，以了解更多關於 **Michelle Kwan** 的資訊：

✓ A picture of Michelle Kwan

✓ A video of Michelle Kwan getting her Olympic silver medal

✓ Figure skating

✓ A video of Michelle doing the change-of-edge spiral

✓ Michelle Kwan's titles and awards

✓ An interview with Michelle

b) 請試著用英文討論下列話題：

1. 你想不想認識關穎珊？為什麼？
2. 你想不想當個職業溜冰選手？為什麼？
3. 你以前有沒有溜過冰？
4. 你比較喜歡看單人花式溜冰還是雙人花式溜冰？
5. 你知道其他花式溜冰選手嗎？你覺得誰最厲害？

解 答

 閱讀理解

2001 Olympics	❸
Public diplomacy ambassador	❻
2006 Olympics	❹
Childhood and education	❶
Her style	❺
Early career	❷

 重要詞彙

artistic feeling	藝術感
bronze medal	銅牌
compete	競爭；爭奪
contest	比賽
fall over	摔跤
figure skating	花式溜冰
fracture	骨折
hip injury	臀傷
hold this position	擔任這個職位
in tears	掉淚的
inspiration	鼓舞
move	動作
public diplomacy ambassador	公共外交大使

qualify for	有……的資格
rumor	謠傳
season	賽季
sign a contract	簽約
silver medal	銀牌
sincerity	真心
skater	溜冰選手
skate	溜冰鞋
skating	溜冰
spiral	迴旋
sportswear company	運動服裝公司
strain	緊繃
stretch out	延伸；伸展
take responsibility for	負責……
technical merit	技術性
title	錦標；優勝
be troubled with	受到困擾
be all set to	做好萬全準備……
withdraw	退出

 填 空

(01) skating

(02) figure skating

(03) compete

(04) signed a contract

(05) sportswear company

(06) skates

(07) fractures

(08) rumors

(09) take responsibility for

(10) season

(11) was all set to

(12) strain

(13) fell over

(14) silver medal

(15) bronze medal

(16) qualified for

(17) troubled with

(18) hip injury

(19) withdraw

(20) contest

(21) titles

(22) technical merit

(23) artistic feeling

(24) move

(25) skater

(26) spiral

(27) stretched out

(28) sincerity

(29) in tears

(30) public diplomacy ambassador

(31) inspiration

Unit 28

Tiger Woods
老虎 · 伍茲

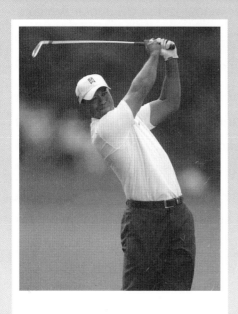

人物速覽

- 世界排名第一的職業高爾夫球選手
- 1975 年生於美國加州
- 史上最年輕及第一位非裔美籍的美國名人賽（US Masters）得主
- 2008 年最高薪的職業運動員

❶ Tiger's father was African American, and his mother is Thai.[1] He has a really mixed ancestry,[2] with Chinese, European and African blood. Tiger was a child prodigy,[3] appearing with his father on TV at the age of two to play with celebrities.[4] At the age of five he was already famous, appearing in golfing magazines. He won the Junior World Championships at the age of eight, which made him the youngest winner ever. He then won it again six times. He is also the youngest-ever winner of the US Junior Amateur[5] Championships, which he has won three times. After studying economics at Stanford University, he decided to become a professional golfer.

❷ He turned professional in 1996. Professional golf players make their money by winning tournaments,[6] and by endorsing products from sportswear companies. Tiger's first endorsement[7] with Nike was worth $40 million. He won his first major grand slam[8] tournament, The US Masters, in 1997, and was the youngest golfer ever to win the title. He won the tournament by a record 12 strokes,[9] and has since won The Masters 20 times. Between 1999 and 2002 he was unbeatable[10] and won every tournament he entered. He won numerous awards and accolades.[11]

Ⓦ Ⓞ Ⓡ Ⓓ　Ⓛ Ⓘ Ⓢ Ⓣ

1. Thai [ˈtaɪ] *adj.* 泰國人的　*n.* 泰國人；泰國語
2. ancestry [ˈænsɛstrɪ] *n.* 祖先；家世
3. prodigy [ˈprɑdədʒɪ] *n.* 神童；天才
4. celebrity [səˈlɛbrətɪ] *n.* 名流；名人
5. amateur [ˈæmə͵tʃʊr] *adj.* 業餘的；非職業的
6. tournament [ˈtɜnəmənt] *n.* 競賽；錦標賽
7. endorsement [ɪnˈdɔrsmənt] *n.* 推薦；背書
8. grand slam [ˈɡrænd ˈslæm] *n.* 大滿貫；全勝；大賽
★ 9. stroke [strok] *n.* 擊球

❸ From 2003 to 2004, Tiger experienced a slump,[12] and did not win so many titles. There were many rumors about why. Some said it was because his marriage was spoiling his concentration; others said it was because of an argument with his coach; still others said it was due to a knee injury. Some said he was making adjustments to the way he swings[13] the club,[14] which is very important in golf. But whatever the reasons, he did not stay away from the game, and soon ranked[15] as the world's number one again.

❹ In 2008 he entered the US Open, one of the top tournaments in the world, which he had already won 13 times previously. His team players noticed that he was not playing so well at the beginning of the game, and that he seemed to be in pain. However, his playing improved during the tournament, and he went on to win the title for the 14th time. After the tournament ended, he announced to the world that the ligament[16] in his leg had torn[17] and that his knee was destroyed. In spite of the very great pain he was in, he continued to play and win the title.

❺ Tiger is one of the most popular players in the history of golf and has increased the popularity[18] of the game, opening it up to many people who

10. unbeatable [ʌn`bitəbl] *adj.* 難以戰勝的；打不垮的
11. accolade [ˌækə`led] *n.* 榮譽；爵位授與
12. slump [`slʌmp] *n.* （聲望）突然衰退
13. swing [swɪŋ] *v.* 擺動；揮動
14. club [klʌb] *n.* 球桿
★ 15. rank [ræŋk] *v.* 位居；位列
16. ligament [`lɪgəmənt] *n.* 韌帶
17. torn [tɔrn] *v.* 撕裂；扯破（tear 的過去分詞）
18. popularity [ˌpɑpjə`lærətɪ] *n.* 眾望；名望

previously had no interest in golf. He always wears a red shirt in the final stretch[19] of a game because he says the color gives him confidence and makes him aggressive.[20] He puts in many hours of practice.

❻ Tiger has written a book about his golf playing style which has sold 1.5 million copies. He has his own company which designs golf courses[21] around the world. With his father he started the Tiger Woods Foundation to help disadvantaged[22] children. Tiger is married to a Swedish[23] model and they have two children.

譯文

❶ 老虎的父親是非裔美國人，母親是泰國人。他是個十足的混血兒，有中國、歐洲和非洲的血統。老虎是個神童，兩歲時就跟父親一起上電視跟名人打球。五歲時，他已經很有名，並出現在高爾夫球雜誌上。他在八歲時贏得了世界青少年錦標賽，成為史上最年輕的得主。後來他又贏了六次。他也是美國青少年業餘錦標賽史上最年輕的得主，並且贏過三次。在史丹福大學念完經濟學後，他決定成為職業高球選手。

❷ 他在1996年轉為職業選手。職業高球選手靠贏得巡迴賽以及代言運動服裝公司的產品來賺錢。老虎幫耐吉的首次代言價值4,000萬美元。他在1997 年贏得他的第一場大滿貫巡迴賽──美國名人賽，並且是史上贏得這項錦標最

Ⓦ Ⓞ Ⓡ Ⓓ Ⓛ Ⓘ Ⓢ Ⓣ

19. stretch [strɛtʃ] n. 渾身解數；最後衝刺
★ 20. aggressive [əˋgrɛsɪv] adj. 積極的；有衝勁的
21. course [kɔrs] n. 場地
22. disadvantaged [ˌdɪsədˋvæntɪdʒɪd] adj. 處於困境的；生活條件差的
23. Swedish [ˋswidɪʃ] adj. 瑞典（人）的

年輕的高球選手。他以破紀錄的 12 桿差距贏得了這場巡迴賽，此後並贏過三次名人賽。在 1999 到 2002 年間，他戰無不勝，打贏他所參加的每一場巡迴賽。他贏得了眾多獎項與榮譽。

❸ 在 2003 到 2004 年間，老虎陷入低潮，並沒有贏得那麼多項錦標，而其中的原因也引起諸多謠傳。有人說是因為他的婚姻破壞了他的專注度，有人說是因為他跟教練起了爭執，還有人說是因為膝傷的緣故。有人說他正在調整他的揮桿方式，這點在高球中非常重要。但無論原因為何，他並沒有遠離賽場，而且排名很快就重回世界第一。

❹ 2008 年，他參加美國公開賽，這是一項全世界頂級的巡迴賽，他過去已經贏過了兩次。和他同組的選手注意到，他在比賽的一開始打得不太好，而且看起來很痛苦。不過，他的表現在巡迴賽期間漸入佳境，並接著第三度贏得了這項錦標。在巡迴賽結束後，他才向世人宣布，他的腿部韌帶磨損，並傷到了膝蓋。儘管感到十分疼痛，他仍持續參賽，並贏得了錦標。

❺ 老虎是高球史上最受歡迎的球員之一，並提高了比賽受歡迎的程度，使過去對高球不感興趣的人也受到了吸引。他在比賽的最後一輪一定會穿上紅襯衫，因為他說這種顏色可以帶給他信心，並使他衝勁十足。他投入了很長的時間去練習。

❻ 老虎寫過一本書來談他的高爾夫球打法，賣了 150 萬本。他有自己的公司在世界各地設計高球場。他跟他父親成立了老虎伍茲基金會來協助弱勢兒童。老虎娶了一位瑞典模特兒，並生了兩個小孩。

閱讀理解

配合題，請判斷下列摘要各屬於文章的哪個段落，見範例。

The slump	❸
Popularity and reputation	
Childhood and youth	
The Tiger Woods Foundation	
First success	
Leg problems	

 重要詞彙

連連看，請為每個詞彙找出它的正確翻譯。

■ confidence · · 榮譽

■ argument · · 爭執

■ championship · · 冠軍賽

■ concentration · · 球桿

■ ligament · · 專注度

■ final stretch · · 信心

■ make adjustments to · · 最後衝刺

■ golf course · · 高球場

■ accolade · · 高球選手

■ club · · 大滿貫

■ golfer · · 膝傷

■ grand slam · · 韌帶

■ knee injury · · 做……的調整

■ put in many hours of •	• 混血血統
■ turn professional •	• 模特兒
■ unbeatable •	• 投入很長的時間
■ rank •	• 排名
■ slump •	• 低潮
■ spoil •	• 破壞
■ stroke •	• 桿數
■ model •	• 揮
■ swing •	• 巡迴賽
■ tournament •	• 轉為職業的
■ mixed ancestry •	• 戰無不勝的

填 空

理解文章大意後，請用前項習題中的詞彙來完成句子，有些字須做適當變化。

■ Tiger has (01)＿＿＿＿＿, with African, Chinese and European blood.

■ He won many junior (02)＿＿＿＿ when he was a child.

■ He showed talent as a (03)＿＿＿＿ from a very early age.

■ He (04)＿＿＿＿ after he completed college.

■ He has won each major (05)＿＿＿＿ title several times.

■ He won the US Masters, a major (06)＿＿＿＿, by 12 (07)＿＿＿＿.

■ He was regarded as (08)_____ from 1999 to 2002, and he won many titles and (09)_____.

■ During 2003 Tiger experienced a (10)_____. Some said this was because his marriage was (11)_____ his (12)_____. Others said it was because of an (13)_____ with his coach. Still others said that he was (14)_____ the way he (15)_____ his (16)_____.

■ He won the US Open in 2008 despite a (17)_____ and a torn (18)_____.

■ He (19)_____ number 1 in the world.

■ He wears a red shirt in the (20)_____ of the game to give him (21)_____.

■ He (22)_____ practice.

■ He has his own company which designs (23)_____.

■ He married a beautiful Swedish (24)_____.

🌐 你還可以學更多

a) 請利用網路查詢下列關鍵字，以了解更多關於 Tiger Woods 的資訊：

☑ A picture of Tiger Woods
☑ A video of Tiger Woods playing golf as a child

⊘ The history of golf

⊘ The Tiger Woods Foundation

⊘ Tiger Woods's prizes and titles

⊘ An interview with Tiger

b) 請試著用英文討論下列話題：

1. 你想不想認識老虎‧伍茲？為什麼？
2. 你想不想當個職業高球選手？為什麼？
3. 你以前有沒有打過高爾夫球？
4. 有人認為高爾夫球不是年輕人的運動。你同不同意？
5. 有人認為高球場對環境有害。你有什麼看法？

解 答

閱讀理解

The slump	❸
Popularity and reputation	❺
Childhood and youth	❶
The Tiger Woods Foundation	❻
First success	❷
Leg problems	❹

重要詞彙

accolade	榮譽
argument	爭執
championship	冠軍賽
club	球桿
concentration	專注度
confidence	信心
final stretch	最後衝刺
golf course	高球場
golfer	高球選手
grand slam	大滿貫
knee injury	膝傷
ligament	韌帶
make adjustments to	做⋯⋯的調整

mixed ancestry	混血血統
model	模特兒
put in many hours of	投入很長的時間
rank	排名
slump	低潮
spoil	破壞
stroke	桿數
swing	揮
tournament	巡迴賽
turn professional	轉為職業的
unbeatable	戰無不勝的

 填 空

(01) mixed ancestry

(02) championships

(03) golfer

(04) turned professional

(05) grand slam

(06) tournament

(07) strokes

(08) unbeatable

(09) accolades

(10) slump

(11) spoiling

(12) concentration

(13) argument

(14) making adjustments to

(15) swings

(16) club

(17) knee injury

(18) ligament

(19) ranks

(20) final stretch

(21) confidence

(22) puts in many hours of

(23) golf courses

(24) model

圖片來源

■ 下列單元圖片由達志影像提供授權：

Unit 2、Unit 3、Unit 4、Unit 7、Unit 8、Unit 11、Unit 12、Unit 14、
Unit 15、Unit 16、Unit 17、Unit 18、Unit 19、Unit 20、Unit 21、
Unit 22、Unit 23、Unit 24、Unit 27、Unit 28

■ 其他：

Unit 1：http://commons.wikimedia.org/wiki/File:Henry8England.jpg

Unit 5：http://commons.wikimedia.org/wiki/File:Wolfgang-amadeus-mozart_1.jpg

Unit 6：http://commons.wikimedia.org/wiki/File:Beethoven.jpg

Unit 9：http://commons.wikimedia.org/wiki/File:Charles_Dickens_-
_Project_Gutenberg_eText_13103.jpg

Unit 10：http://commons.wikimedia.org/wiki/File:Dostoevsky_1872.jpg

Unit 13：http://commons.wikimedia.org/wiki/File:VanGogh_1887_Selbstbildnis.jpg

Unit 25：http://commons.wikimedia.org/wiki/File:Earhart.jpg

Unit 26：http://commons.wikimedia.org/wiki/File:Jesse_Owens.jpg

NOTES

國家圖書館出版品預行編目資料

英文閱讀越好：人物篇 / Quentin Brand 作；戴至中譯. －－ 初版.
－－ 臺北市：貝塔出版：智勝文化發行, 2010. 01
　　面；　公分
　ISBN 978-957-729-766-2（平裝附光碟片）

　1. 英語　2. 讀本　3. 世界傳記

805.18 98020456

英文閱讀越好：人物篇

作　　者 / Quentin Brand
譯　　者 / 戴至中
執行編輯 / 陳家仁

出　　版 / 貝塔出版有限公司
地　　址 / 台北市 100 館前路 12 號 11 樓
電　　話 / (02) 2314-2525
傳　　真 / (02) 2312-3535
客服專線 / (02) 2314-3535
客服信箱 / btservice@betamedia.com.tw
郵撥帳號 / 19493777
帳戶名稱 / 貝塔出版有限公司

總 經 銷 / 時報文化出版企業股份有限公司
地　　址 / 桃園縣龜山鄉萬壽路二段 351 號
電　　話 / (02) 2306-6842

出版日期 / 2010 年 01 月初版一刷
定　　價 / 340 元
ISBN：978-957-729-766-2

英文閱讀越好：人物篇
Copyright 2010 by Quentin Brand
Published by Beta Multimedia Publishing

貝塔網址：www.betamedia.com.tw

本書之文字、圖形、設計均係著作權所有，若有抄襲、模仿、冒用情事，依法追究。如
有缺頁、破損、裝訂錯誤，請寄回本公司調換。

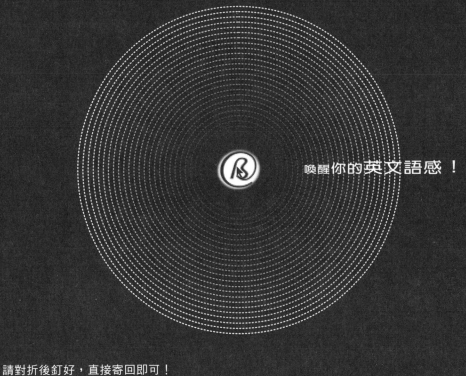

喚醒你的英文語感！

請對折後釘好，直接寄回即可！

| 廣　告　回　信 |
| 北區郵政管理局登記證 |
| 北 台 字 第 1 4 2 5 6 號 |
| 免　貼　郵　票 |

100 台北市中正區館前路12號11樓

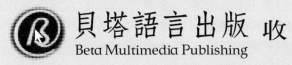

貝塔語言出版 收
Beta Multimedia Publishing

寄件者住址 □□□

貝塔語言出版
Beta Multimedia Publishing

讀者服務專線 (02) 2314-3535 讀者服務傳真 (02) 2312-3535
客戶服務信箱 btservice@betamedia.com.tw
www.betamedia.com.tw

謝謝您購買本書！！
貝塔語言擁有最優良之英文學習書籍，為提供您最佳的英語學習資訊，您填妥此表後寄回（免貼郵票），將可不定期免費收到本公司最新發行之書訊及活動訊息！

姓名：＿＿＿＿＿＿＿　性別：□男 □女　生日：＿＿年＿＿月＿＿日

電話：（公）＿＿＿＿＿＿ （宅）＿＿＿＿＿＿ （手機）＿＿＿＿＿＿

電子信箱：＿＿＿＿＿＿＿＿＿＿＿＿＿＿＿＿＿＿＿＿＿

學歷：□高中職含以下　□專科　□大學　□研究所含以上

職業：□金融　□服務　□傳播　□製造　□資訊　□軍公教　□出版
　　　□自由　□教育　□學生　□其他

職級：□企業負責人　□高階主管　□中階主管　□職員　□專業人士

1. 您購買的書籍是？＿＿＿＿＿＿＿＿＿＿＿＿＿＿＿＿＿＿

2. 您從何處得知本產品？（可複選）
　□書店 □網路 □書展 □校園活動 □廣告信函 □他人推薦 □新聞報導 □其他＿＿

3. 您覺得本產品價格：
　□偏高 □合理 □偏低

4. 請問目前您每週花了多少時間學英語？
　□不到十分鐘 □十分鐘以上，但不到半小時 □半小時以上，但不到一小時
　□一小時以上，但不到兩小時 □兩個小時以上 □不一定

5. 通常在選擇語言學習書時，哪些因素是您會考慮的？
　□封面 □內容、實用性 □品牌 □媒體、朋友推薦 □價格 □其他＿＿＿

6. 市面上您最需要的語言書種類為？
　□聽力 □閱讀 □文法 □口說 □寫作 □其他＿＿＿

7. 通常您會透過何種方式選購語言學習書籍？
　□書店門市 □網路書店 □郵購 □直接找出版社 □學校或公司團購 □其他＿＿＿

8. 給我們的建議：＿＿＿＿＿＿＿＿＿＿＿＿＿＿＿＿＿＿

＿＿＿＿＿＿＿＿＿＿＿＿＿＿＿＿＿＿＿＿＿＿＿＿＿＿＿

＿＿＿＿＿＿＿＿＿＿＿＿＿＿＿＿＿＿＿＿＿＿＿＿＿＿＿

喚醒你的英文語感！

Get a Feel for English !

Get a Feel for English !

喚醒你的英文語感！